I couldn't defeat this demon alone, but I had prepared the people around me for something like this. Would our combined efforts be enough?

Richard dropped down into the burning vehicle. Then things changed. Or actually my perceptions changed, and, as an angel, I could see both the physical side and the spiritual aspect of events clearly. It had happened to me before but rarely when I was in full flesh-and-blood human form.

Time slowed to a crawl, and I could see from both the physical and spiritual sides at once. I was immediately aware that, from this new perspective, the fire changed dramatically. It was no longer just a physical phenomenon but a living being—a demon of such malevolence, rage, hate, and destructiveness that I recoiled and took a step backward.

In spite of it being made of fire, it seemed to me to be a vast darkness, looming above everything, threatening to destroy everything in sight. It wasn't a new experience for me, since I had faced such demons before, but it was never fun. Or safe.

At least now I understood why I had sensed the evil presence around Frank, which had been this evil being working on him to start the fire. This one was a class of being that was especially powerful and dangerous. Tolkien named them well—Balrog, an Anglicized version of the Hebrew for "master of evil." But just then I wasn't thinking linguistic derivations, I had realized the target of his presence and fury—Richard. And Richard had just gone straight into the heart of the fire and darkness.

Even angels sometimes have to act on faith to get the Plan back on track…

Samuel, a secret agent angel on Earth, sometimes has to improvise when things go badly wrong. Over forty years of angelic missions come to a head in a fire at a snowbound truck stop when a fire demon comes to destroy one man's faith—or his life. The only chance for success rests with the spiritual power of the humans whom Samuel has tried to prepare for the struggle, but have they gained enough spiritual strength and awareness…or, if not, does God have a Plan B?

KUDOS for *Secret Agent Angel*

In *Secret Agent Angel* by Ray Sutherland, Sam is an angel who comes to Earth disguised as a human, undertaking missions to help those in need. The story is told in first person as Sam moves from one mission to another, often not knowing what he is really there for or how to go about carrying out his duties. Written like a diary, Sam details over forty years of missions, a different one in each chapter, culminating at a snowbound truck stop, where the real test of faith begins. But have the humans learned enough from Sam to pass the test? A unique, clever, and intriguing story with charming characters, this is a fun, heart-warming read. ~ *Taylor Jones, Reviewer*

Secret Agent Angel by Ray Sutherland is the story of Sam, the angel, who comes to Earth in different disguises to help carry out God's Plan. Sam comes "across," as he calls it, with all the knowledge and skills needed for the particular mission he's on. As he details each mission, one for each chapter of the book, we meet the flawed humans that Sam was sent to help. But the missions never turn out quite like Sam expects them to—proving that God either has a sense of humor, or He switches to Plan B when he wants to shake things up—often forcing Sam to improvise and test his faith that the Boss knows what He's doing. *Secret Agent Angel* is a cleverly told and heartwarming story of love and hope—a message of faith that someone is watching over us and we are never really alone. ~ *Regan Murphy, Reviewer*

SECRET AGENT ANGEL

From the Realms of Glory

RAY SUTHERLAND

A Black Opal Books Publication

GENRE: RELIGIOUS FICTION/SUSPENSE/SUPERNATURAL

SECRET AGENT ANGEL ~ From the Realms of Glory
Copyright © 2016 by Ray Sutherland
Cover Design by Ray Sutherland
All cover art copyright © 2016
All Rights Reserved
Print ISBN: 978-1-626945-72-2

First Publication: DECEMBER 2016

Published by Black Opal Books **http://www.blackopalbooks.com**

DEDICATION

To Regina

CHAPTER 1

AGENT ANGEL

The first thing I knew arriving on Earth was the terrible disorientation of re-entering time. It didn't matter how often you made the transition, it was still a terrible wrench to your mind, almost violent in its effect. I spent a few seconds doing the normal head shaking and shivering to get over the jolt and to get used to being flesh and blood again. And then I got down to business. At least this time, I was undercover and didn't have to wear a goofy robe and those wings that glow in the dark. They could be fun, but they were also cumbersome and a real pain to keep clean.

This time, I looked like a reasonably normal human male, dressed in the regulation shirt and tie like that of a junior manager at a big department store chain or insurance agency. I was in the restroom of a convenience store close to the airport, so I hit the toilet handle to make it seem as if I was in there for the normal reason and stepped out. I bought a honey bun, a chocolate bar, and the largest cup they had of orange soda because one thing I envied about humans was that they got to eat and drink. The Boss sure did a good job when He created that, and I always took advantage of it when I was here on Earth.

I come here pretty regularly. My name is Samuel. I'm an angel.

I sat down at one of the small booths in the store and looked out the window as I ate and drank and waited for my subject to show up. I had timed it right and had just finished the honey bun and half the soda when his car went by, headed home after work, with his three-year-old daughter in the car seat in the back. I dropped the wrappers in the trash and headed to the car which was waiting for me in the farthest parking place. It started right up, which is always a bit of a relief when dealing with a car I've never seen before. We've got good people doing these things, but sometimes the Boss likes to pull surprises, even on us. I remember once when I worked in the fifteenth century in Yemen, I got stuck with a donkey with no training, and that caused me to get stranded in a tiny village where I wound up staying with the local Jacobite priest who had been having a faith crisis. The next morning, he had tried to help me teach the donkey manners while his wife supervised. We were having a conversation about his crisis during a break necessitated by the donkey winning a round, and his wife had exasperatedly broken in with, "You won't get over this unless you get hit with a sign from Heaven!"

Just then the donkey let loose with a kick which sent the priest flying, fortunately with no serious damage to anything other than his dignity. That made him laugh and say that, very much like the story of Balaam, the Boss had again spoken through a donkey. That didn't fix his faith but it seemed to give him the boost he needed, and he went on to be a faithful leader in the Yemenite church, doubts and all.

I cut off that line of thought and got back to the business of following my subject. We didn't have far to go. The store I'd picked to start from was only about a mile from his house, and I wasn't sure he wouldn't stop in for gas or a loaf of bread. Today, though, he went straight home, no stops and without any apparent glances in the mirror, even though a look in his mirror would have shown him a rather dark and nasty trail of smoke coming from his exhaust pipe.

As planned, the last stoplight before his final turn into their subdivision caught him. I pulled up next to him and got a good look. He looked exactly like what he was—a junior level management flunky trying to get on the fast track, with ambitions to reach high and talent to match. But today he looked more than harried and rushed at work, he looked troubled and uncertain. His mind was clearly somewhere else because he didn't notice the light turn green until the driver behind honked. That let me get in ahead of him and slow down so he had to pass me and I got a good look at the girl, too.

Amanda was her name and she was a star pupil at Miss Emmy's Day Care Center and—of course—spoiled rotten by both parents, all four grandparents, and two step-grandparents. She had the sweet look that all three-year-old girls have, even when they're starving in the middle of a plague. I've seen that, too, and I screamed and yelled at the Boss to let me fix some things, but I got the usual answer.

Everything was just as I expected. That was no surprise, since I watched them before I came over, but it was good to confirm it because things look very different when you're on this side and limited by time and space.

Preliminary recon done, I turned off the main road a block before they did and headed to the big department store in the mall where the wife would be finishing her shift as a cosmetics saleslady. They had about decided that she should quit that job since his last promotion, and she was thinking about going back to college, hoping to study art and either be an artist or at least to teach in a high school. But her pay, little as it was, helped quite a bit and she was nervous about trying to do without it.

I parked in the closest spot, which was not very close. I wish the Boss would fix that like He fixed the traffic light but that's one of his inscrutable ways. It's not like I need the exercise since I'm usually a perfect physical specimen when I come over in human form.

I went inside the mall, bought a bag of cashews from the kiosk in the center, and ate them as I wandered around like a shopper until I reached her counter. I timed it perfectly—it generally works that way for us and that more than makes up for the lack of good parking places—and she was about to start closing out her register.

"Excuse me, ma'am," I said, catching her eye.

She looked at me and a little reluctantly came over. She was a good-looking lady with nice hair and a hair band which was distinctly retro but which looked very pretty on her. She was dressed in a cosmetics saleslady's standard business suit and a name tag with the store name and "Audrey" on it. Like her husband, she had a bit of a harassed look, but hers was just from a long shift on her feet, not from any troubled conscience. She smiled the standard saleslady's phony smile. "Yes, may I help you?"

"I'm looking for some Janie Arben perfume in a spray bottle. Do you have any?"

That stuff had been a big seller two Christmases ago, and they'd had trouble keeping enough of it in stock, but now it was old news and not even out on display any more. There were still two partial cases in the storeroom, though.

The phony smile got bigger and phonier. She was in a hurry to get home and those two cases of the type I'd asked for were in the back, buried under several other boxes of stuff. "I'm not sure if we still have any of that," she said hesitantly, hoping I'd give up and go away and let her get out.

"Would you check and see, please? It's important."

I'm a male this trip and men don't take hints very well. Besides, it *was* important, way more than she knew, but not in the way she thought I meant.

She rather obviously stifled a glance at her watch and very obviously looked around for somebody else to palm me off on but the only other lady working then was busy with another customer, a middle-aged woman who was clearly a big buyer, and user, of make-up.

The professional smile turned to one of resignation. "Certainly. I'll have to go to the back for a minute."

"Okay," I said, giving her the Grade "A" Heavenly smile, that would get any of us hired to sell toothpaste.

She walked quickly out from the counter and disappeared into racks of coats.

I ate a few more cashews and looked around at the store and the people in it shopping for clothes. Human senses have always been a puzzle to me and clothing has been the biggest puzzle. I know it's real because I experience it myself when I'm in human form but why the feel of good material on skin causes such pleasure is something I just don't understand. Or why taking on fuel makes a person want to wag like a puppy dog. What is so exciting about heated tree seeds? But I loved those cashews. Or tree bark and dried grass sap? It doesn't make sense, but it's quite real, because I love cinnamon sugar. As I said, the Boss did a real good job at creation, and I know that I couldn't ever come close to doing that. Why Uncle Lucifer thought he could and pulled that stunt, I'll never understand, but I guess I've always known that, which is why I stuck with the Boss, and that sure was smart.

It took her a few minutes but she came back with a

bottle of the perfume—but still too quickly. "Here it is," she said with a real smile this time.

I didn't like what I was going to have to do next because her genuine smile was really pretty, but I had to keep her there for at least four more minutes, maybe more, even if I had to wrestle with her, which I did once on a job in Reformation Germany. That lady was a nun who was supposed to switch over and become a Lutheran pastor's wife but needed some persuasion, which I was supposed to provide. I still get razzed over that one, and it was very embarrassing to get whipped by a nun. The problem was she had grown up a farm girl with seven brothers. She worked in the convent kitchen and laundry, was stronger than me, and outweighed me. But in spite of that little setback, I got the job done. She wound up married with eight kids and a husband who pastored a big congregation and was a stalwart of the Franconian church.

"That's the four ounce bottle," I said. "Do you have a six-ounce bottle?"

Her smile went from pretty to very professional and very strained. "I don't think so." It came out almost as a growl.

I gave her the grade B grin with less teeth but more eye sparkle. "Well, if you don't, could I have two four-ounce bottles?"

Her smile wavered into a near snarl but then went back into place. "Certainly. I'll go get another one."

She was gone three minutes and came back with one large and two small bottles. "We did have one six ounce bottle left," she said. "Do you want it?"

"Yes. That would be great," I responded.

She flashed the real smile and went to the register where the mechanics of the purchase took another two minutes, and we were both home free. I accepted the bagged perfume and went away, while she took care of the business of closing out her shift and hurried to the employee's parking lot.

I drove around the mall just in time to see her run a yellow light leaving the mall lot and race away down the street toward home. I followed more sensibly for a few miles, and we were stuck in a long line of rush hour traffic with me following her about two cars behind when the explosion came. I was expecting it, but flesh and blood still startles. I jumped and had to stifle the urge to shout, scream, or something. There was a fireball reaching up a hundred feet and pieces of something unidentifiable flying through the air. I could see Audrey's car a few places ahead of mine well outside the blast zone, but before I could feel any sense of satisfaction, I was horrified to see one of the big pieces of debris come crashing down, right onto her car.

It crushed the hood and shattered the windshield then, trailing some blue gunk, flipped off into the street, landing against a plumber's truck, denting the side panel.

I let fly with an emotional outburst—no bad words, but a scream of frustration—threw open my door, and ran to her car. But the plumber had beaten me to it and was trying to get the door open by the time I came up. It was jammed tight and even our combined efforts didn't move it. There were times I wished we came here with super strength like the comic book angels, but all I had was normal human muscles, and they weren't enough. The plumber disappeared but was quickly back with a huge pry bar and, with it, we got the latch smashed and the door open enough to see in. Audrey was in one piece and looked all right but was unconscious and a few trickles of blood ran down her face. More alarmingly, there was heavy smoke coming from under the dashboard. As we forced the door farther open, she opened her eyes and looked in our direction but without focus or comprehension. The plumber—Bob, it said on his shirt and truck door—dropped the pry bar and pulled the door open all the way. He leaned into the car right into her face. "Hey, lady, wake up," he shouted. "Stay awake, we need you to help get out."

She looked at him with a little more awareness but was still groggy. I noticed that the smoke was getting heavier, and she coughed several times, having gotten a good lungful of smoke. "I think we'd better get her out of there," I said to the plumber.

As if on cue—and maybe it was, but not my cue—a small flame started from under the crushed hood. The plumber nodded. "You're right, but if her back or neck is hurt…" He grunted and turned back to Audrey. "Can you move your feet?" he shouted at her.

Her head wiggled in an indeterminate way.

"Can you move your feet?" he shouted again, louder.

This time her head moved in a clear nod.

"Okay, let's see them move," he said, stepping to where he could see her feet.

I couldn't see, but they must have wiggled, because Bob reached in to the car and lifted her out. I took part of the load. We carried her over to the grass on the wide median and set her down. By then she was mostly awake and was able to sit up. Bob and I were both huffing and puffing from the exertion and the adrenalin—again I wished for miraculous endurance and strength, and Bob, who looked to be about seventy, was surely wishing for the same thing—and we all took a few moments to just sit and collect ourselves.

After a moment, I turned to Audrey. "Are you hurt?" I asked.

She shook her head. "I don't think so, not seriously," she said, apparently going through a mental inventory of parts. "I got cut—" She touched the bloody part of her head. "—but I don't think it's very bad."

Bob raised himself to one knee. "There will be some ambulances coming. You'll need to get checked out by the medics." He looked at her face. "Most of those cuts look superficial but there's a pretty bad one on your forehead. That one and your being unconscious worry me. You might have a concussion. I think we'd better get one of the ambulances to get you."

She shook her head and wiggled her hands and feet. "I expect there will be more urgent things for them to do," she said. Suddenly she straightened, looking at her burning car. "Oh, my car! And I just got it paid off."

Bob laughed. "Ma'am, you got off mighty lucky. It was nearly you that got totaled instead of just your car. You need to be thankful for being whole. You can get another car."

She smiled, the real one that's so pretty. "You're quite right. And I also want to thank the two of you for getting me out of the car. You were both very brave and nice to do that."

Bob smiled. "No, ma'am, I wasn't either one. I just happened to be close is all." He laughed and looked at his hands. "I certainly wasn't brave. I'm still shaking."

Further conversation was cut short by a police car coming down the wrong side of the street, trying to get to the scene of the explosion but having a hard time getting through the rush hour traffic stopped by the mess. Its siren made any useful talk impossible but the car and siren both stopped as he came past us. The policeman looked at Audrey. "Are you hurt, ma'am?"

"Not badly."

He drove off without answering, his mind and attention apparently already on the scene ahead.

"What happened?" Audrey asked.

"I think a tanker truck got hit and blew up," Bob responded. "But I couldn't see very well. It looks like a big piece of a tanker pump that hit your car and my truck."

Audrey looked at me. "You're the man buying perfume, aren't you?" I nodded. "I was annoyed that you kept me late," she said, "but if you hadn't, I might have been right in the middle of that intersection when the explosion happened."

Then the reaction came over her and she started crying. Bob looked embarrassed. He went to his truck and returned with a small pack of tissues and a cooler of water. He handed the tissues to Audrey who blew her nose and wiped her eyes then had a spell of coughing while he wet a couple of the tissues, cleaned the blood off of her face, and looked at the cut, probing it gently with fingers that seemed to know what to do.

While they did that, I was busy trying to figure out some things and why they had gone wrong. I had done my job. I delayed her the required four minutes and even a little more. But it hadn't worked, she still got caught in the accident. But she hadn't gotten hurt badly, so it wasn't a complete disaster. But my plan had been to follow her home and find some reason to approach them. Well, I had certainly found that, so I decided to make use of it, but before I could do so, Bob the plumber beat me to it.

"Miss Audrey," he said, reading her name tag. "I'd better take you to the emergency room. I don't think you're hurt very bad. It looks like you got a cut from a piece of the windshield, but there could be some things wrong that I can't see. I was an army medic, but that was forty years ago. But I don't see any sign of bad concussion or anything."

He grinned. "In Vietnam, I would have given you a Band-Aid and sent you right back out on patrol. But this isn't Vietnam and you need to be checked out by a doctor."

Audrey coughed deeply again. "Yes, I think you're probably right, but won't the police need me for an accident report?" she asked, getting to her feet as Bob and I both jumped to help her.

"Probably so," Bob said, "but the police will be busy with a lot of higher priorities than your car for a while. They can find you when they need you, and you need to get off the side of the road."

"I guess you're right," she said. Then she looked around. "But can we get out?"

The traffic was backed up behind us as far as we could see, and the fire trucks and ambulances were starting to arrive by coming down the wrong lanes.

"My truck will go right over the median and we can go out that way," Bob said, taking her arm and leading her toward his truck.

I was thinking fast, now. Bob was jumping in and doing what I would have thought would have been my job in this case. So much so that it occurred to me that he might even be one of us, but I didn't think so. He had given no signals of any sort—we've got them, but humans aren't supposed to know them—and it would be highly unusual for two of us to be working the same gig without knowing about it. Although it wasn't impossible. Sometimes, the Boss gets cute even with us. But I was pretty certain Bob was just what he seemed—a good man who was trying to help where he could.

But I couldn't just watch some human pull one of my main projects away so I grabbed her other arm. "You need to let your family know that you're okay and where you're going. Do you have a cell phone?"

She stopped and turned quickly to the burning car. "My purse! I'd forgotten about it."

I went to her car and looked in. There was a purse sitting in the passenger seat and the fire had about died so I wasn't risking much when I reached in, picked the purse up off the seat, and quickly dropped it on the pavement. It was very hot and the vinyl was even smoldering a little, enough that I had blistered a finger getting it. I looked back in and saw a phone in its charging cradle and both were rather twisted and distorted where flames had come from under the dashboard right behind them. That phone had made its last call.

I picked the purse up by the strap, which was cool enough, and carried it over to where she sat in the truck seat. "Watch it, it's hot," I told her, "but your phone is now melted junk."

Surprisingly, she giggled. "It's my day for destroyed machinery," she said. "I hope the hospital doesn't fall down on me."

I smiled back. "If you'll tell me your address, I'll go and tell your family." Actually, I knew her address quite well, but I couldn't let her know that.

"There's no need for that. I'll call from the hospital."

"That could take a good while," I replied. "Your husband will be worried and frantic if he doesn't hear from you soon. Please. I would like to."

She smiled at me. "Well, if you're sure you don't mind. It's just a few blocks away at 337 Evergreen. A brick house with a green roof and a carport. But won't your wife worry about you, too?"

"I'm away from home and a geographical bachelor this week," I said. Actually, I'm unmarried this eternity since we're not made for that, but eternity includes this week. We're not supposed to actually tell an untruth, except under very unusual circumstances, but some misdirection can be very useful and is allowed.

I closed the truck door and Bob carefully worked his

truck through the stopped cars to the median. "Wait a minute," I said "What hospital are you going to?"

"East End General," Bob responded. "It's closest. Do you know where it is?"

I nodded. "Fourteenth Street."

With that, Bob roared off in his truck and I followed more slowly, since my rented sedan had a lot less ground clearance that his 4WD pick-up. I had to go a long way around to their house because of the huge traffic jam centered on the burning truck but it still was only about ten minutes later that I pulled into their driveway.

It was one of those subdivisions that had sprouted like mushrooms in the '60s and '70s with rabbit warren streets and houses seemingly stamped out of cookie cutters so that there were only three of four basic patterns of house. Theirs was one of the smallest houses, but a nice, comfortable one, well-kept with trees that had been there long enough to give some real shade in the summer. I turned onto their street just in time to see a tow truck head out of their driveway pulling his car. Apparently, the exhaust smoke I'd noticed earlier was a bigger problem than I'd thought.

As I pulled into the driveway, I could see Amanda playing on a swing set under the largest tree in the back yard and could see her father though the kitchen door as he stood at the sink and turned to see who was driving up. I got out and by the time I got to the carport he was at the door.

"Hi," I said. "Are you Mr. Steiner?"

"Yes," he said, looking concerned, puzzled, and curious all at once. "I'm Roger Steiner."

"I've just come from up the road where the big explosion was." He managed to look puzzled, concerned, and horrified all at the same time.

"Was…"

"Your wife was outside the explosion but a piece of the truck flew out and landed on her car. She was cut a little and got a pretty good knock on the head and was unconscious, but she seems to be all right now."

"Where is she?"

"She's on her way to East End General. Another man who helped get her out of the car is taking her."

He deflated like somebody who has been hit with too many big problems at once, which was exactly what had happened. Well, I could sympathize and I could help. In fact, that's what I was there for. "I noticed your car being towed. I'd be glad to take you to the hospital. I'm going there anyway."

He perked up a little but was rather uncertain. "No, I'll get a taxi and…"

"Really," I said with the top-of-the line good friend smile, the really trustworthy one. "I'm going there to check on her myself so it's no trouble. And if you called a taxi, the driver would still be a stranger, too, right? I'd like to be of help. It would make me feel like I'm doing something for Miss Audrey."

He gave a little shrug and looked a little relieved. "I guess you're right," he said. "Let me get my daughter inside and we'll go."

"Great," I said. "I'll be in the car whenever you're ready."

It didn't take long for him to get the little girl inside and a bag of something put together, then they were in the car and we were off.

"Hi there, young lady," I said to the girl. "What's your name?"

"I'm Amanda," she said. "What's yours?"

I smiled at her in the mirror. "I'm Sam Mollock."

"And this is Andrea," she said, pulling a doll out of the backpack at her side.

"Well, hello. I'm pleased to meet you, Miss Andrea. And you too, Amanda."

"And I'm pleased to meet you, Mr. Mollow."

"Mollock. K-k-k," I corrected her.

I filled Roger in on as much as I knew about the accident and Bob's Army medic diagnosis.

"So she seemed to be basically all right?" he said, sounding hopeful.

"She was walking on her own and seemed to be completely aware of everything, which Bob thought was a good sign. But he was concerned about her having been dazed so badly, even unconscious. But I'm not a doctor or even a medic, so I don't trust my opinion."

"Daddy, is Mama going to be all right? Will she come home with us tonight?" She was just three, but the worry was clear in her tone as well as the words. Roger turned around and looked at her. "We don't know, honey. We'll have to find out from the doctors when we get there."

The getting there didn't take much longer, and I pulled into the parking lot of the hospital just a few minutes afterward. I went as close as the rules allowed private cars to get to the Emergency Room door, let them out, and then parked the car—again none of the close in parking places were empty.

I entered the waiting room just in time to see Roger go through the automatic doors into the treatment area. Puzzled, I looked around for Amanda and saw her sitting in a chair in one of the triage stations talking to the triage nurse. I also saw Bob the plumber sitting in one of the waiting room chairs. I waved at him as I went to the station where Amanda was sitting and stood in the door. "Hi, Amanda," I said.

"Hi, Mr. Mollock-k-k. This is Mrs. McDonnell, my Sunday School teacher last year."

Just then, Bob stuck his head in the door. "Hi, Irene,"

he said. "I didn't know you were here now. I couldn't see you from my seat."

"Hi, Bob," she responded with a worried look. "Is Bonnie here?"

"No, no, I was close to the explosion out by the airport and I brought in a lady who was hurt by that."

"And this is her daughter Amanda," I said to Bob. "And Andrea is in the bag."

"Hi, Amanda, I'm Bob Dunn," Bob said as she reached into the bag and brought out the doll to complete the introductions.

I noticed a very slightly distressed expression on Mrs. McDonnell and saw that she was looking at an elderly couple waiting to come in and talk with her.

"If Bob and I sit right there where you can watch us, would you let us keep Amanda while you keep working?" I asked. She looked uncertain, so I said, "If it would help, I'll tell the security guard to keep a close watch on us, too." Then I gave her a meaningful look with a little bit of humorous undertone.

She smiled. "He watches everybody so I guess it would be all right. I think Roger would approve."

"I promise I'll be a perfect angel," I replied with a big grin. Sometimes I crack myself up.

We sat in the row of seats right outside of her cubicle where she could see us and settled in for a wait. Bob very quickly began a conversation with Amanda about Andrea the doll which shifted to the books and crayons in her bag and then to daycare.

I looked around and located my quarry then interrupted their conversation. "Would either of you like a drink or a snack?"

Bob shook his head but Amanda piped up with, "Yes, I'd like an orange drink, please."

"A lady of good taste," I replied.

Fortunately, the machine was well stocked, and I got us each an orange soda and a bag of peanuts. When I got back, Bob and Amanda were deep into a discussion of methods of coloring with crayons, with Amanda demonstrating a particular stroke by coloring Sleeping Beauty's face a bright blue, a work which she interrupted in order to take the can of soda.

"Thank you, Mr. Mollock-k-k," she said. "I was getting really thirsty."

"You're welcome. My name is Mollock. Just one 'kuh' sound."

She considered the merits of the suggestion for a moment. "Okay, Mr. Mollock. Did I do it right that time?"

"Perfectly."

She continued her artistic demonstration, and Bob offered the occasional suggestion and so did I, interspersed with some conversation between ourselves. Bob and I each accepted Amanda's invitation to color a page in her book.

It wasn't too boring and, after about an hour, Roger came out of the back.

"Daddy!" Amanda squealed and jumped up to run to him.

Bob and I followed a little more slowly as we both grabbed at books and bag which had gone flying.

"Is Mama coming home now?" Amanda asked after a big hug was administered.

"No, not yet," Roger responded. He put her back down and looked at me. "They've admitted her for at least overnight, for observation and tests. They're taking her to a room now."

I nodded at Bob. "This is Bob Dunn, who got Audrey out of her car and brought her here."

Roger shook Bob's hand enthusiastically. "Thank you very much for that. I'm really grateful to you both for all you did. You've been a huge help with both of my ladies today."

"I'm just glad I was there to help," said Bob. "How is Audrey doing?"

"They took X-rays of her head and neck and didn't see any damage. She definitely has a little bit of a concussion, but it seems to be pretty slight. Her staying here is more caution than real medical necessity. She told me you wanted to give her a Band-Aid and send her back out, and it looks like you were right."

"Well, I'm very relieved to have been right. My skills as a medic are pretty rusty so I wasn't sure."

After a little more such conversation consisting largely of Roger thanking us profusely and our expressing relief at the good report, Bob stood up. "Well. It looks like things are okay here and I need to get home to my wife. Roger, you take good care of your two ladies."

"I certainly will do my best," Roger said as Bob headed out for home.

"Are you ready to head home, too?" I asked Roger. "I can take you anytime."

"Thank you. Yes, I guess we need to get Amanda home for some late supper."

As we gathered up Amanda's books and art supplies, Roger hesitated. "I forgot to find out where Bob lives. I must do something for him after his being such a help today. Do you know him?"

"No, but the sign on his truck door said 'Bob's Plumbing' with a local telephone number so you can probably find him pretty easily."

"Good. I'm going to try"

"Daddy, I'm hungry."

"I know you are, sweetheart, and we'll get something to eat as soon as we can after we get home."

I saw an opportunity and took it. "It's pretty late to

start cooking," I said. "Why don't we stop for a hamburger on the way home?"

Roger made a perfunctory objection, but Amanda squealed in delight. "Ooh! Can we go to Barney's? I want some french fries." She accompanied the request with a pleading look at Roger that would have done credit to the best that one of us could do.

"Now how can you say no to that sweet face?" I said to Roger.

He smiled back in surrender. "It's hard, but to be a parent you have to learn how. But not tonight. Barney's Burger Barn for supper."

Amanda cheered and we gathered her stuff—again! After Roger thanked Mrs. McDonnell, we headed out the door to the car.

"You'll have to give me directions," I said as I backed out. "I've never been to Barney's before."

"They have the best french fries!" Amanda exclaimed.

"Well, I'm looking forward to trying them. If you will point me toward it."

"It's right next to Wally Mart," said Amanda.

Roger and I both laughed.

"Wally Mart I can find," I said and headed toward the big store by the mall.

Much of the rest of the ride was spent discussing french fries and burgers at the various fast food places in town and, while Amanda was obviously familiar with and approving of all of them, she was adamant that Barney's had the best fries. But I noticed that Roger seemed preoccupied and had little to add to our scintillating gustatory discussion of the merits of fatty foods.

I found the restaurant that had the sign with the big purple lizard with just enough individuality to avoid any copyright suits and, for once, got the parking place closest to the door, which made me worry that I was about to have a nasty surprise. We ordered. Amanda got the Merry Meal that came in a purple plastic lizard, and I got the biggest, greasiest double decker on the menu board and a "Super Colossal French Fries" to go with a large strawberry milk shake and apple pie.

When we sat down, Roger looked skeptically at my tray full of food. "How can you eat like that and not be grossly fat?"

I grinned. "I very seldom get to eat like this and I like to take advantage of the opportunities when I get them."

"Meaning your wife keeps watch over your eating like mine does for me."

"Something like that."

He took a bite of his chicken sandwich and Amanda looked disapproving. "Daddy, we haven't said the blessing yet."

We all folded our hands and she recited the "God is great" blessing as she'd learned it at Miss Emmy's Daycare and we all dug in. Amanda ate half of her burger quickly and then started showing us some creative ways to eat french fries, with and without ketchup, mostly involving wiggling them as she put them into her mouth.

I quickly agreed with her that Barney's Burger Barn had some very good food. Amanda and I had a good time comparing the merits of the various food items which we were eating. Roger didn't add much to the conversation, seemed to have his mind elsewhere, and missed out on the fun.

After finishing all the food, we cleaned up and left, briefly delayed by Amanda's inability to find Andrea the doll whom she had set in the window behind her seat. So finally, all present, we headed to their house. Amanda had been through a rough day and promptly went to sleep, and I spent the ride convincing Roger to let me take them to the hospital and to work the next day.

"I know your cars are both out of commission and I'm going by to see Audrey myself so we can just all ride together."

"But don't you have a job to do?" he asked me.

"Yes, but as of right now I don't know how my work will be scheduled." There was no way I could know what my schedule was until I got it set with him, but I couldn't tell him that or that his family was my job. "If there is a crisis I have to tend to, I'll let you know." Of course, his crisis was what I had to tend to, but I still didn't know what I was supposed to do or how to go about doing it. I just had to keep going along with events and watch for opportunities.

He agreed to let me take them in the morning, with some relief, and we carried Amanda, bag, car seat, and Andrea inside the house. After another round of thanks, I headed off. I stopped by a grocery store and bought a bag of chocolate covered peanuts, some little cakes called Strawberry Twirls, and a big bottle of Raspberry Red soda.

Then I went to the motel where there was already a room reserved for me, checked in, got some ice, and settled in for an evening of eating junk food and watching cable television, followed by a long hot shower and a few hours of sleep. I certainly try to make the most of my earthly senses while I'm here. I haven't always had it so nice. Once, in Africa, I spent three weeks in a cold rain sleeping under trees and sharing everything, including my blood, with hordes of insects, leeches, and other unidentified protein seekers. It was well worth it, though. We got a five-year-old girl away from a slave camp and back to her village, where she grew up to be the first convert to the faith, wife of an Abyssinian missionary, and the mother of the founder of the church in that tribe.

But this trip, I had a nice warm, soft bed, and I got to

guzzle sweet soda, eat candy and cake, and watch classic cartoon movies about princesses. I enjoyed every minute of it.

഑ഈ഑

The next morning Amanda was still tired and a little cranky. Roger was little better and still troubled, understandably. We loaded Amanda, her car seat, and bag—with no Andrea the doll—and headed toward the hospital. Given their rather poor moods, it was probably fortunate that there was little conversation.

But that changed when we passed one of the popular fast food joints which sold breakfast.

"Look over there," I said to Roger, pointing at the now-dented truck with "Bob's Plumbing" painted on the door. "Weren't you wanting to see him?"

Roger nodded and Amanda squealed happily. "Can I get an egg sandwich? I didn't get any breakfast yet."

Roger chuckled. "Since I've been reported as a negligent parent, I guess we can stop and see Mr. Dunn."

We stopped and went in. I looked around for Bob. It took some searching, but I finally saw him sitting with a group of several people about his age. He had been hard to see behind a lady in a wheel chair, whom he was feeding very small portions of milkshake in a spoon.

I waited for Roger to get through the line with Amanda's egg sandwich and pointed him toward Bob.

We all went over and waited while Bob held a napkin to the woman's chin to wipe off some leaking milkshake.

"Hi, Mr. Dunn," Roger said when Bob had finished. "I'm glad to run into you here. I want to thank you again for helping Audrey yesterday."

"You're quite welcome, again," Bob said as he put another tiny bite of milkshake in her mouth. "I am just glad that Sam and I were there to help out."

I noticed that the lady he was feeding barely made chewing motions and never moved her head, staring straight forward and showing no sign of being aware that we were there.

"And it was good to get to know Miss Amanda," Bob continued, "so it was all for the best."

After a few more statements of mutual admiration and Roger's promise to call Bob for any future plumbing work, we headed out, but Bob called Roger back. "Would it be okay if I went by to see Audrey in the hospital?"

"She would be glad to see you. Please do."

We headed toward the hospital again with the mood lifted considerably. "I wonder who the lady was," Roger mused. "Probably his wife or a relative of some sort."

"It's a little strange that he didn't introduce us or even mention her," I said. "But did you notice that she seemed unaware of us or of anything else?"

"Yeah. I noticed she ate and drank whatever Bob gave her but didn't seem to make any response to anything else."

"Well, we all have our burdens." I said.

"And our blessings, too," Roger said, smiling. "Like three-year-old girls with egg on their faces."

Amanda took the hint and rubbed vigorously with a napkin on the wrong side of her mouth.

We arrived at the hospital, parked, and went up to Room 1218. Just as we were about to open the door, we heard someone in the room begin to cough deeply and uncontrollably. We all waited with Roger looking worried. When the terrible coughing finally quit, Roger opened the door.

"Mommy!" Amanda shouted as soon as she saw Audrey and went running into the room.

Audrey put down the handkerchief and they were soon entangled in a tight bear hug.

Roger followed more slowly and set the bag he'd brought on the chair. "Hi, honey," he said. "How are you feeling?"

"My head is a lot better," Audrey replied, disentangling herself. "How are the two of you doing?"

"I had an egg sandwich," Amanda announced proudly.

"And I brought you one, too," Roger said, holding out a paper wrapped biscuit. "In case you didn't like hospital food."

Audrey took the sandwich and sat up. "The food has been fine, but I'll eat this, too. Thank you and you're forgiven for not making breakfast for our daughter."

Then she noticed me standing in the door and smiled. "Hello, Mr. Perfume."

"My name is Sam Mollock," I said. "I'm glad you're feeling better."

"Mr. Mollock is taking me to school today. And he took us to Barney's last night."

"Well, Mr. Mollock seems to run quite a taxi service. Thank you so much for everything."

I nodded. "I was glad to get to know everybody and to get introduced to Barney's french fries."

Then she began to cough again—long, deep coughs that obviously hurt and which she didn't seem to be able to stop.

When the spell finally passed, Roger frowned. "How long have you been doing that?"

"I woke up coughing about three this morning. I guess I'm getting a cold."

"Sounds more like pneumonia. Did you tell the nurse?"

"No, it didn't seem important when she was in here. Besides, the doctor came by about six and told me that I was fine and could go home this afternoon."

"*Yay*!" shouted Amanda, bouncing up and down. "Mommy's coming home!"

"Do I need to take the day off?"

"No. I know your meeting today is very important and you would just sit around here waiting and worrying. Go to your meeting and then come get me."

"I hope the car is fixed by then," Roger said.

"If it isn't, I can drive you again," I said.

"I hate to impose and, if the car isn't ready, I need to rent one. We can't impose on you any longer."

"I enjoy it and I don't have anything scheduled today."

"What work do you do, Mr. Mollock?" Audrey asked.

"Please call me Sam. I'm a troubleshooter for the church. Some of our people here need some help, but as yet, I don't have instructions so I'm just waiting at the moment."

"What church?"

"We're a nondenominational agency."

Fortunately, Roger announced that it was time to get Amanda to school, so I didn't have to dance around any more answers to questions. With considerable bustle, hugs, and kisses among the three of them, we were out the door and soon on the road again.

Amanda had a good time giving me directions to Miss Emmy's Daycare, and I was impressed that she knew exactly where to turn and knew the street names, too. Roger took her into the building and was out quickly.

"Are you going to be on time for your meeting?" I asked as I pulled back into traffic.

"Yeah, it's not until nine. Besides, I'm the star attraction today and they can't start without me."

"You're that important?"

"For today's meeting and the project we're meeting about, yeah. I am. And the success of that project is very important to my future in the company."

"Is that why you've been so gloomy?"

Roger looked startled. "What do you mean?"

"You just got really good news from the hospital, and you're still acting depressed and in a bad mood. I can understand why you were feeling down and out yesterday, but today you should be a lot happier."

He shrugged. "The news from Audrey was wonderful, and it certainly takes a big load off of me, and sure, I'm a lot happier."

I smiled and chuckled to take some of the sting away. "Not enough happier for me to notice. Or for Amanda to notice."

Instead of showing anger or irritation, Roger slumped down and folded his arms. After a few moments, he sighed. "Dodging one disaster doesn't mean that you don't have still more bad troubles headed your way."

"I must admit the truth of that statement," I said. "What's the next disaster on the horizon?"

Roger straightened a little. "The project I'm working on. There are some big problems with it, and I haven't decided how to deal with them."

"Will this meeting help you decide?"

"Maybe."

With that statement closing off further questions on that subject, we discussed the weather—nice—and the traffic—bad, and getting worse every year—until we arrived at his office building.

"I'll be right here at five this afternoon," I told him as he got out and retrieved his briefcase from the back seat. I brushed aside a last pro forma objection, and he went inside. I headed back to the hospital.

Inside, I made a quick trip to the cafeteria for coffee and a doughnut. Then, since propriety indicated a wait before going back to see Audrey, I made a couple of random visits to some patients, including one in intensive care where I wasn't technically supposed to be, but I put on a white smock that I got out of a laundry cart and walked right in. I'd long ago learned that if you wear the right things and act like you belong and like you know what you're doing, you can go almost anywhere. If I'd had a stethoscope around my neck, I probably could have performed surgery. At any rate, I was very glad I went in there because the patient was a retired historian who had specialized in England during the Dark Ages, and since I had been there on a few occasions, we had a grand time comparing notes. He was particularly interested in my knowledge of a small monastery in Kent which was mentioned in two texts. I had been there for two months working in the weaving room, but my main focus had been a peasant family on the neighboring manor whom I had to convince to become runaways in the forest in order to get them in place to found a hospice for other forest dwellers, which resulted in the conversion of a young escaped slave named Patrick. Of course, the retired teacher wanted to know all of my sources of information, and I had to be vague, but we both enjoyed a lively hour.

By then it was time to head to Audrey's room and, as the elevator doors opened to let me on, I was pleasantly surprised to see Bob the plumber.

"Hi, Sam," he said. "Are you headed up to see Audrey?"

"Yes, but I'm surprised to see you here now. Aren't you working today?"

"I will be but I had to bring my wife Bonnie in. You saw her at breakfast. She had a seizure this morning, and I brought her in for treatment. She's in the treatment room now so I decided to go up and see Audrey."

"How serious was her seizure?"

"Not very. Normally they're pretty mild, like this one. There's a standard treatment but it takes a while, so she'll be here two days at least. The one today should be no big problem."

"Last night I heard Mrs. McDonnell ask if she was here. That sounds like you two are frequent visitors to the emergency room."

"Not really often but enough to get to know the staff there. Bonnie has a very rare neurological problem. It's degenerative and there are a few treatments for the symptoms like the seizures, but they can't treat the actual problem. In fact, they don't even know what causes it, much less how to treat it. And it's so rare it doesn't even have an official name yet."

I gave a sympathetic look "It must be pretty hard on you, too."

Bob shrugged. "Yeah, but we both vowed 'for better or for worse.' I'm sure she would do it for me. The really bad part isn't the work but having to watch her get worse and worse and to know she won't ever get any better."

"I noticed at breakfast that she seemed pretty unresponsive."

"She hasn't been able to talk for about six months and hasn't responded directly to anything spoken for about three months. She can still eat and drink a little, but mostly gets her meals through a feeding tube. I think maybe she can at least taste the things I put in her mouth but I sometimes doubt she actually knows she's eating, and she's getting slower at it and less able. I don't think she'll be doing that much longer."

The elevator stopped and we went out into the hall, giving him the opportunity to cough and wipe his eyes without being obvious.

I pretended not to notice. "Do you have any help with her?"

"Oh, sure. I couldn't handle it alone and still work. Her brother's widow lives down the street from us and spends the day with her most days, and when she can't, one of several ladies from our church will come and stay for a while. Thank Heaven for church folks."

"Amen."

He knocked on Audrey's door and we heard a rather weak, "Come in" in response. When we went in, we saw why the response was weak. Audrey was laying back against the slightly raised bed, pale and obviously weak and tired.

Bob frowned. "Hi, Audrey. Are you okay?"

"I don't know. I've been coughing and can't stop. It hurts to breathe and coughing hurts bad."

"Did you tell the nurse?"

Audrey nodded. "She said she would bring me some cough medicine, but I haven't seen her since."

I moved up to the bed. "Do you want me to check on it?"

"I hate to be a bother."

Bob shook his head at her. "You should hate worse to be sick and hurting. We'll see what can be done."

He took her nurse call button and pushed it.

Just then she started coughing again, deep harsh coughs which obviously hurt badly and deeply. But the coughs grew weaker and weaker as though she couldn't take in enough air to cough any more.

She finally stopped. "Every time I do that, it hurts worse," she said in a very weak voice. "And I'm coughing up blood, now."

"That's serious," Bob said. "You should make a fuss about it until they check it out."

She began to cough again, but slowly, as though she had no energy or air.

Suddenly she stopped, her eyes rolled back, and she fell back against the pillow, unconscious.

Bob, looking very alarmed, reached for her, straightened her out on the bed, checked her eyes, put his hand on her chest which wasn't moving, and quickly checked her pulse. "Get the nurse! Quick!" he shouted after only a couple of seconds, jumped onto the bed, and began to administer CPR to the inert Audrey.

But before I could get to the door, a nurse came in, apparently in response to the call light. "Respiratory arrest and no pulse!" Bob shouted at her without stopping. "Get a doctor in here!"

The nurse hurried out and, in a few seconds, we heard a bell begin to ring insistently. Bob continued to keep pumping on her chest. "Can you do mouth to mouth?" he asked me.

"I think so."

"Then do it," he barked in his best army sergeant voice.

This was a first for me, but I knew the theory. I went to the bed and did the best I could for a few minutes until a team of three people and a highly equipped gurney burst through the door. I moved away but Bob kept at it until they had the gurney lined up next to the bed, then he moved aside as they very efficiently moved Audrey to the gurney and began hooking various tubes and devices to her even as they wheeled it out the door being held open by the nurse, who followed after them, letting the door close.

In the sudden calm, Bob and I stood in near shock for a moment, then he went to the chair and flopped into it.

After a few moments of recovery, he rubbed his eyes tiredly. "This has been a really bad day." He ruffled his hair. "And it's not even ten o'clock yet."

I sat on the bed. "There's a good side to it," I said. "If you hadn't been here, it would have been a lot longer before she got any help."

He opened one eye and looked at me. "I guess you're

right. In fact, I expect she'd have died before they found her."

"So actually, I think you could say it's a really good day, and you were here for a reason," I suggested with a comforting look.

He smiled tiredly. "Maybe. But it's not been good for Audrey. Or Bonnie, my wife."

We sat silently for several minutes while our heartbeats got back to normal and the adrenalin went out of our systems. Bob was half reclined in the big chair and was so still that I thought he might have gone to sleep. If I had been in a more comfortable seat, I could have gone to sleep myself.

But he opened his eyes and looked at the ceiling. "We need to let Roger know about this. But I have no idea how to get hold of him. Do you?"

"He works at Cedar Crossing Financial Services, and their offices are in an office complex on Redmond Street, just past the airport."

He looked questioningly at me. "A two-story brick building with four big white columns and a drive-through on the left side?"

I nodded.

"I know it. I did some of the plumbing during the construction a few years back and have been back once since then to replace a sink."

He sat up, opened the drawer of the nightstand beside the chair, and began to search through it, taking out a phone book. He looked at the cover. "Only two years old. Close enough." He flipped through the pages. "Here. Cedar Crossing Finance Company on Second Street. They seem to have moved up in status since two years ago." He took out his cell phone and dialed the number. "Let's see if they still have the same phone number." After a few seconds wait, he said, "May I speak to Roger Steiner, please." Another few seconds. "I see. When will the meeting be over?" He chuckled. "Yes, ma'am, I understand. My crystal ball is in the shop this week, too. Can I get a message to him?" Again a wait. "Certainly. After the meeting would be okay. Would you tell him that he needs to come to the hospital? There's a problem with Audrey."

He clicked it off and put it away. After another couple of minutes of gazing at the ceiling, he sat up. "It will be a good while before he gets here. I think I'll go get a cup of coffee from the cafeteria. Would you like one?"

"Sure. Do they still have some doughnuts, too?"

"Let's go find out."

Fortunately, the cafeteria had doughnuts and cherry pie. I couldn't decide which looked better, so I got both. And a Twinkie for good measure. At the register, I was very glad for the invention of credit cards. They certainly were handier than a bag of coins, especially the heavy gold ones and they were not nearly as attractive to thieves, like happened to me once in Greece where I spent half a day running and hiding from a gang of robbers.

We come over with a full set of defensive skills and some other tools which I'm not supposed to reveal but using them is a last resort since it's not often our job to hurt people, even ones who deserve it. Besides, one of the robbers later turned around and became the bishop of Salonika and the father of an important missionary. That kind of thing helps me to remember that the Boss's main business here is to help people repent to keep from getting punishment they deserve.

We sat at a table and ate and drank in silence for a minute.

"I'm glad you knew how to help me with CPR," Bob said after finishing his doughnut. "Where did you learn?"

"I've never done it before," I replied.

"Well, you seemed to know how. Are you certified?"

"No. I just learned the basics somewhere along the way."

"Everybody ought to learn. Was it part of your job training?"

I shrugged. "I guess you could say that."

"What is your line of work?"

"I'm a troubleshooter for our church headquarters."

"What brings you here?"

"We're interested in some possibilities in this town, and I came to investigate and help out where I can." This conversation was getting troublesome, and I didn't like getting backed into a corner so I changed the subject. "What church are you a part of?"

"New Market Independent Presbyterian."

"They're the folks who help you and Bonnie out?"

"Yep. They have been great about a lot of things. What denomination do you work for?"

"We're nondenominational, or rather cross denominational. We work with anybody."

Fortunately, I've got a battery of standard answers to counter most such questions, but we're supposed to stay away from such conversations as much as possible, and, again fortunately, I got the conversation turned to his experiences as a Sunday School teacher and plumber.

After telling me a funny story about a ten-year-old's strange concept of Moses at the Red Sea and another about a man's cat who got stuck in a pipe, he stood. "I think we should go to the front lobby and watch for Roger. Do you have time to wait around some more?"

"Sure," I said. "I don't have anything scheduled for today. Don't you need to be at work?"

Bob shook his head. "The job I was going to do today is a construction site where nothing else will get done until next week, so if it doesn't get done until tomorrow, it's not a problem."

"Good. I think Roger might need some moral support today."

We sat in the front lobby for about an hour with half-hearted conversation and less than halfhearted watching of the sports channel on the television. But I noticed that most of the time, when we weren't talking, Bob would stare at me, as though he were trying to figure something out.

After about an hour, we saw a station wagon pull up to the front door. Roger got out of the passenger side, waved to the driver, and hurried in. We met him and he seemed nearly frantic, on the verge of losing control.

"What's going on?" he asked.

Bob quickly explained what had happened while leading us to the patient information desk.

"But since we're not family, they aren't allowed to tell us anything more, but you can find out," Bob told him.

Roger explained the situation to the lady behind the desk. She dialed a number and handed the phone over the desk to him.

After a brief conversation, he grew even paler. "Okay," he said, handing the phone back to the lady. "Where is the waiting room for surgery?"

She pointed and started to give directions but Bob interrupted. "I'll take him. Thank you very much, ma'am," he said and led the way down the hall, up an elevator, and into another waiting room, which was empty except for us. Roger picked up the special white phone which had no buttons, identified himself, and hung up.

A couple of minutes later, a nurse came into the room. "Mr. Steiner?" she asked.

We all stood up and went to her.

"That's me," Roger responded.

"Your wife is in surgery. They have her heartbeat going again, but she isn't breathing. She's on a respirator and they're doing tests and some other procedures to try to find out why her lungs have shut down. The surgeon will come talk to you when he gets finished."

Roger nodded and would have turned even paler, except he was already as far as he could go in that direction.

He blindly backed to the closest seat, fell into it, and then he did lose it, crying uncontrollably and sobbing. Bob looked embarrassed for a moment but then sat down next to Roger and put both arms around him in a big hug. Roger responded with more sobbing and leaned into Bob. I got the box of tissues off the table and set it down beside them.

Roger continued to cry for a while and then straightened up, took the tissues, and began to clean up.

After a couple of minutes of nose-blowing and sniffling, he shook his head. "I am very embarrassed now. That wasn't exactly movie tough guy material."

"Don't worry about it," Bob said, passing a waste can over to him. "I've done the same thing myself a couple of times. In this very room, as a matter of fact. And I was blessed enough to have some friends here to hug me, too. So I'm glad to have the chance to pass it along to you. There are times to be tough and times to let it go. This was a time when being tough wouldn't have helped a thing."

"I guess," Roger said, getting another tissue and working on his face some more. "At least I can hope I've gotten that out of my system, now."

He leaned over, his elbows on his knees, and put his face in his hands. "This has been a really bad day."

He looked up, surprised and a little shocked when Bob and I laughed.

Bob quickly explained, "Those are the exact words I

said right after Audrey was taken to surgery. And we're both quite right. It's been a terrible day."

Then I explained to Roger that Bob had brought his wife in for treatment and how he had administered CPR to Audrey and probably saved her life.

After sitting silently for a few moments, Roger sighed. "That's certainly one bright spot in the really bad day. I seem to be letting the two of you take care of things for me while I brood and mope around."

"Everybody needs some help every now and then," Bob said. "I couldn't handle things with Bonnie and work, without several people helping me out a lot. So just pass it along to somebody else when you get the chance."

"While we're on that subject," I put in, "you certainly have been brooding. You brushed me off this morning, but what's this big crisis at work you've got cooking?" Of course, I'd been brushing off even more questions than he had, but I decided a direct approach was needed. "Tell us about it."

Roger looked a little indecisive. "This morning at work I got a phone call from the insurance company. The truck that exploded was an illegal hauler, wasn't regis-tered or insured, and was hauling toxic waste. The driver was burned up so badly that they're having trouble find-ing enough pieces to identify him. So we may not have any coverage for the car or the hospital stay."

Bob grimaced sympathetically. "You're right again. 'This has been a really bad day.' And I know what that's like. I'm in a little bit of the same fix. Just before I was going to retire from a factory job seven years ago, we found out that some crooked dealings had wiped out the company, including the pension fund. The crooks got caught, but the company went bankrupt so I was left with no job and no pension. That's why I'm crawling under houses fixing pipes at my age."

Roger looked up at Bob as if he'd gotten a shock. "What happened?"

Bob shrugged. "I don't know much of the details. Somebody made some risky loans with the pension money, and it went into bankruptcy. Turned out the loans were crooked and some folks got the money and kept it. There are a lot of lawyers working on it for us. Maybe someday I'll get a little something out of it. Not as much as the lawyers are getting, though."

"Aren't the regulators on it?"

"They are now, but that's closing the barn door after the horse is already out."

"So what are you doing now?"

Bob chuckled. "Working hard most every day and scraping by. Fortunately, Bonnie had a pretty good hospitalization plan so that helps a lot but it doesn't pay everything. But thankfully business has been good, and I'm keeping my head above water. But sometimes just barely."

Just then the door opened and a man in rather well-used surgical scrubs came into the room. "Mr. Steiner?"

Again all three of us got up and went over to him, but this time both Bob and I pointed to Roger.

"Yes?" Roger asked, a little nervously.

"I'm Dr. Holt. Your wife's heart is beating on its own now, but she's not breathing. She's on a respirator getting oxygen, and that's helping some but she's still unconscious." He grimaced. "It doesn't look very promising. We can't be certain but there is probably some brain damage from lack of oxygen. Right now, the main problem though is her lungs. They're very badly damaged, basically destroyed, and are only functioning at a very low rate, not nearly enough. The only real hope would be a lung transplant, but the waiting list is long, and there isn't any way…" He trailed off with a sigh. "Right now the oxygen and respirator are keeping her alive, but that will only last for a few days. Her lungs are showing some kind of extreme reaction, as if they had been burned, but it's not typical flame damage. Did she breathe any flames in the accident?"

"I don't know. I wasn't there, but both of these gentlemen were."

The doctor looked at us.

"There was a fire but it was small, and she certainly didn't breathe any flames that I saw." He looked at me and I shook my head.

"There weren't enough flames to breathe if we had tried," I said.

"But there was a lot of smoke," Bob went on, "and I'm sure she got several good breaths of it. She was coughing some right after we got her out."

"Could you tell what was burning?" the doctor asked. "Cars don't normally burst into flames from an impact."

"The piece that fell on the car was full of some kind of blue liquid and some of it ran into the engine compartment of her car," Bob said, clearly remembering the same thing that I had. He turned to Roger. "And you were told that the truck was carrying toxic waste."

The doctor nodded. "That fits. Where is the car now?"

"Mitchell Towing hauled it." Roger said, "It's probably in their impoundment lot. They can tell us."

The doctor headed for the door. "I'll send a crew out there to see if we can determine what that stuff was." He stopped and turned to us. "Will you be around here for a while?"

We all nodded.

"Good, we may need to ask some more questions." And he was gone in a hurry.

Roger sat down, put his face in his hands, and began to cry again, quietly. Bob sat next to him and put a hand on his shoulder. I did the same. For several minutes, we just sat there, silently. Then Roger stood, walked to the window, and looked out for a long time. While he was doing that, Bob and I kept silent, but I noticed that Bob would stare at me, as if he was still trying to figure something out.

After a while, Bob suggested we get some lunch, with which I am always in agreement, but Roger replied that he wasn't hungry.

"Doesn't matter," Bob said. "You need to eat. Not eating won't help anything. So let's get some food."

"What if the doctor comes back while we're gone?" Roger asked.

"They'll page us and we can hear it in the cafeteria. Let's go."

So we all trooped to the cafeteria and had fried chicken, mashed potatoes, and broccoli, which I topped off with chocolate cake. And a big cup of cherry-pomegranate soda. Although Roger had denied being hungry, once he got started, he polished it all off.

Lunch conversation studiously avoided the main subject on our minds and devoted itself to baseball scores, about which I knew nothing; stock performance, about which I knew even less; and local politics, which were a total mystery to me. I guess I was less than a wonderful conversationalist, but they seemed to do all right without me.

We had just gotten back to the hall outside the waiting room when we heard the loudspeaker ask for "Roger Steiner to the surgical waiting room, please."

By the time it had repeated the announcement, we were in the waiting room and Roger picked up the white phone.

"Yes," he said and identified himself. "Where is it?" Then he hung up and turned to us. "Dr. Holt wants to see me in the surgical office. I'm scared to death. You two come with me."

"Sure," Bob said and led the way out.

The surgical office was down a long hall, around a corner, and well marked so that it was easy to find, but apparently Bob had been there before and knew the way. Roger knocked and we went in. Dr. Holt was behind the desk with two very thick books open in front of him and a computer screen behind him showing some meaning-less—to me—but very complex looking chemical formu-lae. He told us to have a seat. We did.

"I just got the report of the material that was burning on Mrs. Steiner's car. It's a very rare compound with a name about three lines long. The bad news is that it's ex-tremely toxic and corrosive, and smoke from it is equally nasty. It's clear that your wife got a large amount of it into her lungs, and every breath she took, and especially every cough, spread it further." He rubbed his face. "I'm afraid I can't hold out any hope for her. There isn't any treatment that will reverse the damage. I'm very sorry."

Roger nodded and looked down, already numb emo-tionally.

"How did that stuff get there," Bob asked. "Was the truck full of it?'

"No, otherwise, we'd be evacuating the whole city. We've got enough trouble handling the burns and smoke inhalation from the gasoline the truck was hauling. We're not sure but apparently there was just a little of the nasty blue stuff in the truck's pump and that was what hit her car. The truck tank was full of contaminated gasoline. It had apparently just hauled a load of the blue compound and had just a little of it still in the pump. Only two com-panies use the compound and both of them are reputable companies who are cooperating completely. The EPA is already checking into who did the disposal of the stuff, but that doesn't help Mrs. Steiner. I'm very sorry."

Roger looked up. "Will she regain consciousness again?"

Dr. Holt looked sad and shook his head. "With the extremely low level of brain function possible on the amount of oxygen she's getting, that's not a realistic hope. She will continue like she is for a few days but beyond that—" He shook his head again.

"So she's effectively already dead," Roger said without expression.

"Not yet, but short of—it won't be long."

Bob grimaced. "Sam and I were right at the car and the smoke, are we going to have lung damage, too?"

"Not likely. If you had gotten enough of the smoke to do damage, you would already be showing symptoms. You both need to watch carefully and, if you show any symptoms of respiratory distress, get it checked out immediately. But if it hasn't shown up by now, it probably won't."

"Good. Thank you," Bob said, obviously relieved.

We went back to the waiting room, with Roger showing all the life and awareness of a rock, something which continued for some time after we sat on the couch.

"I have to get Amanda from daycare," he said suddenly.

I stood up. "All right, let's go."

Roger stood up and headed for the door like an airplane on autopilot. Bob got up, too. "Mind if I tag along?" he asked.

Roger kept moving, unhearing.

"We'd be glad to have you," I replied, and we all headed to the parking lot.

The drive to Miss Emmy's was carried out in almost complete silence. Roger was apparently in complete emotional overload. Bob and I just let him sort out his own thoughts. At the daycare he went inside, still on automatic, but after a longer than expected wait, he came out with Amanda clasped in a big bear hug, and he was crying again. Instead of putting her in her seat, he opened Bob's door, set her in Bob's lap, went off a ways, and stood with his back to us.

"What's the matter with Daddy?" she asked, sounding a little frightened.

Bob got out and put her into her seat. "He's sad because some bad things happened today," Bob told her as he tried to figure out the straps on her seat. Finding the right combination, he buckled her in. "But don't worry. Your daddy is going to take good care of you because he loves you an awful lot."

"That's right. I certainly do," Roger said, coming up behind them, having regained control. "And for a special treat, you're going to spend the night at Carolyn's house tonight."

Amanda smiled uncertainly. "But can't I stay with you? Mommy's coming home tonight, isn't she?"

Roger got into the back seat next to her and looked out the window. "Mommy's not getting to come home, after all. But you'll have fun at Carolyn's, and her mom has promised to make popcorn."

"I love popcorn," Amanda said with a big smile, but the smile quickly went away. "But I want to see Mommy."

Roger reached over and squeezed her hand gently. "Well, tonight, you go have fun at Carolyn's house. Okay?"

"Can I go see Mommy before I go to Carolyn's?"

Roger sighed heavily. Bob and I traded a look at each other. I knew this was very hard for Roger but neither Bob nor I could offer any help.

"No, honey. Mommy's too sick to have any company

right now. So you just go have fun with Carolyn."

"Daddy, why is Mommy so sick?"

Roger sighed again. "That's real complicated and I don't know all of the answers myself. But part of it is that some people did something bad that they weren't supposed to do that made a big fire and the smoke from the fire made Mommy sick."

"Well, didn't those people know they weren't supposed to make that fire?"

"Yes, they knew that."

Amanda shook her head in indignation. "Well, if everybody would just do what they know is right, everything would be a whole lot better. Doing bad things hurts people."

Roger smiled. "You're absolutely right, sweetheart. A lot of grown-ups need to hear what you just said."

Bob and I were both quietly chuckling at her three-year-old wisdom.

"Mr. Mollock, would you please take us to Carolyn's house?" Roger said.

"I certainly will, if you will give me directions."

"She's our next door neighbor," Amanda answered. "And she has a spotted puppy."

We all laughed.

"Well, between popcorn and puppy, I think you should have a good time tonight," Bob replied.

We drove to their street while being entertained by Amanda's account of her day, which had included a visit by a policeman who had shown them his police car and even turned on the siren for them. "And it was loud!"

Roger carried Amanda and her seat into Carolyn's house, then went over to his house to pack her bag. It took a little longer than we expected, but he delivered the bag and Andrea the doll and came back to the car. "I'm sorry to take so long. While I was in the house, I got a phone call from my boss who needs me to come to his house for a few minutes. I hate to ask but would you mind taking me?"

"Not at all," I replied. "Bob, do you have any pressing engagements at the moment?"

"No. Do you?"

"Well," I replied, "somewhere in this town there is a steak with french fries waiting for me, but steaks are extremely patient, I believe. It can wait some more. Where is his house?"

 C/SC/S

The sun had set while we were driving. Bob and I sat in the car in the growing dark, again talking about nothing much. Roger's boss had a large house in an upscale neighborhood, an impressively sized pool in the back, and a more impressively sized car and SUV in the garage.

After a little while, the conversation dwindled to nothing. I was looking in the big window of the house at the impressive furnishings.

"You told Roger he was evading questions, but you are the world champion question evader," Bob said, breaking the silence and surprising me. "Who are you really?"

Being in human form has some distinct disadvantages and the cold, sinking feeling I got in my stomach then was one of those disadvantages. Not fun.

"What do you mean? I'm Sam Mollock, with a church agency."

"Which tells me nothing, and I think you mean for it to say nothing. What church? Where? And what are you doing here specifically?"

That cold feeling came back, colder and deeper. Right then I wished the Boss had made human emotions less hormonal and that adrenal glands were voluntary. "I explained all that," I said, still looking out the car window.

"You haven't explained anything. Like why everybody, including me, takes to you like a long-lost brother, and until now, we all just accept your non-answers as though they meant something."

I turned to look at him. "Do you think I'm a con artist?"

"That's occurred to me, but I don't think so. Neither Roger nor I have enough money to put much of a con on us, and I don't think a con artist of your skill would bother with such a small-time scam. I also remember several years ago, we had a pastor who was in seminary and all on fire to teach us in church everything he knew. He even taught a class in Hebrew which I went to. I don't remember much of the very little Hebrew I learned but one word has stuck with me. Malach—angel. Now, Sam *Mollock*, who are you really?"

The cold feeling went completely berserk then, and I felt myself go as pale as Roger had earlier. This was a first for me. I had come here openly several times, but on those occasions I had the wings and robe, so people would know immediately who and what I was. This time I was undercover—no wings, no robe, and no plan for this shock.

"Why can't I just be what I say I am?"

"I guess you might be that, but right now I don't believe it. You've been everywhere right where you need to be and right at the precise time you need to be there, and nobody questions it."

One of the things I liked about working on this side was the utter unpredictably of humans and events in time, but all of a sudden, I wasn't enjoying the unpredictably. In fact, I was terrified.

After all the trips I had made into time, this was the

first one where I had ever felt this particular human feeling—helplessness.

"What do you mean?"

"You're hiding something. Something important. But you're careful."

"So you think I'm intending harm?"

Bob laughed. "No, actually I'm convinced you're here to help. I'm just wondering if you're more high powered help than any of us expected. Tell me this and let's see if you can lie. Where were you before you came to our town?"

Now I was in a real fix. We're not supposed to actually lie except under extreme circumstances involving somebody being harmed and this wasn't one of those. To tell where I came from would violate my instructions to stay unrevealed, so I said nothing.

After a few moments, Bob laughed again. "So you can't tell a lie. That means you're not just a normal human. What is your mother's name?"

Again the best I could come up with was silence.

Bob chuckled. "Several years back I read the book of Tobit. That man spent a long time in the company of another man who turned out to be the Archangel Raphael. Is your real name Raphael?"

The cold sinking feeling came back and I had to take a deep breath. "No, my real name is Samuel. Raphael is my…uncle…I guess you could call it."

"Uncle?"

"He's a senior member of my family not in direct lineage, so 'uncle' is the best I can do. I'm in Uriel's legion."

"Where are your halo and wings?"

"We only use them to impress people. I'm not here to impress anybody."

"What are you here for?"

I shrugged. "I still don't know for sure. If you figure it

out, let me know. You seem to know as much as I do."

"In the Bible, the first thing angels usually say is 'Fear not.' How come I'm not afraid of you?"

"If you came across me suddenly, with wings and halo, glowing in the dark, and ten feet tall, you'd be afraid. As it is, you've had some time to get used to the idea and figure out that I'm not here to burn the city down."

"Was that you at Sodom and Gomorrah?"

"No, they were my cousins, from Michael's outfit. I'm not mentioned anywhere in the Bible. Except for the 'multitude of the heavenly host' who sang to the shepherds. We were all in on that."

Bob rubbed his face and sighed. "Wow. This is unreal. Either you're about to say 'April Fools—I gotcha,' or I'm about to wake up and find myself at home in bed. I really expected you to have normal answers and turn out to be a normal person. I have no idea how to deal with this."

I laughed. "Well, neither do I. But at least you don't have to go back and explain how and why you got discovered."

"Are you in trouble?"

"Not like you think. I've had things go wrong before. Once in Slovakia in the 1700s, I came over in full robe, wings, and halo and was a real Christmas angel on Christmas Eve, which was a lot of fun. I was there to give a young lady a special message. While I was announcing, her two year old son came up behind me and pulled my robe so hard that I lost my balance and almost fell down. Took most of the dignity out of the moment. Especially when the lady laughed so hard. But it all worked out. I still delivered the message, got to hold the boy and play with him for a while, and he went on to be an important teacher in the university and was an influence on Pasteur and Jenner."

"Can't you just snap your fingers and make everything all right?"

"I don't have a red 'S' on my shirt. The only power I have is what is specifically given to me. Which right now is nothing more than you have. If I need more, it will be given, but I don't know if that will happen. On a job like this one, it's not likely. My task this time is persuasion, not power. Right now, I'm flesh and blood like you and have about the same limits. "

"'About the same'?"

"I have some more information, but not everything, and I don't know the future any more than you do. The big worry I have right now is what's got Roger so upset at work. I've got a feeling that is a big part of my job here."

Bob looked at the house. "Well, I think this meeting tonight is a crisis point for it. Why else would he leave Audrey to go to work? It has to be a critical point for something."

Just then Roger and another man came into view in the big window. They seemed to be arguing about something and both were obviously agitated.

We could see Roger take a big breath, calm himself, and say something to the other man. Whatever he said, the other didn't like it. He got very agitated and started jabbing his finger at Roger several times. I couldn't tell but I could easily guess that his face was very red.

Bob stirred and reached for the door. "Maybe I should—"

"No, wait," I said. "I think this is one Roger has to handle himself."

So we sat still and, in a few minutes, Roger came out and got into the back seat.

Bob turned around. "I think today just got even worse."

Roger sighed and deflated. "Yeah. Sam, would you mind taking me back to the hospital?"

I started the car and pulled out.

Bob sat back and buckled his seat belt. "But before you get out of this car again, you're going to tell us what's going on. You've danced around it and hemmed and hawed but now you're going to talk. So spill it."

Roger sat in silence for a couple of minutes. I stopped at a red light and turned around to look at him. "This might be something you have to do yourself, but you don't have to do all the worrying and thinking by yourself. Some loads can be shared."

I went back to driving and Bob took over. "As you said it's been a really bad day, and we can tell that you're undecided about something important. Is your problem anything that it would help to talk about?"

"You're right about my being undecided. I'm a project manager of a very large financial account…"

The rest of the explanation, which went on for several minutes, involved financial words and concepts that I wasn't at all familiar with, surprisingly.

I generally had whatever human knowledge I needed to do my job, once including detailed knowledge of the spice trade and Italian banking in thirteenth-century Genoa, where I was helping to get a university started, mostly by begging for money from wealthy spice merchants.

But apparently my job here didn't involve finance, because I had no idea what "receivership" or "Chapter 11" meant, and I would have expected a "court-appointed custodian" to sweep up in the jury room.

"Bob," I interrupted, "Are you understanding any of this?"

"Unfortunately, yes. It's some of the same type of things we're dealing with in my own case. They're basically asking you to loot the insurance company and transfer the funds to a shadow corporation?"

Roger nodded. "And it's at least arguably legal because I have court-directed authority."

Bob grunted. "And since the company is already on the ropes, you can probably make it look legitimate."

"Right. It would actually be legitimate."

Bob grunted again, disgustedly. "But it wouldn't be right."

I expect he was thinking about his own bankrupt pension fund.

We drove in silence for a couple of minutes.

"Amanda said earlier today that 'if everybody would just do what they know is right,'" Roger said very softly, as if to himself, "'everything would be a whole lot better. Doing bad things hurts people.'"

Bob grunted again. He was getting good at it. "Amanda seems to be a lady of great wisdom."

"But it's not as simple as it looks to a three-year-old. If I don't do it, my company can get the court to take me off of the case, appoint one of them. It still happens, they all get rich, and I get fired, having accomplished nothing."

Expecting another grunt, I looked at Bob. Instead, he turned around and looked at Roger. "Why *isn't* it as simple as it looks to her? She was exactly right. 'Doing bad things hurts people.' And you're thinking about doing a bad thing that will hurt some people. What's so complex?"

"It's complex because I'm broke, no car, a huge hospital bill, my wife is dying, and I can't see how losing my pretty good job is going to help anybody." Roger was angry now, and sounded it.

I pulled into the hospital lot. "Visiting hours are over. Will they let us in?"

Bob pointed to a loading dock. "Park by that dock. It stays unlocked and we can get in that way."

It was good to have somebody who knew the ropes. Even if the ropes involved unauthorized entry.

The loading dock was littered and smelly from a large trash can but the door was unlocked. We went in and made our way up to the surgical area. Instead of going into the waiting room, Roger went down the hall. "I'm going in to see Audrey," he said.

So Bob and I went into the waiting room. Conversation was preempted by an elderly couple who were watching a news channel on the television. Since it was rather late in a hard day, both Bob and I leaned back and were soon dozing.

⁊

I was awoken abruptly by Roger bursting in excitedly. It took a few moments to collect myself and make any sense of his babbling.

Bob, who couldn't make the claim of being a perfect physical specimen, appeared to take even longer. "Wait. Slow down and start over," he said when he was finally somewhat aware. "What files and disks?"

"All of the information about the Consolidated Key Corporation that I'm responsible for is on a series of computer disks and hard copy paper files. If the finance company doesn't have them, they can't do anything. Since I have authority over them, I can remove them from the office, and the company is blocked from transferring the money out." He looked around at the room that was now empty except for us. "Let's go out to the car and I'll explain."

And he about ran out of the room. Bob and I followed a little more sedately.

"Do you know what he's talking about?" I asked.

"Not really," Bob shrugged. "But I think he came up with some idea about the financial records. He lost me somewhere in the explanation, but that might have just been because I was still half asleep."

"Yeah, me, too. But I didn't understand any of it."

We finally caught up with Roger, but only because the car was locked and he couldn't get in. But by then, Bob and I were both awake and functioning.

I started the car and noticed that it was half past midnight. No wonder we had been asleep. I started to stifle a yawn but decided to let go with a big one, which turned out to feel pretty good. "So where are we going?" I asked.

"To my office," Roger replied. "I'm going after the files."

"For what?" Bob asked. "Aren't there duplicates? And triplicates and…others?"

"Sure, but mine are the official ones. And as long as I have physical possession of them, and the computer codes, I can prevent any tampering. You were right. It is simpler than I was realizing." He was calming down now and talking slower. "Amanda was right. While I was in the room with Audrey, watching her just lying there, and listening to a machine breathing for her, I realized she was there because somebody had done something wrong so they could make a lot of money. Well, they got their money, and Amanda will grow up without her mommy. And Bob, you're in financial difficulty because somebody else did something wrong to make a lot of money. Most of the time in the room, I kept hearing Amanda. 'Doing bad things hurts people.' And I decided that I'm not going to hurt somebody like that just so I can make money. I'm glad she said that. She was an angel from Heaven, today."

Bob and I traded a look and he grinned. "She is an angel from Heaven, all right," he replied. "And there are more of them around than you would expect. But didn't you say your company could get you taken off the case?"

"They can ask the court to do that. But that threat was only effective when I was going to go along. If I go into court and reveal their plans, I'll at least have a chance to keep it from happening. The bosses know I'm not much in favor of the plan, but they don't expect me to actually fight them on it. That's why this could work. It's unexpected."

"So they trust you and you're going to betray their trust," I said. Bob looked at me strangely, surprised, with an expression that seemed to say, "Whose side are you on?" I grinned. "How often do I get to play Devil's advocate?" I whispered. "And he's got to think it through."

Bob shrugged then chuckled and shook his head.

Roger thought for a while. "That's only a little bit of it. It's not so much that they trust me, as it is that they think I'm greedy enough to go along with it. And, unfortunately, my work there gives them reason to think so. I've been too willing to cut corners. And anyway, the trust of the shareholders and the court outweighs the trust of my boss that I'll help him steal."

"Good thinking," Bob said.

"Besides, I think the main trust I need to keep is Amanda's trust that her daddy is one of the good guys who will do the right thing and not hurt people."

By then, we were at the turn off of the main highway onto the street where Roger's office was. It was visible from the highway.

"Don't go into their parking lot," Bob said just as I was about to turn into the empty parking lot. "Go to the next one. We'll park in it and walk over to the office."

"Won't that look like we're doing something illegal?" I asked.

"It's better not to be seen so that nobody knows we're there," Bob replied. "Then it won't matter what it looks like. Roger, do you have a night watchman?'

"No. There's nothing in our offices that's valuable to a thief. We can go in the back delivery door which can't be seen from the street."

"We seem to be making a practice of sneaking in delivery doors tonight," I said, as I turned into the neighboring parking lot.

"Park next to that van," Bob instructed, pointing toward a white delivery van parked in the line closest to Roger's building.

I pulled in beside the van and turned off the engine. "Now what?"

"Now we go get the stuff," Roger said.

"Wait a little," Bob said. "Let's just watch for a few minutes to see if anybody is around."

That was such an obviously good idea that nobody replied. We just sat and watched for about ten minutes, during which a few cars went by on the main highway, but nothing else moved.

"Let's go," Bob said.

We all got out, waited for the car's interior lights to turn off, and walked furtively across the way to the back delivery door. It reminded me of the time when I had come over as a soldier in the Austrian army during the Napoleonic wars. My subject was a Tyrolean farmer who'd been drafted, and we'd been assigned to go on a patrol to find the enemy's flank. Sneaking through woods, fields, farmyards at night had felt about like tonight's furtive trip, but fortunately, tonight's trip was a lot less than the twenty miles in the snow we'd gone in Europe. That was one of the few times I've ever been shot at. It wasn't any fun. Especially since I wasn't allowed to shoot back because we were being fired at by one of our own patrols who had gotten lost. But I had done my job and kept him from getting shot, even though he'd tried to be a hero. I had to trip him and sit on him to keep him from getting out of the ditch we were in and killing some of his own army. I was glad he was a little fellow and not a Franconian nun.

Roger had his key out but stopped before inserting it.

"Something's not right," he said. "This door should be locked." Instead, it was open about an inch. "And the inside hall light should be on but it isn't."

"Be very quiet and listen." Bob put his ear against the crack. After a minute of listening, he shook his head. "I don't hear anything except a leaky water cooler."

Roger looked at the door uncertainly. "It may just have been left open by mistake."

"How likely?" I asked.

Roger shrugged. "It's not something I normally pay much attention to."

"Wait a minute," Bob said, bending over to look at the door lock. "Look at this."

Roger and I looked but didn't see anything noteworthy.

"There are some scratches on the lock. It might have been picked. Or somebody could have been careless with a key."

We all stood uncertain for a moment.

"Well, let's do something," I said. "Standing here isn't helping."

Roger opened the door and went in. "I came to get the files and I'm going to get them."

Bob looked at me and winked then followed Roger. We made our way through a hall, up a flight of steps, and into another hall, walking as quietly as we could and not talking. The halls were all dimmed with only one small light in each, but not nearly dark enough to hide us.

We passed a door stenciled with *Howard, Fine, and Howard* and then came to a door with *Cedar Crossing Financial Services* on it and it was standing open.

Roger stopped. "That door should definitely be closed and locked," he whispered very quietly.

Bob again put his ear to the open door. "There's somebody in there," he whispered after a moment. "They're being quiet but they're moving things around, and I heard a drawer close."

"Would any of the employees be in now?" I asked.

Roger shook his head. "If they were, they wouldn't be sneaking around."

"You are," Bob whispered, smiling.

"I've got reason to. Let me go in and see if I know them."

"Be careful," Bob said unnecessarily. "Does the door squeak?"

Roger shook his head and pushed on the door, which promptly squeaked, but very quietly. Roger shrugged, grimaced, and went into the darkened office. He was back in less than a minute. "I know one of them but he's not a company employee. He's a shady character who calls himself a private detective, but he's more of a crook. He does some work for my boss on occasion. But the good part is they're in my desk and filing cabinet, taking everything out. I guess they were more worried about me than I thought and had the same idea I had. They're taking all the records. That gets me off of the hook. Now I can't do anything. Let's go."

"Wait a minute," Bob whispered crossly. "You're going to just walk out and let it happen."

"Yeah," Roger retorted equally crossly. "Now I'm not responsible."

"You are if you know about it," Bob retorted.

"I can't stop everything bad from happening," Roger whispered a little too loudly.

Bob frowned and put a finger to his lips. "You're responsible because you know about it and have a chance to do something. 'All that is required for evil to triumph is for good men to do nothing.' Maybe we should ask Amanda about that."

Roger said a bad word under his breath. "What can we do?"

"Keep them from getting the files," Bob said. "He pulled out his cell phone and held it out to Roger. "Go out where they can't hear you and call the police. Sam and I will keep an eye on them."

Roger hesitated. He looked like he really wanted to be someplace else. Well, so did I. I still hadn't gotten that steak. "They might be armed," Roger said.

"I've been shot at before," Bob replied.

Yeah, and you spent six weeks in Long Binh hospital and a year in physical therapy, I thought. But I didn't say anything. Roger had to decide for himself.

Roger looked uncertain for another moment. But he nodded and took the phone. He was soon down the stairs and out of sight.

"Now what, ex-Sergeant Dunn?"

"I don't know. I hoped you would have some ideas. Can't you consult the oracle or something?"

I shook my head. "My job is persuasion, remember?"

"Then why was I doing all the talking just then? Never mind. I still don't know what to do, but I'll make something up."

And he quietly went through the door, crouching. I followed, rather nervously, and the cold feeling came back. I tried to remember what I'd known as an Austrian soldier, but the precise details of that knowledge didn't seem to be there anymore, so I just crouched like Bob and went in as quietly as I could.

The room was a medium-sized one with three desks in it and very dark, but there was a double-door-sized opening on the right into a larger room with ten or so desks in it which was dimly illuminated by a couple of *Exit* signs that gave it an eerie orange glow. Near the other end of the large room, three men were stealthily filling up some boxes with something. Bob motioned me to hide behind one of the desks in the first room. I ducked behind the farthest one, from which I could see into the larger room. Bob got onto the floor, crawled into the other room, and went behind the first desk. Before I could start to wonder what he was up to, I saw him reach up onto the desk, pick up a stapler, and throw it against the far wall behind the three men. They, of course, jumped and turned toward the crash, two of them pulling out pistols. That cold feeling in my stomach came back again. Bob then threw something unidentifiable against the desk next to him. The three men jumped again and turned toward us, just in time to see Bob run through the door into the first room where I was.

The larger man motioned to the other with a gun. "Check that way. I'll check that one." They set out in opposite directions while the third just watched.

Bob ducked behind one of the desks and picked up something else to throw.

We waited tensely, watching the man come into our room. Just as Bob was tensing for another throw, this time at the gun, the man went by the open front door. Roger stepped into the room unexpectedly and hit his gun hand with some kind of metal rod, causing the gun to fall and the man to yell in pain. He reached into his pocket with his other hand. Roger swung the rod like a ball bat against the other man's shoulder, and we heard something crack loudly. The man went down, screaming. The other man with a gun took that moment to get out. He ran out the door at the other end, and we could hear him charging down the stairs. The third man tried to run too, but tripped over one of the boxes and sprawled into the aisle between the desks, then scrambled to hide behind one.

Bob made a quick leap, grabbed the pistol which the injured man had dropped, opened the cylinder, checked the load, and closed it.

"Roger, watch him. If he makes trouble, break his skull."

"Okay."

Then Bob motioned for me to follow, and we crept into the big room toward the last thief. We could faintly hear from outside an engine start up and roar off in a hurry. I realized that it was the van we had parked by and briefly wondered where Bob had learned to think like a professional burglar.

But we were in for another shock when the third thief spoke.

"Mr. Dunn, please don't shoot me. I didn't mean for anybody to get hurt."

Bob stopped in great surprise and ducked behind a desk. He looked over at me with a puzzled expression. I shrugged. It was as much a surprise to me as it was to him.

Bob shifted over a few feet and came up from behind the desk with the pistol pointed toward the voice. "Who are you?"

"I'm Darrel Waters, Mr. Dunn."

Bob searched his memory for a few seconds and then looked puzzled again. "One L Darrel? From my Junior Sunday School class?" he asked, rather incredulously.

"Yes, sir."

Bob looked at Roger then at me. I shrugged again. "Not my doing," I whispered at him.

"Stand up so I can see you," Bob called out.

A young man about twenty stood up from behind a cabinet, his hands held up in the air. "Don't shoot me," he said rather timidly. "I don't have a gun with me."

Bob peered at the young man. "Darrel, what in the world is going on here? Come out to where I can see you better."

Darrel walked over to the aisle between desks. "I don't really know, Mr. Dunn. I just came along to open the door and help carry boxes. I didn't think they'd really shoot at anybody."

Bob and I stood up. "Didn't you know they were stealing?"

Darrel hung his head. "Yes, sir, but it was just papers. And they said nobody would be here."

"Did you help them break in?"

Darrel's head dropped a few more degrees. "Yes, sir. That was the main thing they wanted me for. I'm a pretty good locksmith."

"Who are the other two?"

"That was Walter Unger who ran away. I don't know the other one. Just Johnny. I never saw him before tonight."

Bob glanced at me and then back at Darrel. "Sam, would you check him for any weapons, please."

I went to Darrel, changing directions when Bob cautioned me not to get between them, and frisked him as well as I knew how, which was far below expert level. "I can't find any. That could be a pocket knife in his pocket."

"Yes, sir. It is," Darrel said.

"Take it out and drop it on the floor," Bob told him. "Sam, back up."

Darrel took out a medium size knife and let it drop. "Now, step up two steps." Darrel did so. "Sam, pick up the knife." I did. Bob relaxed a little. "Put your hands down, Darrel."

Darrel did so with obvious relief.

Bob called, "Roger, how's your man?"

"He's being good."

"Because you broke my shoulder," the man growled with a nasty epithet.

Just then we heard a police siren headed in our direction. Bob had Darrel walk over and stand a few feet from the injured man so he could watch them both. "Darrel, how did you get into this mess? You know better."

"Yes, sir, I do. But Walter is a friend of my mom's, and he's been real good to me. So when he said he needed my help, I didn't want to look bad to him. So I came."

"Getting you in legal trouble isn't exactly being good to you."

"No, sir. But being interested in me and letting me hang around with him is. And he did all that."

Then we heard somebody in the hall outside, and Roger looked out. "We're in here," he said and shortly two policemen came into the room.

The first one in looked around and held out his hand for the gun which Bob handed over. "What's going on? Darrel," the policeman said. "What are you doing here?"

"Hi, Officer McCready. I'm in trouble, I guess."

Bob arched an eyebrow. "You know him, too?"

"Officer McCready was my American Legion Baseball coach for three years."

"Darrel was a good first baseman. And a good boy. Now what's going on?"

Roger and Bob told the story, assisted by Darrel. Officer McCready called an ambulance for Johnny. I tried to stay unobtrusive and hoped that the police wouldn't ask my address. Johnny insisted that they had been hired by the company president to be there and that they were completely legal.

"Oh?" Officer McCready said. "Then why did you bring a gun and break in at midnight?" Then he looked at Roger and Bob. "But he might be right. If the company president backs him up, then the only crime is brandishing a pistol, a misdemeanor. But right now it looks like breaking and entering and attempted burglary."

After getting statements from all of us and loading Johnny into the ambulance, the police took Darrel to their car. "I'm not going to put Darrel in confinement for the night, since we're not even sure his actions were illegal," Officer McCready said to Bob as they went out. "I think we'll have to charge him, but I expect he can go home then."

"Good," Bob said. "I hope it's not too serious for him."

"Me, too," Officer McCready said, "and I hope he learns something from it."

We went back to the car. It felt good to be just walking instead of sneaking for a change.

By then it was too late to go home for the night so we went back to the hospital. We went in the delivery door again, up to the surgical waiting room, collapsed on the couches, and were soon asleep.

⌘

When I woke up, it was still dark outside, but I was alone in the room. I checked my watch and it was still a couple of hours before normal hospital wake up time. I wondered where Roger and Bob had gone off to, but quickly figured that out. I washed my face in the bathroom and went searching. It didn't take me long to find the surgical intensive care ward, and even less to find Audrey's room. I waited until the night nurse went into the back and sneaked into Audrey's room. As I expected, Roger was in there. He was sitting by the bed, holding her hand, being careful not to touch either of the two needles in it. He looked up at me. "Hi," he said tiredly. "I'm too keyed up to sleep, but too tired to stay awake."

I nodded and stood by the bed. She was hooked up to several tubes, wires, and machines, most of which were beeping or gurgling. Roger put her hand back onto the bed, very gently, sat in the big chair, leaned back, and seemed to go to sleep.

I looked again at the rather pitiful sight of the dying woman in the bed but before I could get too emotional, it came over me like a bright light and I let loose with the biggest Hallelujah! I could think silently in my mind, followed by the biggest Thank You! I could manage.

I had gotten the message—or rather orders for my next move. I hadn't gotten to do many of them. They were usually done by Raphael's crew, but the few I'd done had all been great blessings for me, and of course great blessings for the subject. Grinning from ear to ear, I moved to the head of the bed. I put both of my hands on her head, avoiding the shaved places with electrodes, and closed my eyes.

I could feel the healing power go through me, and like before, felt it come back. But this time with a big difference that made me jump, it startled me so. What I felt come back wasn't through one person, but from two. I grinned even bigger and sent up another silent Hallelujah! Sometimes I love this job. Most of the time, actually.

Then Audrey moved very slightly, and I felt a tremor, but I couldn't tell if she was shaking or if I was. It didn't matter, because her eyes opened and she tried to say something but couldn't because of all of the stuff in her mouth and throat. But it came out as kind of a moan and Roger heard it. He dashed to the bed—in what almost amounted to teleportation, it was so quick—and was looking amazed into eyes that unexpectedly looked back. She groaned again, something that probably was intended to be his name. He said her name very clearly. I decided it was time to get out, not that either of them was noticing me. As I left, I saw the nurse hurrying toward the room, having seen the displays go haywire. She looked at me briefly, but was too intent on her crisis to bother with me and was quickly inside. Then some alarms started going off.

So I went looking for Bonnie's room. I found it after a half hour's search on other floors only to find it right around the corner from Audrey's. I knocked softly.

"Come in," Bob's voice answered.

I did and saw him in the same position Roger had taken, sitting by the bed holding his unresponsive wife's hand.

"Hi, Sam," he said. "Did you get any sleep?"

"Not enough," I replied. "Did you."

"Some, but I was too excited to sleep much."

"It has been an exciting time, at that," I agreed.

"Tomorrow, I guess I'll be back to normal old plumbing work."

I smiled. "You'll be okay."

"Yes, indeed. I'm actually looking forward to not being excited. But you didn't come here to sit around and be bored, did you?"

I shook my head. "No, generally when we're sent over, it's for some kind of excitement."

"There was some excitement down the hall a little while ago. Do you know what it was?"

I nodded. "Yeah."

Bob looked a question at me and I grinned.

"Well," he said, "did you have anything to do with it?"

Grinning bigger, I nodded.

Bob smiled back. "And is Miss Amanda going to get her mommy back?"

Grinning still bigger, I nodded again. "A completely healthy mommy."

Bob leaned back with a happy look. "I sort of expected that. I figured you were here for something more than persuasion."

"Well, you were right. Besides, as you pointed out, you did all of the talking when persuasion was needed. I didn't do anything. And Amanda is getting more than her mommy back. She'll soon have a little brother, too. A healthy one."

Bob laughed. "That's wonderful. Do they know?"

"Nope. You're the first."

Bob smiled and looked at Bonnie. "Do you have any more healings in you?"

I shook my head sadly and he sighed. "I guessed not. Well, we had come to terms with this a while back. But it still hurts."

We sat in silence for a few minutes, then he chuckled. "I suppose my blessing out of this was to get to watch an angel at work. Very few people get to do that, I guess."

I nodded and, after a moment's thought, smiled at him. "You're right. Getting to watch an angel do his work is a real blessing. And I'm very blessed to have gotten to see one this trip. You. Thank you, very much."

Bob looked puzzled for a moment and then smiled. "Maybe. But I think Amanda did more on that score than either one of us." He frowned a little. "I wasn't much of an angel to Darrel, was I? If I had done more for him when I could have, maybe he wouldn't have been taken in by a crook."

"Possibly," I agreed. "But you can't undo the past, you can only learn from it."

Bob nodded. "Well, I think I learned a lot from this experience. I'll try to put what I've learned to work. How much of this should I tell Roger and Audrey?"

I shrugged. "Whatever you want. They might not believe you."

"After her near death experience, I expect they will. Aren't you going to see them again?"

I shook my head. "I'm going back as soon as I leave here. They've still got a lot to deal with that I can't fix. I expect Roger will be looking for a job, and they will have some big financial troubles. But the biggest problems are behind them. I think they'll have a new perspective on the troubles they still face."

"I'll miss you. It's been a blessing to get to work with you."

"Thank you." Then another order came through and I smiled again, less celebratory, but still good.

"I can't heal Bonnie, and I can't tell you why," I said. "Because I don't know why," I said in response to the look that came over Bob's face. "But I do have a gift for you, too, even though it's a very temporary one."

Bob looked puzzled and then shocked when we heard a woman's voice say, "Bob!"

He turned to Bonnie and rushed back to her side.

"Hello, Bob," we both heard again clearly, even though her mouth didn't move. But her eyes looked at him.

Bob looked up at me. "What—"

"It will only last for a few minutes," I replied. "Don't spend it asking me questions that don't have answers."

He turned back to Bonnie and took her hand. "Honey, can you hear me?"

"I can always hear you, darling. I'm still in here. I just

can't get out any more. Please don't stop talking to me. Keep on."

"Oh, I will, I will," Bob said tenderly.

"I love you," I heard both voices say as one.

Then it was time for me to get out again, though again I didn't think they noticed me leaving.

On a whim, since I didn't have to hurry anything now. I waited outside the room and after about an hour, Bob came out, wiping red eyes. He looked a little surprised to see me. "Thank you, Sam," he said. "That was a wonderful gift. We talked for about half an hour. One of the most precious half hours of my life. Thank you."

"You're welcome," I said. "And I wanted to say goodbye. It really has been a blessing to work with you. And also offer some advice. Keep track of Darrel. Now I'm wondering if he wasn't my real subject all along."

"I definitely plan to do that," he replied. "And you keep an eye on us, too. We might need some more help."

I smiled. "For the most part, you're supposed to do things the normal way, but the normal help you have available all the time is enough if you'll use it."

"Yes, that's true, isn't it?"

"Yeah, it is." I nodded. "One thing you can count on absolutely is that you are never all alone."

Bob smiled. "Yes, that's certainly one thing I've learned out of this."

Then I remembered, took the small bottle out of my pocket, and handed it to Bob. "Put some of this on Bonnie. I hope she likes it."

Bob looked puzzled but took the bottle of Janie Arben perfume and said he would.

I nodded. "Tell the Steiners goodbye for me."

We shook hands. I headed out to the car and, since it was so early, I had a huge greasy, syrupy breakfast instead of steak and fries. Then I parked the car in the same spot I had found it in, went inside the store, hesitated, gave in, and bought a small orange soda and a pecan roll, sat down, ate, and thought for a little. I had accomplished my primary goal, which was Roger and his ethical dilemma, but I couldn't help wondering if there hadn't been a deeper hidden purpose aimed at Darrel, or Bob, or…

Well, sometimes the Boss gets cute even with us.

I stood up, disposed of the evidence, went into the back room, and…

CHAPTER 2

The old man wasn't going to make it. We could all see that. He lagged behind constantly, and, at the end of every day, he just dropped onto the ground, exhausted. Even after adjusting our loads and giving him the lightest one of only sixty pounds or so, he still was wearing down fast. Whoever selected him as a porter for this trip down the Ho Chi Minh trail did a bad job.

That was why I was here, to take care of him, to convince him to keep going, and to keep him from dying of exhaustion or being killed by one of the guards. I had come over just in time to get picked as a porter for this trip and, even though the trip had been grueling drudgery up and down steep hills on the jungle trails, I had gotten to know most of the porters at our end of the line and had learned which guards to avoid if possible—all of them, basically.

By the time we had gone a mile on the first day, we knew it was going to be rough. The guards had hurriedly picked several men from the Vietnamese villages in the region where the old man lived and rushed us on trucks to the depot about twenty miles away. The dirt roads were very rough, making the ride very bumpy and uncomfortable. The rattling of the trucks being driven too fast for the rough roads and the less than efficient mufflers made attempts at meaningful conversation difficult, but I made the acquaintance of the man standing next to me who was named Danh and learned that this would be his second trip down the trail, his first having been four years before. When I asked him if this was normal procedure, he shook his head emphatically. "No! My first trip was as a teen-ager and we formed up and trained in our home village for several weeks before we were sent off on the trail."

The man next to us nodded in agreement. "There must be a big emergency down south that requires such a rush."

The trucks stopped. We were unloaded and rudely hustled down the road on foot, while the trucks turned around and went back the other way. Although the guards discouraged talking, they couldn't stop it completely and soon the word spread through the group that we were headed toward a truck depot which was about five miles farther down the trail.

Before we came in sight of the depot, we knew it was there by the sound of many trucks. The smell of truck exhaust, mixed with the odor of rice cooking in fish sauce and inadequately tended latrines, assaulted our nostrils. The depot was primitive, consisting mainly of packed dirt areas—where cargo was moved between trucks and stacked—and a couple of sheds for maintenance, with even more trucks being worked on underneath the trees of the thick forest. The trees had all been left in place with only the lowest branches having been removed, making it very difficult to spot from the air. It was a place of bustling busyness, and we were hurried to one line of trucks where we were put to the task of unloading them and stacking crates and various pieces of military equip-ment into piles as directed by a couple of the permanent staff at the depot, with our guards "encouraging" us with threats, curses, and blows.

As usual, I had a body which was a perfect physical specimen, so the work wasn't terribly difficult. But the screaming and harassment by the guards got tiresome. I could understand why humans sometimes wanted to strike out at somebody. Of course, I wasn't allowed to do that kind of thing on this trip. Those kinds of jobs were generally handled by Michael's crew. As one of Uriel's group, my line is more persuasion and encouragement.

Even though nobody took the time to explain anything to us, the number of trucks, the amount of cargo, and the hurried urgency of all the uniformed people made it clear that something big was in preparation. I wanted to ask one of the other porters if this level of activity was normal, but every time one of us tried to talk, the guards would scream at us to get back to work. Obviously, somebody was in a big hurry. We unloaded the one truck and were halfway through another when two soldiers came and had a quick conversation with our guards, who then had us reload the truck with the stuff we'd just taken off. Then we were rushed to a large stack of empty carrying frames which we were told to pack up with the stuff laying on the ground around us.

With that, we had to talk a little, and I slipped in a question of one of the men who seemed knowledgeable and friendly. "This is my first trip as a porter. Is this normal for a pack train on the trail?"

He shook his head. "I've never seen it so rushed and awful like this," he said. "Most things are carried by truck now, but some smaller side trips are on trails that trucks can't use, so we still have to use backpacks and carrying poles on those routes."

Just then the big loud guard came over and screamed at us to get to work. So we did. We got the packs loaded with a heavy load of various military things, tried them on, adjusted straps, ropes, and arrangement of our loads to get the very heavy packs as comfortable as possible. The bamboo pack frames we carried were marvelously engineered and padded so that the weight of the load wasn't as bad as I would have expected. After a couple of adjustments, the load was manageable, but very heavy.

It was quite unlike the time I'd been a packman hauling sand for the building of the big cathedral of Cologne. There the loads had been much heavier and carried in a sack over my shoulder, walking up narrow planks to the top of the wall a hundred and fifty feet in the air. But there, every work day had started with prayer and the mid-day meal was thick slices of pork and a big chunk of rye bread. I spent six weeks doing that just so I would be there to convince the foreman to try his hand at the stained glass. He did. He was wonderful at it and made two of the most beautiful panels in one of the nave windows, which unfortunately were destroyed in the bombings but which had made an impact on many people prior to their destruction.

This time, we didn't get ham and bread, but a sack with several rice balls cooked in fish sauce which we were told would have to last us the first three days of the trip. We also received another set of the black pajama type clothes to supplement the set we had been given before we started.

As soon as we were loaded and ready, the guards spent several minutes explaining the march rules. "Stay in your place in line, stay within two meters of the man in front of you…"

There were severe penalties for infractions—no food, beatings, and even summary execution. Then they lined us up. I worked it so that I was right behind the old man who was right behind Danh and, as soon as we were all in line, the guards set us off on a narrow trail headed east.

It was certainly not a leisurely stroll through the woods. The guards set a very fast pace and enforced it with screams and blows. With our heavy loads and the fast pace, we were all soon huffing and puffing and had little wind for conversation or attention for anything except keeping our footing on the narrow, steep, and rutted trail. Which was a shame, because I did notice that the country we were in was beautiful.

We kept at it without a pause until midday when there was a brief stop to eat a rice ball from the food sack each of us had been issued.

With the break and the guards eating as well, there was some opportunity for conversation.

"What is your name?" I had asked the old man.

"This trip is so awful that we are mere animals without names," he responded.

"Then let's change that," I said. "At least between us. I am Samuel."

He looked at me skeptically. "Like the prophet in the Bible?"

I nodded. "It's unusual, but it's my name."

"Somm yool." he repeated, making it sound very Vietnamese. "I am Loc."

"This is my first trip," I said, "but I didn't expect this. Aren't we all 'heroes of the revolution' or something and so deserve better treatment?"

Loc grunted disgustedly, and Danh scowled, holding up his rice ball. "My last trip began with a big feast with speeches that called us heroes and promised that we would do great things and how wonderful we all were." He took a bite of his rice and snorted. "This is not a banquet."

Loc finished his rice and lay on his back. "On my trip, we had one army officer with us who encouraged us and tried to keep us safe and at each way station guides would lead us to the next one. This time there are twenty guards and permanent scouts. Do you know what that means?" He raised his head and gave us a glare. "It means we're on a trail that isn't used much, so there are no way stations, no guides, and a great likelihood of being ambushed by the enemy. And no food supplies along the way. Look at the last several men in the line. They aren't carrying military supplies, they're carrying food—our food. The normal losses on the trail from malaria, injury, and the enemy will be offset by our eating the loads of those men."

Much too soon there was a large, loud, and mean guard, yelling at us to get back on the trail. He was one to avoid, but that was seldom possible.

After that, we started off and spent all of our energy keeping the fast pace with little energy for talking, a situation which continued for several days. During this time, a pattern of sorts worked out. We learned each other's names and the names of the two guards who stayed with our group of the pack train. The large mean one was woefully misnamed An—Peace and he had a great natural talent for petty cruelty. The other one, named Thanh was quite loud and pushy but was less of a naturally cruel person and much less quick to hit us with his stick or rifle butt. Still, he would do so, especially when An or the captain was in sight.

The second night was when Danh, another porter named Binh, and I switched loads to give Loc a lighter one. Loc ended up with two sacks of rice and I got his mortar tube and a machine gun tripod. My load was now heavier, but thanks to those wonderfully built pack frames, the extra weight wasn't as big a burden as I expected.

The next morning, after our breakfast of half-cooked

rice in fish sauce—followed by mid-day meal of partially cooked rice in fish sauce, and then supper was half-raw rice cooked in fish sauce—the less awful guard Thanh noticed the change but said nothing. When An also noticed and started to curse, Thanh stopped him. "It is better this way," he said.

An scowled at him. "Changing loads is not permitted. Besides," he added with a wicked grin, "it's fun to watch him struggle."

"And if he collapses, who will carry his load? You?"

"Maybe we should ask Captain Nguyen," An said.

Thanh shrugged, walked off, and prepared to get started.

I turned and was a little surprised to see the old man kneeling by his pack with his eyes closed. I went over to where I could hear and was again surprised to hear him reciting the Creed, and he was even more surprised when I joined in on the Lord's Prayer. When we finished, he smiled at me as I helped him get his pack settled.

"I thought I was the only believer," he said. "But it's best not to let the authorities know about it, at least not too openly, so there may be more but who are keeping it quiet."

I nodded and then we moved out. As usual, we had little energy for any but the briefest comments.

While we had very little time, opportunity, or energy for socializing, Danh, the porter just ahead of Loc became the unofficial leader of the men in our end of group. I barely ever even saw the people at the back end.

Loc and I began to take a moment each morning for prayer, usually silent but sometimes he again said the Lord's Prayer aloud, and I joined in. He was careful to do so when no guards were in sight, wisely. Contrary to what some believe, the Boss seldom wanted martyrs. It happened enough without looking for it. Once in fourth century Syria, I had been sent to help get a young man out of a prison mine. He had decided to become a martyr, and I had to convince him that he could do more good alive than dead. I hadn't made much headway, and he was about to make an irrevocable step when I was allowed to tell him that if he didn't become a martyr, he would return to his home village, get married to the shoemaker's daughter, and have a big family. Since he'd been madly in love with her all along, he gave up the idea of martyrdom and was ready to help in the escape plot which succeeded. Later, his son became a soldier who played a big role in preventing a pagan-led attack on the Christian community in the city of Hippo.

So Loc and I continued to pray in semi-secret, and that grew to be an important bond between us. If any of the others noticed the prayers, none of them made any comments to us. Encouraging believers is always a secondary mission for any of us when we come over, and it's frequently the main mission, so I wanted to help Loc stay faithful.

The eighth day on the trail had started off wrong with an unseasonable rain which had struck just after midnight. It had drenched us and kept us from sleeping well, making most everybody a little testy. When it got light enough to start, it got worse because, after our normal breakfast of half cooked rice in fish sauce, the old man was even slower to get going than usual. I had half expected it since, the day before, a shiny, large airplane had flown over the trail very low, and we all had to scramble off the trail to hide. Loc had fallen pretty hard into a ditch, and a couple of us had to help him up. We half carried him the last half mile.

He was obviously very sore that morning and, after a shorter prayer than usual, he had real trouble getting his load slung and then nearly fell when he took a step. I reached out, steadied him, and lifted his pack while he got it all adjusted better.

"Thank you," he said.

Fortunately we had not attracted the attention of any of the guards, and we got started without any of the screaming, threats, or blows which were delivered on any pretext, or for no pretext.

"Be strong," I responded. "We'll make it," I added, more in hope than in knowledge.

He shook his head doubtfully and set off up the trail.

As the morning went by, we were fortunately on a generally level section of the trail, so the old man was able to keep up, even though just barely. Through the occasional break in the trees, I could see that we were coming to a tall ridge. I knew that the afternoon would bring us to the uphill part of the day's march, and that it would be tough on the old man.

Fortunately, we stopped for the noon break at the foot of the hill, just after crossing a slow moving stream. After checking ourselves and each other for leeches and removing a few, we all stopped and sat down to eat our rice ball, but the old man had just collapsed and didn't even try to get out of his pack or check for leeches. Danh and I went over to him, took his pack off of him, and helped him to sit up against it. After removing two leeches from his leg, I sat next to him and he slowly ate. "It's getting pretty bad, isn't it?" I said.

He frowned. "It has been bad from the beginning, and it is getting unbearable."

"This is my first trip down the trail," I said. "Is every trip like this?"

He shook his head disgustedly. "No. This is my third, and the others were nothing like this. Before, we had shorter days and every seventh day, we stopped at noon and rested the afternoon. And the guards weren't nearly so cruel. Evenings were enjoyable times of storytelling and socializing. These guards have something wrong with them. But I haven't made the trip for ten years so maybe it's different now."

"Please forgive my nosiness, but how old are you?" I asked.

He smiled. "Yes, I'm old. Too old for this. I'm forty-six."

"Why did they pick you for a porter?"

"It was me or my youngest son who just got married. I volunteered in his place."

He leaned back against his pack and closed his eyes, so I took the hint and left him alone, starting a conversation with another porter who also was more interested in resting than in talking. After several minutes of that, we could hear the guards begin to stir, signaling the start of the afternoon's march.

The next couple of hours saw the trail grow steadily steeper. Loc grew more and more unsteady and slow. He tried hard but kept letting the gap grow between him and Danh, just in front of him in the line. I lagged with him and finally got behind him and pushed until we had caught up to our normal place. But it didn't last and before long, he had slowed down again. Fortunately, the next several men in line were sympathetic and went around us so it wouldn't be obvious that there was a gap, but shortly after mid-afternoon, An the guard—in one of his meanest moods unfortunately—noticed that the old man and I were out of place. He came running up, screaming at Loc to catch up, get back in his place, and stay there or else. We tried to speed up and get back, but it wasn't going to work. The guard wasn't just mean but impatient, too, and after about a half hour of agonizingly slow progress back toward where we were assigned to be in the line, the guard completely lost patience. He ran up and, with a foul curse, pushed the old man off the trail and down into a gully.

"Stay out of the way and join the back of the line," the guard screamed.

It was risky, but the old man was my job, so I went down into the gully to where he had fallen, He was just lying on his side and breathing hard. I knelt beside him and was surprised when I heard him laugh softly. "This was a painful thing, but at least I get to rest here for a moment."

I smiled back. "Maybe so, but don't rest too long. The end of the line is already in sight back there."

He sighed. "Then let's get going again."

He needed my help to stand back up under his load and now, in addition to his bruises from the fall the day before, he had a nasty cut and bump on his forehead. He tried, but he simply couldn't climb the bank with his load, so I helped him take it off and carried both packs—one at a time—up the bank. Then he still needed help getting up to the trail. By that point, I was about exhausted, too, and we might both have fallen back down the gully if one of the last porters hadn't noticed, grabbed my belt, and pulled.

"Thank you." I gasped and began to put my pack back on.

Fortunately, the other porter helped the old man put his on and we were able to stay with the line.

As we trudged along, I watched our new friend some and came to the conclusion that he wasn't of the same cultural group as the rest of us. There was nothing I could identify exactly but something was different. So I decided a direct question might work.

"Are you from our village?" I asked him.

He smiled. "My family has lived there for twenty years, but we came from Kachin in Burma after the army wiped out the rest of our village. We are Jingpo." His Vietnamese was unaccented, but still he had a slightly different inflection which was distinctive. We had no more time for talking, however, as one of the guards came up then and informed us that we should redouble our efforts at maintaining proper march formation and, if we did not, he would be forced to administer corrective action. Although he didn't say it in those exact words.

With the exertion of getting back on the trail, neither Loc nor I had any energy to spare for talk anyway. The old man made a great effort to keep up, but it didn't work, so I grabbed his pack and pushed. After about half an hour, I was very tired, but our new friend noticed and took my place. After about ten minutes, we crested the hill and it was downhill the rest of the day, which was less physically draining but equally bad, in that we had to constantly watch our footing and avoid ruts, sticks, and other such things which could cause a fall.

By stopping time, everybody in the train was exhausted, and Loc was so red faced and sweat soaked I feared he would fall over dead. As soon as we stopped, he did fall over, but just asleep, not dead. Our new friend helped me get Loc's pack off and laid him out a little more comfortably, then we both collapsed ourselves, spending several minutes just lying still and trying to recuperate enough to get the energy to eat our rice ball. When I regained enough energy to eat, I noticed that everybody was about as bad off as we were. It had been a really rough day coming up the steep ridge and then down the other side. Nobody did any more than eat and roll out their mats for sleep, so I quickly followed suit.

When I awoke the next morning, I immediately noticed that something was different. It took me a moment to realize that it was beginning to get light and we hadn't been awakened very loudly an hour before dawn as normal. It was a pleasant surprise, but I was afraid that we'd pay for it later. Still, I figured it would be best to enjoy it while I could, so I lay my head back down and dozed again. About half an hour later, Thanh, the guard who could be bearable when he wanted, came and rather quietly announced that it was time to begin the day.

Seeing everybody's puzzlement at the relatively late hour, he smiled. "Yesterday was such a hard day that Captain Nguyen decided that some extra rest would be good," he said to the line in general.

Another guard came by with a sack and gave everybody a small can of meat paste. I opened mine, ate it very hungrily, and thoroughly enjoyed it, even though I couldn't tell what kind of meat it was. Maybe better that I didn't know. I always enjoyed eating when I'm here in human form, but this trip was turning out to be a real disappointment as far as gustatory delights were concerned.

Then An, the mean guard, came into sight and Thanh's tone changed., "Rest is over," he shouted. "Get up and get moving. Soldiers are waiting for your loads. Get going."

An shouted even louder with several curses thrown in but, except for noise, they did nothing, so we had an unrushed breakfast of rice ball and meat paste and even a few minutes for conversation. As usual, Loc and I took a few moments for a prayer and we were both surprised when our new Jingpo friend joined us for the Lord's Prayer, even though he ended with a few words in a language neither Loc nor I understood.

"Was that the Jingpo language?" I asked. "And what is a Jingpo?"

"That was a traditional Jingpo blessing, and I am a Jingpo," he smiled. "My name is Seng."

"Seng?"

"I am named for two of the great heroes of our fight

for independence from the Japanese and the central government."

"And you pray with us."

"Indeed. I did not know there were any other believers here, but I am glad."

"Are all Jingpo believers," I asked.

"No, but many of us are, as are our neighbors the Kren."

Both Loc and I introduced ourselves, and we all agreed that the extra rest was nice.

"Apparently, the captain has some better nature, after all," I said.

Loc snorted. "Maybe, but that's not the only reason we've stopped. We're getting close to the area where the enemy sends patrols and raids. The captain is probably waiting for scouts to check out the trail ahead and see if it is clear. We will have to hurry more to make up the time."

Seng smiled ruefully. "Maybe so, but it is still nice."

As if to validate Loc's guess, the guards began to move and we hit the trail again. We moved a little more slowly at first, but just before the mid-day break, a guard from the line in front of us appeared on the trail, signaling to An who began to rush us, and the pace became very fast. Apparently, Loc had been right and, with the scouts finding the trail clear, we were expected to make up the lost time.

The noon break was much shorter than normal and the afternoon was so fast paced that it was difficult for all of us and worse on Loc, who could barely keep up. Several times, I helped him by pushing on an uphill stretch. Twice Seng also helped by grabbing Loc's pack and pulling. When it began to get dark, we didn't stop immediately, but kept going. Fortunately, we were at a level spot beside a slow creek, and it wasn't as dangerous as it would have been on a rutted slope, but we still had trouble. I heard several people trip, and once somebody ahead fell. When it became completely dark, we stopped and spent an uncomfortable night, since we had to eat and set up our mats in the dark.

Next morning, we were awakened earlier than usual and, without even time to eat, we were started out in the dark. That whole day was torture. We kept up a very fast pace, and the old man couldn't match it. An was even meaner than usual. He came by us several times and yelled at Loc to keep up. Once he emphasized his anger by hitting him in the legs with his staff.

"That's not helping," Seng said angrily.

An, in response, whacked him, too. "Keep moving and be quiet," he snarled.

On one uphill stretch, when both Seng and I were pushing Loc up the hill, Thanh, the better guard came up behind us. I had been so intent on struggling to keep up that I didn't notice him until he grabbed Loc's belt and helped pull him. When we reached the top, Loc took a deep breath. "Thank you," he said to Thanh.

Thanh nodded in reply and went on ahead.

Fortunately, there was a halt about half an hour later and, after a few minutes, we were hurriedly moved off of the trail into the brush. We found out why when an airplane flew over the trail, very low. We got to stay in the brush for several minutes, which gave us a little rest and gave the mosquitoes a good meal.

After a bit, Thanh came by. "Stay undercover and eat, but be quiet," he said and moved on back up the trail.

I broke out my rice ball and was surprised at how good it tasted after no breakfast. Then I wiggled over to Loc. "How are you doing?" I whispered.

"The hills are getting steeper and I am getting weaker. It is not good."

Seng noticed us and wiggled over, too. "Keep going," he said. "It's all we can do in this situation."

The old man shook his head. "Soon I will be unable to keep going. Then the mean guard will kill me. I am a patriot, and I am proud to do my duty. I fought the Japanese and the French, and I would be glad to do my duty on the trail, but when the time comes, I will try to kill him first."

"Don't start thinking like that," I said, laying back against a tree. "We will make it."

"I will not," said Loc. "I can feel it. Within two days, I will no longer be able to continue."

"We will help," offered Seng.

Loc shook his head. "It is too much."

Just then Thanh came back up the trail. "All is clear now. Let's go."

He went on up the trail calling all of the porters out. In a few minutes, we were back on the trail and moving, but the pace was a little slower and twice more we stopped and got under cover, but no more airplanes came over.

In spite of the slow pace, Loc struggled to keep up. I pushed a little, Seng helped some, and all of us worried. Just before normal stopping time, we were motioned into cover again, but this time there was considerable activity by the guards, several of whom ran past us up the trail toward the line ahead of us.

After a few minutes, we heard a great commotion up the line, and most incongruously, a clearly feminine scream, followed by a masculine bellow of pain.

Shortly afterward, a cluster of the guards came past, half dragging a strangely dressed woman who was very short, even by Vietnamese standards.

She was struggling but to no effect. Her nose was dripping blood, and one of the guards' hands was bleeding, too.

Another guard held a primitive looking crossbow.

The captain met them just behind our place on the trail and the guards dropped the woman.

"This scout found her hiding beside the trail a half mile ahead," the ranking guard in the group said. "She had this." He held up the crossbow.

The captain nudged her with his foot. "I suppose you were hunting," he asked sarcastically. She made a rude sound.

"Tie her and bring her along," the captain directed. "We will—question her."

At that, Seng jumped and was about to go out into the trail, but I grabbed his arm and stopped him. "There are six guards with rifles," I pointed out. "Just what do you expect to accomplish?"

He looked at me angrily for a moment then slumped. Loc reached out and grabbed his ankle. "Think it through. There may be something you can do, but just getting hurt or killed on an impulse will gain you nothing."

Seng sat back down, but his glower didn't go down, and, after a few minutes, we were back on the trail, again at a very fast pace.

In the late afternoon, Loc fell. He hadn't tripped nor had he hit a rut. He just fell. It happened just as Thanh was passing him, and surprisingly, Thanh helped him up. "Be careful, old man," he said in a friendly tone. Loc nodded.

An hour later Loc fell again, also for no obvious reason, but this time when An was around. An's response was quite different from Thanh's. He ran at Loc, cursing, and he hit him twice with his rifle butt. I hurried up to help Loc get up and was able to catch the third blow on my pack.

An looked at me as if he would hit me, too, but he stalked off. "Keep him going. Or else," he ordered.

Seng and I got Loc going again and, fortunately, we stopped again a little later.

There was an unusual amount of activity by the guards and, shortly after we stopped, we saw one of the scouts run by to report to the captain.

"Apparently, there is reason to expect enemy activity," Loc said from his place where he had collapsed. "At least we get a rest because of it."

Seng didn't reply, but looked back down the trail, toward the place where the captain and his crew maintained their normal place. After a few minutes of that, he helped Loc get his pack and mat situated, then he headed off into the brush, away from the trail. I took a step and tapped his back. "Where are you going?"

He looked at me with a frown. "I'll be back."

"Let me come with you."

"Are you a hunter? Can you move through the brush with no sound?"

Yes, I came over with great skills for both since I knew I'd be in the jungle, I thought, but I said nothing.

He smiled. "So stay here. I'll be back. I just want to listen."

I gave him a skeptical look with encouragement undertones.

"I'll be good," he said, then he disappeared into the dusk.

I gave him a minute's head start then followed, as silently as he had been. I'd been a scout several times, including once as a native scout for Dr. Livingston and another when I helped a missionary in Ecuador find his way over the mountains into the Amazon valley in the 1700s. There, we had to help the locals defeat some robbers who were looking for slaves. We had done it by sneaking into their camp at night, sinking all their boats, and dumping their gunpowder into the river.

So I was quite able to move quietly through the brush behind Seng until I saw him lying in some bushes watching the group around the captain. I moved up right behind him without being noticed and touched his foot. He jumped. He was startled, such that I feared we would be discovered, but nobody noticed. I silently got beside him and got a dirty look. The captain and two guards were quietly discussing the condition of the trail. The prisoner lay on the side of the trail with her hands and feet tied.

Then An and a uniformed scout came to the captain and we heard the scout say, "We found signs of their having been here within the last two days. Mostly wearing sandals just like hers and two more wearing European or American boots."

"Which way were they travelling?" the captain asked, and the scout pointed east, ahead of us. The captain nodded. "Good, maybe they've given up on finding this one and left the area."

An frowned. "Or maybe they're setting an ambush."

The captain nodded again. "Send a squad on a night patrol on the trail ahead," he said. The scout nodded and went back toward the front of the pack train. An turned to go but the captain stopped him. "Your group has slowed us all. You must make them go faster. Especially now that we are in a dangerous area."

An frowned. "It's the old man. He can't keep up."

"What is he carrying?"

"Two rice sacks."

The captain thought a moment then frowned. "Kill him then. That much rice is less important than speed now." He pointed at the prisoner. "Kill her, too. In the morning. Quietly."

An grinned wickedly, nodded, and left as the captain went back down the trail.

Seng and I silently backed out of our places and made

our way back to our packs. When we got there, Seng began quietly but intently muttering in a language I didn't know but which I guessed was cursing in Jingpo. He smacked the ammo can on his pack so hard that Loc woke up.

He listened a moment and when Seng didn't seem inclined to wind down any, Loc looked at me. "He seems upset," he said a little wryly.

Seng switched to Vietnamese and called the captain, An, and all of the guards several vile names.

Loc raised an eyebrow. "He *is* upset."

"As you will be when you hear why," Seng told him. He turned to me. "We have to get away. Tonight."

"'We?'" I said. "Why are you going?"

"I'm getting the girl and we're all going together."

Loc and I looked at each other a moment then, after a moment's silence, Loc frowned. "Why are you so interested in the prisoner? She was almost certainly intending to disrupt our journey and very likely would have killed you if she had had the chance."

Seng considered a moment. "Because she is of the mountain people, not Viet. Because I know what it's like to be a stranger who doesn't fit in. She's not my enemy. We're both strangers in a land not our own and neither of us have any reason to hold any love for the government which I supposedly serve now, however unwillingly. The same government which is going to have her abused and killed is also the one which prevented my family from owning any land and which prevented us from going anywhere else."

They both sat lost in thought for a few moments. So did I. This was a surprise. My job was to watch over Loc and now I had two more people in the equation. Unexpected events were part of the job, however, and I was sent over to take care of whatever happens. Like once in fifteenth century Silesia, I was to make sure a low level nobleman made it on time to a meeting, the purpose of which I was never told. I was to drive him to the cathedral, but he never showed up. I had to search all over the whole valley, trying to find him, and never did. But in the process of searching, I helped a young farm couple find a lost milk cow which turned out to be the foundation of their fortune which their grandson used to good effect in the Hanseatic League, through which he founded a major charity in Konigsberg. The noble got to the meeting somehow, on time, without my help, and I never found out what went on there.

"So what's your plan for getting her away?" I asked.

Seng frowned. "I don't know."

Loc raised up and looked down the trail toward the prisoner, then he suddenly got up and walked down the trail in that direction. Seng looked horrified and upset at the same time. "What does he think he's going to do?" he whispered.

"I don't know. Let's watch and see."

But before we could get into position to see, Loc came back, carrying the girl over his shoulder, and put her down in a patch of brush where she couldn't be seen from the trail.

"What—" Seng hissed

Loc held up his hand for quiet, took out a very small folding knife, and cut the cords around her wrists and ankles. "There was nobody watching," he said.

Seng smiled. "But now we've got to go immediately, before she's missed." He turned to the girl. "We're leaving the pack train and taking you with us. Do you know this country?"

She looked skeptical for a moment but then shrugged. "Pretty well. We is to go in south," she said in heavily accented and ungrammatical Vietnamese.

"That's across the trail," I said. "We'll likely be seen going across."

Loc again stood up, went out into the trail and across, then quickly turned and motioned us to hurry across. We helped the girl stand up, but her feet and ankles were so bad from lack of circulation from being tied too tightly that she couldn't stand alone. Seng picked her up and went across quickly. Since nobody shouted or gave any other sign that they had been seen, I went on across, too.

We all went several yards back into the brush and stopped to confer. "We go south?" Seng asked the girl.

She nodded. "We go as fastly as we can."

"But we must not leave a trail," Seng objected.

She nodded. "But come dark soon. They good no follow us in dark. Now go. Go fastest."

Seng picked her up, got her onto his back with her arms around his neck, and we set out. It was fortunate that I had brought across the jungle movement skills, because as Seng had already shown, he was an accomplished sneak, and Loc was very little less skilled.

So we maneuvered our way carefully through the brush, making very little noise and disturbing almost nothing.

After about ten minutes, we heard somebody shout behind us on the trail, somebody else shouted back, somebody else called for quiet, and the shouting stopped, but we could still hear the sounds of a frantic search being carried out.

Another ten minutes of making our way through the brush brought nightfall and also the sound of search parties going through the brush in several directions.

Then we came to a very small, narrow, and faint trail which led in a general southeastern direction.

"Now we run," said the girl. "Run like never before."

"We will fall in the dark," Seng cautioned.

"We be capture if we no run," the girl responded. "And that be big worse."

So we ran down the trail in the dark. We certainly didn't run at full speed since Seng had the girl on his back, all of us were already near exhaustion, and Loc was a little unsteady. But we ran. Aside from our fatigue, running down a trail in a thick rain forest is dangerous at best, and in the dark it is foolhardy. Seng's prediction proved quite accurate, and we all fell several times within the first hour, but fortunately with no serious injuries. At least not serious enough to stop us. Loc had what would become a black eye; the girl got a cut on her forehead from a sharp branch; and I had a variety of bruises, aches, and pains from encounters with rocks and sticks by the side of the trail. It was difficult even to stay on the trail at all in the dark and we, all too frequently, had to stop and search for it. A few times, we even backtracked until we could be sure we had found it.

It was a night of misery and terror. After Loc's third or fourth fall, I grabbed his wrist and pulled him along.

He tried to get loose. "I can do it."

"Shut up," I said rudely. "I don't have breath and energy to argue."

After a bit, Seng stopped and we all followed suit. "Listen."

We tried to breathe quietly but weren't very successful, so Seng set the girl down and moved back up the trail several yards to hear better. He listened and we all rested for a few minutes, then he rejoined us. "I hear no sounds of pursuit," he said. "I think we can walk for a little."

"No, no." the girl said excitedly. "Run! I run now." She tried to stand and managed it but when she tried to walk, it was only a limping hobble.

"We will walk a while," Seng said and turned around for her to get back on.

"Let me carry her a while," I said and moved between them. Seng made a weak objection, but didn't offer to wrestle me for the job.

She was a very small lady, but heavier than she looked, and I was impressed with Seng's endurance and determination in carrying her so far on a run in the dark. I had come over in a very strong, well-conditioned physical body, and I couldn't imagine what it was like for Loc who had forty-six years of back-breaking work, intestinal worms, malaria, and no medical care. After a while more of carrying her through the dark, the slightly larger than half moon got high enough to provide a little illumination and we made better progress.

But as it turned out, the moon wasn't our friend because others made better progress, too, and we could hear the sounds of our pursuers coming down the trail behind us. We stopped for a few moments to make sure and we clearly heard voices.

"We must run again," the girl said.

Seng nodded and we ran. Now the moon was our friend again and, thanks to its dim help, we could make better time than before. We made our way up a ridge and, just past the peak, we were stopped cold. The trail went onto a rocky outcrop and simply disappeared. We spent a few minutes casting about looking for the continuation but could not.

"It's probably here but invisible in the dark," Seng whispered a little angrily.

"We go now," the girl urged.

"Yes, we go now," Seng said wearily and headed down the slope through the brush.

I followed but very carefully. Hurrying down a steep hill in the dark with no trail and carrying somebody on my back could be a disaster so I had to move very carefully. Fortunately, we reached the more level place without disaster but with a new set of bruises and scratches. Still, we kept going southeast as best we could.

I noticed that Seng was pulling on Loc's belt and Loc staggered frequently.

Seng stopped. I set the girl down gratefully. In the moonlight, Loc looked completely exhausted, and I doubted that I looked much better. I certainly didn't feel any better.

We put our heads close together so we could talk in whispers. "Should we keep going, or try to find a hiding place?" Seng asked.

Loc shook his head. "I can go no further."

"No, no," the girl whispered urgently. "We must get away."

Seng looked at me and I shrugged. He looked indecisive and started to say something, but before he could, we heard the sound of voices above us. We couldn't make out what they were saying, but it was rather clear that they had come to the outcrop where we had lost the trail. That meant that they were gaining on us.

But fortunately for us, they had flashlights and found the trail as it led off the rock. They headed down the trail and went past us, missing us by about a hundred yards.

Then it began to get light and Seng looked hopeful. "Maybe they've missed us."

"No," said Loc. "In the light, they will soon notice that we have not been on that trail and come back to find our tracks.

The girl stood up and took a few steps. "I better now. We must run. Go this way." She pointed due south, away from the trail the guards had followed.

Seng sighed. "Very well."

So we went through the brush some more, trying hard to leave no trail, but four people cannot help but leave some sign which can be read by a skilled tracker.

The girl was right. She could walk fairly well now, and it was a relief not to be carrying her. She led the way and, after about an hour of brush busting, we ran across another trail, this one even smaller than the last, leading due south.

"We go this one," she said and started running.

But her ankles weren't that good, and she fell twice in a hundred yards. Seng picked her up, looked at Loc who basically looked like he had died the week before.

Seng shook his head. "They can't run, and if we carry them, we can't out run the guards. We have to find a place to hide." He looked around. "Maybe a cave—"

Just then we heard a shout from behind us. "Here!" An's voice called.

That sent us all running down the trail into a small creek valley, but after only a little, the adrenalin ran out.

Seng came to me. "Keep them going," he whispered and moved to the side.

I started to object but he motioned for silence and pushed me down the trail.

I went. After about five minutes, we heard a commotion behind us, a short cry of distress cut short, and then silence. In a couple of minutes, we heard the sound of footsteps running quietly down the trail in our direction. With few options now, we moved off the trail to hide in the rather sparse brush.

Then I saw Seng come running into sight with a patch of blood on his shirt and carrying a rifle and two ammo magazines.

We came back onto the trail and hurried. In only half a mile the girl suddenly stopped. "I know this place," she said excitedly. "Come with me."

We hurried down the trail to the stream. She waded in and moved upstream where we soon came to the sound of a waterfall.

"There is place behind water," she said and went into the pool at the base of the falls.

We followed and she took us right into the falling water. In the stories, it would have been a large cavern with furnishings and a fireplace and maybe a joint of beef on a spit. But it wasn't a Robin Hood story and there was barely enough room between the waterfall and the cliff for us to have space to breathe. At that point, I didn't care. We all sat down in the pool, leaned back against the cliff, and just breathed deeply, enjoying the sensation of rest. But in only a few minutes, after we got our breath, reality set in. The water was cold, and the rocks we sat on and leaned against were very uncomfortable. As a temporary hiding place, it would do, but if we tried to stay all day, hypothermia would set in.

But the immediate suddenly became very important when we heard voices. They came nearer, and we could hear two guards arguing about how to check the area.

"I know how," one voice said.

That was followed by a burst of rifle fire on full automatic. The bullets struck the cliff right above us, right where our chests and heads would have been had we not been sitting. We all jumped and then ducked but no damage was done.

We heard a voice angrily tell the shooter to quit. "You just announced where we are to everybody around."

Then silence. For about an hour there were no voices and no sound except the water and some birds. Loc had gone to sleep. We were all shivering, miserable again.

Seng looked at me with a question in his expression. I shrugged in response.

So we sat and shivered some more. I had been cold before, even colder than this. Once I had come over as an Aleut in order to get the village chief to let a Russian priest start a church on the island. The villagers had had a very bad set of experiences with Russian hunters and were of a mind to kill any Russians they saw. Fortunately, this Russian had been different—very compassionate—and had some medical knowledge. When he saved the life of one of the young men in the village by simply lancing an infection and keeping it clean, the chief had given in and that island had become the center of a great mission. In addition, that priest and his successor had done much to ameliorate some of the abuses that Russian trappers had visited on the Aleuts.

But, there, I hadn't been soaking wet and sitting in a waterfall. I had the thought that sitting shivering in a waterfall wasn't doing much persuading, but my next thought was that we all had to be alive for persuasion to do any good. Finally, we had to come out or die there. I leaned forward until I could just barely see out past the water and stayed still for several minutes. I saw nothing suspicious so I stood up and came out into the wonderful, beautiful, and warm sunshine, followed by the others. We walked out of the water to find a very faint path which the guards had been on.

"Now what?" I asked of the group in general, feeling relief that leeches didn't like cold moving water.

The girl pointed to the east, and set out. But before we all took a step, a harsh voice called out, "Halt!" and we heard the sound of the rifle's safety clicking off.

The girl's eyes grew as big as the moon had been last night. "Run!" she yelled and gave an excellent demonstration of what she meant.

I ran, too, but decided that it was time for some more direct intervention in the form of an old trick. I concentrated briefly and heard the guard who had spotted us gasp in surprise as he lost his sight and was blinded temporarily.

I felt a big sense of relief which quickly went away

when I saw another guard rise out of the brush several yards to our left and point his rifle right at me. I felt a momentary burst of hope when I saw that it was Thanh, the better of the guards. That hope was totally misplaced, as Thanh proved by firing a burst. I winced, but felt nothing and, with relief, ran on unhurt. But the relief was equally short-lived when, behind me, I heard Loc grunt. I looked back briefly and, in horror, saw him on his knees with blood coming from his mouth, then he fell completely.

In total shock, I stopped and started to go back, but the girl grabbed my wrist and pulled. "Run!" she urged again and her urging was punctuated by the whine of a bullet passing close by my head.

Knowing she was right, I ran, but my mind was in complete overload. This had never happened to me. This couldn't happen to me. I was sent to protect Loc and I just saw him die. *This can't be real*, my mind screamed, but another short burst from Thanh's rifle convinced me. Then Seng stopped, dropped to one knee, took aim up the trail, and another bullet whizzed past, but this time not meant for me. Still in shock, I saw Thanh fall, and then a turn in the path blocked it all from view.

In very little time, we heard the guards return to the pool and start running after us. In spite of our weariness, shivering, and shock, that spurred us on, and we drew a little ahead.

Then surprisingly, the girl slowed and looked into the tree tops. She gave an odd cry which could have been a bird call. Then she pushed me. "Run!" she said yet again. She had gotten stuck on that word.

Still, it seemed a very good idea, so I ran. Once more she gave that odd call and, in a few minutes, she slowed to a fast walk and motioned us to do the same. Just as we were about to come out of the jungle into a small clearing of elephant grass I heard "Stop right there," in something totally new to me—Vietnamese spoken with an Alabama accent.

The girl said something in a language I didn't understand—surprisingly, because I usually came over with all the languages I need. I guess the Boss decided I didn't need that one.

Then the strangely accented voice said "Get off the trail into the bushes and hide," which we quickly did.

After a minute or two of near silence, we heard our pursuers come up the trail behind us. But before we could get very scared, we heard a tremendous explosion and several rifle shots. There was more silence and, after a couple of minutes, fourteen men came up the trail, carrying the guards' rifles, ammo, and knives.

The men were rather short and all of them looked a lot like the girl, a resemblance heightened by their clothing, which was identical to hers, and their near total lack of facial hair. The strange voice with the accent appeared then and turned out to be a very large man with very dark skin like an African but who was wearing an American army uniform with sergeant's stripes on the sleeves and carrying a rifle identical to the guards' rifles.

He gave some instructions in the strange language—he didn't have the Alabama accent when speaking it—and we all headed down the path into the elephant grass.

We went about a mile and stopped in a very dense thicket. I wasn't sure about our companions and whether they were our rescuers or captors, but at least they shared their food and water with us. Their food was quite good, especially after so many days of nothing but rice balls in fish sauce.

They gave me a rice ball but one with seasoning and peppers in it along with chunks of spicy meat which made it very good. I also received a strip of some dried meat which was unidentifiable until I tasted it and found it to be monkey.

The American sergeant had a conference with two older-looking short men, with several glances in our direction. They called the girl over for part of it and, afterward, she came over to us. "My people, of the Jarai, thank you for your rescue of me from the—" She used a word that wasn't Vietnamese but she said it like a really ugly insult. "Since you cannot go up to your homes, you are asked if you wishes to come by us to us home."

At that Seng perked up. He stood and bowed. "I am honored, and would like to accept." He followed that with a look at the girl which made her blush.

The large sergeant came over. "You are getting a very unusual honor," he said to Seng. "These people very seldom accept outsiders, but the young lady is the daughter of a very important elder, and she told us of what you did for her. Their invitation is a tremendous expression of gratitude." He looked around. "We need to move. There may be Cong in the area. But I don't think any of you are up to traveling far today. We have a bunker about five miles away. Can you make it that far?"

Seng nodded nonchalantly, not wanting to be outdone by his new lady love.

With no other business pressing, I nodded assent.

The sergeant turned and gave an arm signal and the group moved out. Two of the men walked right behind Seng and me, obviously to keep an eye on us.

The trip to the bunker was accomplished in silence and haste. I spent the time brooding over my failure to protect Loc. Halfway up a ridge, the whole group stopped and hid in the brush beside the trail.

I sat on a handy rock. I was still in shock. Loc was my job and he was dead. I could only hope—well, actually, I knew—that the Boss had a backup plan.

He was obviously going to need one since I had failed in my main mission.

After several minutes of waiting, our escorts came back onto the trail and motioned for us to continue up the trail. Just around a turn we came to the rest of the group standing looking in all directions. One of the older men went to a vine covered bank, grabbed the carpet of vines and pulled it aside, revealing a wooden door which he then opened.

We hurriedly went into the bunker, except for the last two men who went back down the trail to serve as security after putting the vines back in place.

The bunker consisted of three small rooms connected by tunnels. Each room had a firing port, well camouflaged from the outside and there was a rear entrance. Seng and I were ushered into the last room and told to sit on a bench against the back wall. The sergeant checked every firing port and the occupants, apparently encouraging them and eliciting a laugh or a grin from each of them. Seng and I sat in silence for a few minutes, then one of the older men of the group came into our room and sat on the floor opposite us.

He stared at us with no expression for about half an hour, then he got up and come over to sit cross-legged right in front of me. He stared into my eyes some more, then cocked his head to one side.

"You seem distressed," he said in Vietnamese.

"I am indeed. My friend Loc is dead."

"We have all lost many friends in this war."

"That is true, but Loc was my responsibility. I should have protected him and I failed him."

I noticed Seng turn his head to look at me.

The Jarai elder cocked his head the other direction. "How was he your responsibility?"

I shrugged. "It was a responsibility that I took upon

myself. At the least his death should have counted for something."

Seng stirred in agitation beside me. "Did you not see what happened?"

I nodded. "I was there."

"Apparently you did not see. His death was not for nothing," Seng said emphatically. "After Loc fell and you started running, he rose back up with a rock in his hand. Thanh was about to shoot the woman and me but Loc threw the rock at Thanh, hitting his arm. That made Thanh's last burst miss us. Without Loc's help, we would all be dead. His last act saved all of our lives."

My mind went briefly into overdrive again, but I settled it down. Things were beginning to look different. "So you are alive only because of the actions of Loc as he was dying?"

Seng nodded and I leaned back against the wall in confusion. At least this news put my failure in a very different light.

The elder tapped my knee with a calloused finger. "Sometimes what you think you are meant to do is not your real task." He leaned forward to tap the other knee and a necklace with a cross braided out of a black bootstring fell out from his collar. "Sometimes when we are assigned a task we don't know what the real goal is."

Then it clicked. I had failed Loc, but as he frequently does, the Boss took something that was bad and transformed it into something good. It was a failure on my part but the Boss's success. He was being devious again.

Seng nudged me with his shoulder. "You did very well. I was very glad to have had you along with me."

"Thank you."

Then the lookout in the front room said something which the elder translated for us. "The scouts are back."

The sergeant and eldest went to the first firing port and

held a conversation through it with the scouts which the elder summarized for us, "There is no pursuit. It is safe to go home."

So we vacated the bunker and gathered on the trail as the last man out replaced the vines.

I was standing between Seng and the sergeant and the sergeant looked at me. "You are coming with us, aren't you?"

I shook my head. "I have relatives in the area," I said, which was true, even though they were not earthly relatives. "I will go to them. I thank you for what you have done for me and for my friends."

The sergeant and Seng looked surprised, and the sergeant's look quickly turned to suspicion.

"Don't worry," I said to the sergeant. "I'm not Cong, and I won't tell anyone for a long time about what I saw."

The sergeant nodded skeptically, but one thing we do well is to inspire trust. It worked this time and the sergeant went off to see to the march.

The lead pair of the Jarai moved out and we were out of time. "Thank you," Seng said.

"You are welcome, and thank you," I said, then he was moving out, too. I was trying to figure how to explain this one when it all went away.

CHAPTER 3

Coming over is always a shock, and this time I came out in near pitch darkness, which made the shock and disorientation even worse. I put my hand out to steady myself and touched a brick wall which was all that kept me from falling. I shook my head and shivered then looked around. I was in a near-proverbial dark alley with no lights, and I could just make out the mouth of the alley a dozen yards away. I was glad that I had picked the spot carefully, and that I knew no one was in it, or I would have been leery of the place. I walked over to the alley mouth, where there was more light from a dim streetlight about a hundred yards to the north. I looked around and saw a warehouse district with several low buildings in differing states of upkeep, with most of them being on the lower end of that scale. Definitely a part of Memphis that the tourist bureau didn't publicize.

I was again a typical human male, in rather rough clothes of a type which were about normal for someone down on his luck, but who was hoping to do better. I started off toward the light and, before I had gone far, I saw another man come out of one of the buildings, which looked to be completely unoccupied. He headed for the light as well. I had expected him to show up soon and come to the light—a standard gathering place for men looking for work loading or unloading the trucks which came in and out of the various warehouses in the area. I had expected to be the first one since it was still a couple of hours before sunrise, but he beat me there.

"Good morning," I said, from far enough away that it was obvious I was announcing myself and not trying to surprise him.

He nodded. "Mornin,'" he replied, a little warily.

He was several inches below average height and so thin that he looked malnourished, which he was. He was also in the latter stages of recovering from a case of mononucleosis, which he had sweated out in an abandoned office in the warehouse which he'd just left and he still hadn't gotten his full strength back. He was wearing old-looking jeans and a tattered old army field jacket with several pockets. I knew that those pockets held his entire worldly goods.

"You're here early," I offered.

He nodded again. "Couldn't sleep. Worried that somebody would come in and find me. And more worried that I'd miss out on a job and a ride." He took off his cap, revealing some fiery red hair in need of a comb and a barber, in that order. He produced a comb from his pocket, but the barber wasn't forthcoming.

"This is my first day here," I said. "Do you get much work?"

"It's my third day, but I had work yesterday and the day before. Enough to eat, but not to get a fancy hotel."

I grinned. "Well, maybe today is the day we hit that jackpot."

He smiled back. "If I did make that much, I'd spend it on a bus ticket instead. I'm called Red," he told me, extending a hand.

"I'm Sam," I said, taking it.

After a few more minutes of conversation about nothing much, we stopped and watched a truck and trailer pull into the street.

The truck pulled to the light and stopped with several emphatic hisses from its air brakes. The driver rolled down the window. "Good. I was afraid nobody would be here yet, it's so early. Need a job?"

"Yep. You got one?" Red replied.

The driver nodded. "In fact, I need both of you, if you're both wanting work."

"That's what I'm here for," I said.

"I'm trying to get to Omaha," Red stated. "Do you know of anybody headed that direction?"

The driver raised an eyebrow. "Omaha, huh? Well, you'll need some money before you get there, so come on and help me load."

"You pay cash?"

"That's the only kind of money I've got."

Red nodded and we both climbed onto the flatbed trailer. The driver headed off with a roar and dual clouds of diesel smoke coming out of the exhausts.

He drove around two corners, then he slowed, pulled up to the door of one of the better-kept warehouses, and stopped with the engine idling. We all three jumped to the ground.

The driver, who was a big hefty man, produced a key from his pocket. "Come help me with the doors," he commanded.

He unlocked the big padlock, and we pushed the heavy doors aside with loud squeaks from the rollers.

"What's your name, Red?" he asked, inadvertently hitting on the right name.

"I go by Red."

Mike laughed.

"I got it right by accident. There's a big breaker box on the left just inside the door. Throw the switch, please." Then the driver headed to the truck cab. Red and I went into the warehouse and, in the dim light from the street-lights, found the box. Soon a string of lights in the ceiling came on. Red and I watched as the driver backed the rig into the warehouse and into a loading pit beside which was a large mass of filled plastic bags. The truck engine stopped. Red and I went over, stood by the bags, and waited. After a minute, the driver came out, having given us a chance to read the bag labels and to learn that we would be loading bagged cow manure.

"Cow manure?" Red asked with a grimace.

"Yep," the driver said with a grin. "But don't worry, it's dried and in plastic bags. You can't smell it, and it won't get on you. Unless a bag busts open. Which might happen." He laughed at Red's expression. "What's the matter, Red? Got something against cow manure?"

Red grinned back. "Not if I get paid for it. I just didn't expect it…uh…"

Taking the hint, the driver extended a hand. "I'm Mike. You'll get paid for it. And you'll earn it. It's not on pallets, so we have to load the whole thing by hand. This stuff is used as mulch and fertilizer by gardeners." He looked at me. "What's your name?"

"Sam," I replied.

"Sam, you hand the bags to Red, and he'll hand them to me, and I'll stack them."

So we did. The bags were lighter than they looked, and the loading went pretty quickly. Mike had obviously done this many times before and was quite fast at it. Red seemed to be pretty experienced at truck loading, too, and was a hard worker.

My job required no knowledge, except to pick up a bag and pass it along. Which was good, since the Boss had sent me without any knowledge of truck loading. We come over with whatever we need to know—I did hernia surgery once in a rural clinic in Honduras—but I was an unskilled worker this trip, so stevedore skills were lacking. But I could hand off bags with the best of them. It took almost as long to tie down each tier as we finished it as it did to stack it. From a financial standpoint, it didn't take long enough since we were both getting paid by the hour.

When we had finished tying off the last rick, Mike stretched and turned to Red. "You two did good work. That's not always the case when I pick up a helper from the local job market. Not all of them are like you two seem to be—folks who are trying to get ahead and willing to work hard for it."

Red grinned. "At least we're both sober," he said.

Mike counted out our pay and handed it to each of us. "So, Red. You're going to Omaha, you say?"

Red nodded. "Yep."

"What's in Omaha?"

"A job. I've had a run of bad luck, but I've been offered a job sweeping up in a tire store with a promise of learning the shop end of things and maybe moving up. So if I don't get a ride from here today, I'm headed to the interstate to try hitch hiking."

"Well, Red, you're in luck. This load is going to Omaha, and I'm going to need help unloading it. Are you open to another job late tonight?"

"In *Omaha*?"

"That's where I'll be. Are you coming?"

"Sure!"

"I wanted to make sure you were a decent worker and not crazy or a drunk. But I guess you'll do, Red."

I poked Red. "What's your real name, Red?"

Red turned to me and grinned. "If he'll take me to

Omaha, I don't care if he calls me Pokeweed. Red is fine."

I shrugged. "Okay, Red."

Mike looked at me. "Where are you headed?"

I shrugged. "Trying to get to Fargo. Or Boise. Or Willamette. But I'm in no big hurry." Actually I didn't know if I was in a hurry or not. My only instructions this time were to find Red at the light and look for opportunities. What opportunities would come weren't included in my instructions but I didn't think that the Boss's plans included having me wave goodbye while they headed off to Nebraska, so I said, "I see that you've got only two seats, but I'll ride in the sleeper if you'll take me."

Mike considered for a moment. "If you two don't mind switching off between the passenger seat and sleeper, I'd be glad to have the help unloading tonight when we get there."

So to Red's very visible relief and excitement, we were off to Omaha. There was a little bit of getting the warehouse in proper order, then Mike drove the rig out, we got the lights out and doors locked, and we were ready.

As we were heading to the truck cab to get in, Mike frowned. "How about some breakfast before we head out?"

Red looked uncertain "Ahhh…well—"

"I'll buy," Mike interrupted. "Call it a bonus for working hard this morning."

"You already paid us for an extra hour," Red pointed out.

"That's because we worked a part of an hour. And like I said, you two worked hard and good. Some folks I get for this would have loafed to make it take longer and not tried to do a good job. I come out cheaper and better, paying you more and buying you breakfast."

"Okay," Red replied.

Mike looked at me. "Sam?"

I grinned. "I'm always ready for a good meal."

So we loaded up, with me in the sleeper shelf—a padded platform behind the seats, just long enough and wide enough to lay down on, mostly. Mike would have been a little cramped in both directions. We headed for the main road and Becky's, which was where Mike said he was taking us.

"I like to eat at Becky's whenever I'm in here," Mike said. "Ever eaten there before?"

Red shook his head. "Never been here before. I'm here because it's as far as the last ride was going toward Omaha."

Mike grunted. "You sound like you're from somewhere close. Not meaning to be nosy."

"No problem," Red replied. "I'm from east Texas, just outside Killeen. That area was settled by folks from right around here so our accents sound about alike."

The rest of the conversation centered on Texas, cotton, oil, cattle, and "The Oilers chances this year," which I thought might be a reference to an antique railroad but from the rest of the conversation, I learned it was about some game or other. I could have talked to them about east Texas but my knowledge was badly out of date. I'd last been there during the depression when I'd come over to help a rancher who owned what he accurately called, "A worn-out worthless pile of dust with worn-out starving scrub cows and some worn-out swayback nags," in order to help convince him to hang on for another year. With the help of his neighbor, who was also a cattle man, and the part-time pastor of the local church, he stayed, "One more year so's I can go broke in a big way," as he put it, just long enough for a wildcatter to make a big oil strike and make them both very wealthy. He'd then used some of his money to fund a major charity drive by that church, which made a big difference in that section of the state.

But I would have a hard time explaining my days as a roustabout during the depression, since I had made a point of looking no older than either of them did—early to mid-twenties.

We got to Becky's, and the food was as good as Mike's word of mouth advertisement. Pancakes big enough to cover the plate and almost light enough to float away, enough butter to fill a churn, molasses-flavored corn syrup, real smokehouse sausage, and a homemade cinnamon bun which was wonderful but had about two days' worth of fat and sugar.

To my great surprise, though, the coffee was awful. But the rest of it made up for it. Mike noticed my face when I took my first sip of coffee and laughed. "Yeah, it's not very good. Becky says bad coffee keeps you awake better than good coffee."

"Not if you don't drink it," Red retorted, putting his cup down with a grimace. But he attacked a gravy covered biscuit the size of a saucer with a very different attitude.

Mike paid the waitress, who hadn't learned her sassy attitude in a fancy restaurant, and we headed back to the truck.

I offered to flip a coin to see who got first turn in the seat, but Red shook his head. "If you don't mind, I'll take first shift in the sleeper. I didn't get much sleep last night and between that and the lifting and loading, I'm beat."

"That's fine with me," I said. "If I'd won the toss, I'd have taken the seat."

So Red climbed in first and squeezed into the sleeper. I took the passenger seat. Mike pulled out and headed toward the big road and the big triple bridge. It was just starting to show hints of light in the east, but even in the dark, the bridges and the Mississippi were quite impressive. I wished I could have crossed in the light but there was enough of a view to be awed by the size of the river, the bridges, and the dozen barges in sight. Red missed the whole thing, having gone to sleep almost before we were out of the parking lot at Becky's.

Mike turned the radio on low, and we rode mostly without conversation. I watched the light grow and enjoyed the music coming from the big long-range Nashville station. Merle was proud of Muskogee, Charlie wanted to get to San Antone, and then in an "Oldie," Johnny fell into a ring of fire. Then we heard that the army's air mobile, infantry, and the armored cavalry had crossed into Cambodia and serious protests were taking place in Connecticut.

Mike reached over and turned the radio off with a word which I'm not supposed to know —at least I'm not supposed to use it.

"What do those morons think they're going to get done by waving signs and calling the police bad names? Is the war going to go away because they get themselves on the six o'clock news?" he said.

I didn't really think he expected an answer, but I gave him one anyway. "I think those protests were about some courtroom business, not the war."

"Same thing and the same morons," he snorted. "There are some good reasons to oppose our being over there, but that bunch manages to miss all of the valid ones."

It turned out his views were more than just being opinionated. He'd been to Vietnam while in the air force, and he hated the communists there, plus his experience with an anti-war group which "welcomed" him back in San Francisco had been appalling.

"And my youngest brother is mixed up in that mess, with long hair and dressing like a peasant." He made an obvious effort to calm down. "Let's talk about something else. You got a girl?"

"No. You?"

He grunted, a little disgustedly. "I guess."

I laughed. "That's a lot less definite answer than I expected."

He chuckled. "My girl—Charlene—and I are weird. She's being difficult lately and then tries to tell me that I'm the one being difficult. We've been dating since high school, but it's been an off-and-on thing ever since. We'll do real well for a while, then we'll fight and stay away for a little, then we get back together. We seem to be headed for an off-again point lately." He shrugged. "It'll pass."

"Which will pass? Your difficult time or your being together?"

Mike gave me a skeptical look. "Who knows? And right now I think, 'Who cares?'"

He looked a little startled at having said that, not sure if he should have. We tended to have that effect on people. They'd tell us things they would never admit to anybody else. Lots of times, I'd heard things from people that they'd not even admitted to themselves until they told me.

Once in fifteenth century Austria, the village cobbler's daughter had admitted to me without thinking that she was madly in love with the village priest, which was of course a no-no at that time. But once she admitted it to herself, she decided to tell him in confession. Then he admitted to feeling the same way about her. So he went to his bishop, who was secretly delighted to permit him to leave the priesthood because he was a really poor priest and pastor, but turned out to be an excellent blacksmith, husband, and father. But to get the bishop to agree, I still had to make a wings-and-halo appearance to him. And the new priest was a great one.

Mike looked like he was in a similar situation where he hadn't really admitted something to himself until he told me. He quickly changed the subject, and we discussed airplanes, trucks, shipping schedules, church, preachers, farmland, kids, Sunday School, and several other things for a couple of hours.

Then Red woke up and looked out of the sleeper. "I think I'm going to need to stop pretty soon," he said.

The idea met with general assent and, within a few minutes, we came to a truck stop where we took care of the necessities and grabbed a snack. I ate a cookie which was wonderful and Red had some fudge. Then we were back on the road, with Red in the seat and me in the sleeper.

I wasn't very tired. I normally come over as a perfect physical specimen, and the loading of the truck had been no more than a very light job, nothing like some times I've been over. About the worst in terms of physical labor had been the time I was a porter on the Ho Chi Minh trail during the big rush build-up before Tet, and being an Indian slave miner in a Mexican silver mine under the Spanish. In the mine, I had carried baskets with over a hundred pounds of ore up a pretty steep mineshaft for about half a mile and then up a forty foot ladder, and we did it for fifteen hours every day. I was there for only nine days. The others were there for a lifetime, which wasn't as long as it sounds. But when I left, I took three other men with me. We evaded the Spanish cavaliers and the even-harder-to-lose Indian trackers and got into eastern Sonora where one of my companions had grown up. All three of them made a life with that tribe and were instrumental in the start of that tribe's church.

So I propped my head on my hand and watched as much scenery as I could from the less-than-wonderful vantage point the sleeper afforded—although I had a great view of the back of Mike's head—and took part in the conversation. Red turned out to be a big talker, and Mike did fine in the conversation with Red being the instigator, so we were well entertained with conversation and, for a little while, the very impressive view of the arch and the river as we went through St. Louis. But mostly we were out of sight of the river, and the view was pretty but not exciting. So we talked until it was time to stop for a noon meal. Mike offered to pay again, but Red and I both thought we should pay for our own. Mike didn't argue very hard.

He stopped at a big chain truck stop where the food was cheaper but not nearly as good as Becky's. I still enjoyed it, especially the banana pudding which Red and I shared for dessert. I really wanted to get one of the pieces of coconut pie behind the glass counter, but it cost more than I thought I should pay. On this trip I was supposed to live on whatever I could get legitimately here, so I had to take good care of the pay I had gotten from Mike that morning. But that pie sure did look good.

Then Mike fueled up the truck and did some maintenance-type things here and there on it, checked the load and tie-downs, all with the assistance of Red who seemed to know what he was doing, and we were off again. It was Red's turn in the sleeper, and he talked for a little while but within half an hour, he was sound asleep again.

Mike chuckled when Red started to snore. "I guess being a hobo is a hard life."

"Yes, it is," I agreed.

Which I knew to be true. I wasn't an experienced one in this setting, but I had been the medieval equivalent several times in Europe. I had come over several times as a wandering friar, who were much more respected than the wandering homeless but led a similar life, and a few times I had come over as one of the wandering homeless. On one of those, I had to convince another rootless man to settle in as part of a small village which was short of people and willing to take him in. Most of the rootless would have jumped at the chance, but Cloveg had been pretty badly wounded, both physically and emotionally, on his last attempt to rejoin society, and he was reluctant to make the commitment.

With the help of the local priest and his son and daughter, we finally convinced him. He cleared some land, married the priest's daughter, and was the grandfather of one of King Karl the Great's biggest supporters in the area. I still snort when I hear Karl called by the French name Charlemagne, since he was as German as could be. But he really was the Great. Several of us came over frequently during his reign and for some time prior because, as you can imagine, the Boss took a great interest in Karl's work. And fortunately for the world, Karl took a great interest in the Boss's work, too.

I got Mike to tell me about the area we were going through. We had headed west and left the river and were in the prairie now. This was Mike's home region. He had travelled extensively in it, and was pretty knowledgeable about the history. I had taken this general route once before, when it looked a little different. I had travelled to the high plains with a party of buffalo hunters in the 1870s, so I had met a couple of the people that Mike was telling me about.

They were a much rougher bunch than Mike made them sound, and they had less high-sounding purposes. "Gonna get me a bunch of money and never work no more," was the way one of them had put it.

I remember hoping that he'd spend some of that money on a bath, although I didn't really smell any better at the time. One member of the party was going to Denver to try mining, but never got there, instead taking up residence in a village of the Arikara Indians and was able to start a church there.

The afternoon went rather slowly and as expected, dark fell before we made it into Omaha, so I missed my first sighting of the bluffs, which I'd missed on my last trip, too, due to a thunderstorm that spooked our horses. They ran twenty miles south, and we had to chase them on foot. Of course, I had seen the bluffs from the other side, but that's very different.

We did get to see two big air force bombers take off into the night as we drove by the air base, and that was an impressive sight, even from a mile or so away. Then we went to a part of town which probably wasn't in the tourist brochures, but again we went to one of the better maintained warehouses. This time there was a guard to unlock the door and turn on the lights, but no loading pit.

Mike pulled into the warehouse, shut the truck down, and we all got out and stretched. Then Mike headed toward a large doorway. "You two start untying the ropes. I'll be right back."

Red climbed onto the trailer, and I started loosening the knots while he coiled the ropes. We finished that job in just a few minutes, and Mike still wasn't back so Red got down from the trailer and fastened the ropes to their places on the back of the truck cab. He seemed to know how it was done, and I didn't, so I just handed the ropes up and watched. Then we leaned against the fender.

"Did you get all rested up?" I asked.

"Mostly," he agreed. "But I'll be tired again after this. It's been a rough few days lately, and I haven't completely recovered from a bad case of the flu. I'm not really cut out for this kind of life, and I really hope this job works out. It would be mighty nice to feel like a real person again."

"I guess so," I said, suppressing a smile. "But I've never been enough of a regular person to know what it would feel like."

Red looked at me strangely, but before he could reply, we heard an engine start up, and then a fork lift with Mike driving it came into sight through the doorway he'd gone out. He drove it to a stack of wooden pallets, picked up the stack on the fork, very carefully drove the precarious-looking pile to the truck, and lowered it to the ground, shutting off the engine.

"Do you know how to stack a pallet?" he asked us, getting down.

Red nodded, but I was clueless and shook my head.

"It's not complicated or hard. Red, start handing me some bags." Then Mike took the top pallet off the stack, set it on the ground, and showed me how to arrange the bags on the pallet so they would make a stable load. He was right and it was neither complicated nor hard. "Seven bags high. No more, no less," he told me then got another pallet down.

Red kept us both going by handing the bags off.

We quickly had both pallets finished with "seven bags high, no more, no less." Mike started the forklift and moved them to the wall.

I got another pallet down and had it nearly finished when Mike was ready to move it, so he just waited on the fork lift until it was complete. But instead of taking it away, he pointed me toward the stack of empty pallets. "Now there's room to work on the trailer, so put a pallet up there."

Working on the trailer was simpler and, that way, Mike could pick the pallet off the trailer, so the work went pretty fast.

Soon we had finished, and Mike was coming back from parking the fork lift against the wall. "Well, I promised you supper as part of the deal, so let's go to Trailside, okay?"

I nodded and Red shrugged. "I'll take your word for where to go since you're buying."

Mike backed the rig out of the warehouse, dropped the trailer in a line of similar ones, with help from Red, who knew how it was done, and none from me, who didn't.

There was a truck stop just a mile or so away at the edge of the warehouse district, and it was a local one, not a chain.

We filled up the tanks with Red doing the honors at the pump, and Mike taking care of the finances, including paying Red and me, again with a slight bonus. My contribution was in hoping the truck stop's food would be good. I never found out, since Mike loaded us back up into the truck cab, and we drove about half a mile away to a small burger joint with a neon sign that said *Trailside* on it.

"I like this place," Mike said, "but it doesn't have a truck parking lot, so I can only come when I'm bobtailing—without a trailer," he said in response to my questioning look.

We went into the rather small and crowded place, which was apparently a converted filling station. It looked like it had been better decorated and cleaned when it was a filling station—a real dive. And noisy from the crowd and from Kitty and then Loretta on the juke box.

We sat at a booth where the table had once been chrome and linoleum but wasn't anymore. The waitress—Shirley, it said on her name tag—turned out to be even sassier than the one at Becky's, but she got us our water and took our orders quite effectively as she called all of us "honey" about three times apiece.

"You're a brave boy, honey," she said to me when I ordered a Bulldogburger—cheese, onions, jalapenos, and special barbecue sauce. "Nobody's ever figured out what's in that sauce."

The burgers arrived, and we all got called honey again. "Check yours for dirt, honey," she said to Mike with a wink. "I think Tom dropped it on the kitchen floor."

There must have been something special about living in a stockyard town—the burgers were wonderful.

"You have to eat a piece of Tom's great homemade apple pie," Mike told us. "They're really good and really homemade, right here in his kitchen."

So we all got a piece and it lived up to its billing from Mike.

While we were there, the crowd thinned out. The few who were left ran out of dimes to feed the jukebox, so conversation became a practical option again.

Mike looked at Red. "So, are you going to stay with your cousin tonight?"

Red shook his head. "I don't know where he lives. He's not expecting me, and I don't really know him very well. He's giving me this job because his mom owes my mom a big favor from 1944."

"Then you're lucky they've both got long memories," Mike said with a smile. "So do you have any ideas about where to stay?"

Red shrugged. "Last night I stayed in an unlocked warehouse. I expect there's one here."

Mike frowned. "That can be dangerous." He looked thoughtful while Red shrugged again. Then Mike looked like he had just made up his mind about something. "I've got a trailer. It's little and it's a dump, but if you want, you can stay on the couch tonight. Then I'll take you to work in the morning."

Red looked shocked, but he didn't even pretend to

think about refusing. "That would be great. Thank you very much," he said eagerly and gratefully.

Mike looked at me. "What about you?"

"I guess I could head for the highway and try to hitch a ride."

Mike looked at the clock over the cash register. "Not much chance after dark. It's 10:30 at night. Besides, any moron who'd pick up a hitch hiker this time of night is probably somebody you don't want to ride with. You come on to the trailer, too."

"In for a penny, in for a pound, I guess, huh? Thank you. A lot." My gratitude was as real as Red's for a different reason. Not only did I now have a place to stay for the night, I had a means of staying connected to them, which was my purpose here. Now if I could just figure out what the Boss's purpose was, I'd be set.

Shirley brought Mike the bill and a sassy, "Hope that pie doesn't make you too sick, honey," then was off to sass another table.

Mike paid at the register, leaving a healthy tip for Sassy Shirley, and we loaded back into the truck cab, my turn in the sleeper.

"Is Shirley always that nice?" I asked.

Mike laughed. "Her name's Jessica, but for some reason she always wears that name tag. And yes, that was typical Jessica. And I think as many people come because of her as for Tom's cooking. Tomorrow is Saturday and I meet Charlene there for breakfast every week that I'm in town. Do you two want to come eat with us before I take Red to work?"

"Won't we be intruding?" Red wondered.

Mike shook his head. "Nope, we bring friends with us pretty often."

"Okay," Red responded, "but only if I pay for my own."

"Me, too," I added.

We rode in silence about two miles to a residential area which was somewhat below average. Mike pulled into the dirt driveway of an old, small, and slightly decrepit mobile home and stopped behind a twenty-year-old pickup truck.

Mike got a bag from the compartment under the sleeper and led the way inside. The trailer was quite small and decorated in early antiquated bachelor style—a dump. No two pieces of furniture matched, the curtains were ragged bed sheets, and the whole thing had a general sense of decrepitude. But while it was far from neat, it was clean, surprisingly so.

This late in a long, hard day, we were all tired, even this perfect physical specimen. While Red took his first shower in a couple of weeks, Mike put a sheet on the couch and from a back room produced an air mattress stamped *US Air Force* which he quickly blew up with a small pump. A sheet went on it, too, and after trips down the hall by each of us, Mike went to the bedroom. Red took the couch, I took the air mattress, and we were both quickly asleep.

෧෨෧

Charlene was already there at the Trailside when we arrived in Mike's pickup and, true to Mike's statement last night, I didn't notice any sign of her disapproving of our presence. We all introduced ourselves and went in. Shirley/Jessica wasn't there. Our waitress was a tired-looking older lady who didn't seem to enjoy her work as much as Jessica/Shirley had, but she was equally well known by Mike and Charlene, who called her Mrs. McLain, and she was equally efficient since our biscuits and eggs were delivered promptly and correctly. And politely. They weren't quite as good as Becky's, but close, and the coffee was wonderful. Mrs. McLain should teach Becky how to do it. But she didn't call any of us honey.

Somebody had turned down the volume on the juke box, and Conway was crooning at a level which allowed conversation.

"I'm glad to be here," Red told the couple, "but I'm afraid we're intruding."

Charlene laughed. "Not at all. A lot of our Saturday breakfasts are social outings. It's not at all unusual for us to sit with another couple from our Sunday School class. Besides, Mike takes in quite a few hard luck cases and they come with—" She gasped and covered her mouth with her fingers for a moment. "Oh! I'm sorry, I didn't mean—"

Red held up a palm and laughed. "Nothing to be sorry about, ma'am. I certainly qualify as a hard-luck case at the moment. And I am extremely grateful to Mike for 'taking me in' as you said. Without him, I'd probably still be looking for a ride here. And hungry. Which, thanks to his hiring me, feeding me, and driving me here, I'm not." He looked at me. "What about you, Sam. Are you a hard luck case?"

I shrugged. "Not really. I'm just the independent sort with very few needs."

He started to ask another question, but Mike interrupted. "I've found that in dealing with 'hard-luck types' that it's best not to ask too many questions, but to listen when they feel like talking."

"Okay." Red looked at Mike. "I'm still new at the hard-luck life. And I hope I don't get the chance to get more experienced."

Between bites, we learned that Charlene was in the child care business and kept a roomful of three-year-olds at Mrs. Bronson's Kiddie Kastle, that she loved her job and her charges, and that she was less than real happy with Mike at the moment, and vice versa, although we got that from their tone more than from anything they said.

After one rather testy exchange between them, Red tried to change the subject. "You mentioned your church. Where's that?'

Mike grimaced slightly, and Charlene sighed. "We're members at State Street Baptist. It's a middle-sized church, about eighty people there most weeks."

I pointed a forkful of eggs and sausage at Mike. "Mike, you looked unhappy then. What's going on?"

Mike smiled a little wryly. "Red was trying to find a safe subject, but he happened on the thing that's got us worked up right now."

"There's nothing to be 'worked up' about," Charlene said, primly. "It's a simple decision to make."

Mike frowned. "A simple decision with big implications," he said.

I arched my eyebrows at her and she smiled. "I've been asked to take over the five and six year old Sunday School class, and Mike doesn't want me to take it."

"That's not the case," said Mike, a little testy again. "I said you shouldn't take it just because people expect you to."

Charlene turned to Red. "I'm already the substitute teacher in that class, and I teach it once a month. Ron, the regular teacher, is in the National Guard and I teach for him on his drill weeks. So I already know all the children and how things are done."

"And somebody else can learn," Mike put in. "She already told me that she wouldn't like to be out of our own class all the time, but she feels obligated. She works with kids all week, and she'll tell you she's not sure about having them on Sunday, too."

Just then, it came to me what I was there for. The Boss wanted Charlene to take that class, and my job was to help get her into it. From the looks of things, I was facing some resistance, but otherwise, why would I have been sent?

Red, playing peacemaker, changed the subject again, this time to the safely neutral subject of the tire store to which he would soon be reporting. Both Mike and Charlene were somewhat acquainted with Red's cousin the owner, having gone to the same high school but a couple of years apart. Mike thought pretty well of him and his business and had bought tires there several times. "He's honest and knows his business. I think you'll do all right there. If you work as hard for him as you did for me, you'll do fine."

"I hope so and intend to," Red replied. "But I don't intend to spend my life pushing a broom. The reason I came this far for a janitor's job was the chance to learn the business and move up. I certainly hope that part works out."

Mike grinned. "If you can mount a tire as well as you stack a pallet, you've got nothing to worry about. And being late for your first day's work wouldn't be good, so let's get going."

We trooped to the cash register, paid our bills, and I went back to leave a quarter for Mrs. McLain and couldn't resist telling her, "Thank you, honey" as I went out, earning a reproving look. But not a puzzled one. She knew Jessica/Shirley.

Mike kissed Charlene goodbye. She got into her Volkswagen beetle. We piled into Mike's old pickup and headed to "Terry's Tires" at the edge of town.

Terry's Tires was a standard-looking tire store—white concrete block building with big windows in the office area, five bays, several racks and stacks of tires for many types of vehicles, and a large lot in the back with tires taller than me, which were obviously intended for some very heavy machinery.

Mike pulled into the parking lot. "It's a little far to walk back to my place," he said. "If you'll come back out and tell me what time you'll be getting off, I'll come back and pick you up, and you can stay a couple more nights with me."

"I'm very grateful," Red responded.

He got out and went into the office part. It was about 8:30 in the morning, and it looked like the work crew was just showing up to prepare for the day. Through the front window, we saw Red go to the front counter where another man came up and shook his hand, rather happily, it seemed.

"That's Terry," Mike said. "So far, so good."

Red and Terry talked for a couple of minutes, then Red came back out and up to Mike's window. "It's off to a good start," he said. "I've got the job and after I sweep the floors, I'm going to be helping on the tire mounting machine. We'll close at four."

"Sounds great," Mike said, smiling. "I'll be here at four fifteen."

"Thank you, very much. I'll pay you back for all of this."

Mike shook his head. "I've gotten a lot of help over the years," he said, "and several of those times when I offered to pay, I was told 'Just pass it on when you get a chance.' So that's what I'm doing, and that's how you can pay me back."

Red nodded. "Well, thanks. A lot." And he headed for the broom rack.

I expected Mike to pull out of the store lot, but instead, he turned to me. "Are you open to a short term job?"

"Sure," I said. "I told you I'm in no hurry to get any-where."

"A friend of mine is in the construction business and needs a few days' work from somebody. Minimum wage, and hard work, but work."

"Sounds good," I replied.

Then he pulled out and drove a few miles to an older residential area where a very large old brick house was in the process of being demolished. "Part of Jimmy's busi-ness is that he tears down old houses and salvages the materials for specialty jobs. Do you know where we are?"

"Yep," I said. "We're about a mile from your place thataway." I pointed southeast. I had a near-perfect sense of direction and knew exactly where we were.

Mike nodded. "So it's close enough to walk back. If you stick with the job, you can stay with me again to-night, too."

I grinned at him. "You're willing to help me out, as long as I'm willing to help myself and work at it, right."

"Exactly right. I'm glad to help folks who are trying to do better, but I have little sympathy for lazy leeches. I've got a feeling you're not a leech, and you can help me make up my mind by taking and keeping the job."

I opened the door and got out.

Mike pointed. "That's Jimmy standing by the front steps. Go prove to us that you can move up from being a bum."

I grinned. "Who says I'm not more than a bum al-ready?" I said as I shut the truck door.I introduced myself to Jimmy, who had seen Mike let me off and had figured out what was up. "I'm Sam Mollock. Mike says you can give me some work," I said.

Jimmy looked at me a little skeptically. "Yeah, but it's hard work." He looked at my hands, which fortunately were suitably calloused and rough, as though they'd been doing manual labor. "Come over here."

The job turned out to be turning a pile of rubble into a stack of bricks, cleaned of mortar and whatever else was on them. He showed me what looked to be a small hatchet with a hammer head on the back, a chisel, and a wire brush, and how to use each one. "If you can't get a brick clean with these, it's past using so just put it in the trash pile. Okay?"

I nodded. "Seems pretty simple."

"It is. Just takes sticking with it. We take lunch break between twelve and one. There's a store in walking distance down that street, and I've got bread and bologna you can eat for free. There's a water jug on the back of the truck, and an outhouse in the back yard. Any questions?"

"Nope."

"I'll be around if you have any later, or ask Hank if you can't find me. That's Hank on the front porch. So let's get to work."

So I got to work. It wasn't really very hard work and certainly not intellectually demanding. It was a little like the job I'd had for two weeks working on the walls of fourteenth century Darmstadt. I had been an assistant to a stonemason who needed some convincing to take up sculpture. But most of my time there was spent chipping little pieces off of big rocks with tools about like the ones I was using on the bricks, but here I was chipping mortar, not rock

It wasn't bad, even though it got pretty warm and several of the other workers took off their shirts. At noon, I decided to take Jimmy's offer of free food, which turned out to be bologna and mustard sandwiches, potato chips, and brownies which his wife had made. I noticed nobody went to the store to eat. The bologna sandwiches were mediocre but the chips were good and the brownies were wonderful.

The afternoon went about the same, except that around mid-afternoon, Jimmy opened a cooler and everybody got a soda. Mine was grape. It was good.

At quitting time, Jimmy came over, looked approvingly at the substantial stack of clean bricks, and counted out my pay. "Good work, Sam. Can you come back Monday?"

"Same deal?"

"Same deal."

"I'll be here."

I started walking toward Mike's trailer, having turned down the offer of a ride from Jimmy, since I knew he went the other direction, and it wasn't very far for me to walk.

The way to Mike's went past a day-old-bread store, so I went in, spent a quarter on a box of twelve slightly past-their-prime honey buns, and ate one of them as I walked the rest of the way.

When I got to Mike's, nobody was there so I sat on the front step, ate another honey bun, and went to the faucet for a good long drink of water.

Then Mike's pickup truck pulled around the big truck and Mike and Red got out. Red went to the back of the truck, took out a bicycle, and pushed it to the porch.

"Well," Mike said to me, "I hear you stuck it out for the whole day."

"Yep, no problem," I replied. "How did tire store janitorial work go?"

Red shrugged. "Okay, I guess. It's a job and a big step up for me. The best part was operating the tire mounting press. If Terry will promote me out of janitor work, I think I'll like this job. And if he doesn't, I'll get some work experience."

"What's with the bicycle?" I asked.

Red patted the seat. "I can ride it to work so Mike doesn't have to take me. I saw it for sale at the junk store close to Terry's so we stopped, and I spent three dollars on it. Now I can get to work without depending on somebody else."

"Good for you," I said. "Mike, how did you know I stayed the whole day?'

"I stopped for gas and saw Hank so I asked him. He said you stayed and did good work."

I smiled. "So, am I a lazy leech?"

Mike laughed. "Not today anyway. You two come help me carry groceries in."

We went to his pickup and each of us had a brown paper bag to carry in. We took it all into the kitchen and unpacked a bunch of cans, boxes, and bananas. One of the large cans was spaghetti, which Mike heated up for our supper, along with some garlic toast made of light bread. Compared to one meal I remembered from the sixteenth century where the best chefs of Toulouse made their best stuff for a troop of visiting Italian dignitaries—including me—the canned spaghetti was pretty bad. But once in northern Luzon during World War II while running from the invaders, I had a meal which consisted entirely of raw insects, one of which tried to crawl back out, and compared to that, Mike's spaghetti was wonderful. Perspective does matter.

The conversation mostly was about our new jobs, and then Mike and Red started talking incomprehensibly about the Royals—in America?—and how Lou and Amos, Dick and Paul made things look promising. Somewhere in the conversation I figured out that they were talking about baseball, but it seemed to bear little resemblance to the game we'd played in the pasture in 1880s Florida on our days off from digging to enlarge a sugar plantation. As we finished and started to clean up, Mike hesitated.

"It isn't a requirement in order to stay here but I'd very much like for you to go to church with us tomorrow. I'll be leaving about 9:30."

"I'd love to, but these are the only clothes I have."

"Well," Mike said, considering, "you'd be welcome however you're dressed, but you'd probably feel a little better if…" He turned to me. "Are you going?"

"I'm going to church somewhere," I replied, "so, sure, I'll go with you."

"Then let's wash your clothes, and I'll loan each of you a better shirt to wear to church. He went into the back room and came out with two sets of gym shorts and shirts. "Change into these," he said, tossing them in our direction, "and I'll wash your clothes."

We emptied our pockets, put on the gym clothes, and laughed when Red's shorts immediately fell to the ground. Sized for Mike's rather ample middle, they didn't quite work for skinny little Red. Mike went to the kitchen counter and handed Red a clothespin to take up the slack then went out the door to the neighbors', telling us that he kept her car running and got to use her washer and dryer in return.

So we watched television while the clothes got clean. Mike turned out to be a fan of "westerns," and it was fun and entertaining to watch Matt and Festus chase the outlaws. Then we finished the evening off with a cartoon which had even less to do with real cats and mice than the westerns had with the real west.

Then back on my air force mattress and a good night's sleep.

⌧⌧

The shirts Mike loaned us the next day were fairly

standard dress shirts. Mine was blue and Red's was white. It threatened to swallow him, but he rolled up the sleeves and tucked it in here and there, and it didn't look too ridiculous.

He laughed at the situation. "I'll have to buy some clothes before next Sunday," he said.

Mike shook his head, smiling. "Get the right size this time."

Then we loaded up in his pickup and made the short drive to State Street, where Charlene was waiting in her Beetle for us—for Mike, anyway. It was Rob's drill week, and Charlene was teaching her class of five and six year olds, so Mike took us to their Sunday School class made up of other twenty-somethings, and taught by an older man about fifty, who did a good job.

As we left the room after the bell rang, Mike turned to us. "Charlene takes the kids into the sanctuary, and I help her out. You can go on in if you want."

Red smiled. "Can I come help?"

Mike shrugged and smiled. "Sure, if you can take it."

So Red and I helped them herd a group of eight children down the hall, up a short flight of steps, and into the big sanctuary where most of them fanned out to sit with their parents, but one group of three went to the second pew and sat with a lady who was by herself until then.

"That's Mrs. Shilton who brings several children from her neighborhood," Charlene explained. "It's one of the poorest parts of town, but the kids like her and seem to like church."

We sat together in a pew about halfway back. Charlene turned to Mike. "Did you see that bruise on Jerry's neck?"

Mike nodded. "Hard to miss it. How'd he get it?"

"He said from playing ball."

Mike frowned. "That is a bad bruise for ball playing."

Red leaned over. "Which one's Jerry?" he asked.

"The five-year-old in the red shirt," Charlene said, pointing toward the front rows.

I looked and saw it was a really cute kid whom I'd noticed as having a really sweet smile for Charlene as he left the classroom.

Further conversation was cut off by the organ music starting, and I was carried away in worship.

After the service, we helped Mrs. Shilton get her charges into her station wagon and in the process, I noticed Red get Jerry over to one side and talk to him, obviously asking a question, but Jerry only shook his head and looked at the ground.

But the kids all finally got into the car, and Mrs. Shilton was off on her bus route.

Mike turned to Charlene. "What did you cook for dinner?"

She snorted. "Bologna and crackers is what you'll get from me. You didn't say you were coming for Sunday dinner."

"Well, don't we usually eat Sunday dinner there?"

"Usually isn't always. So where do you want to eat?"

"Your place."

"What's second choice?"

"Ronnie's."

"Okay."

Mike looked over at us. "Would you two care to come with us?"

Red frowned. "Is it expensive?"

Mike shook his head. "About like Trailside. A little more."

Red still looked uncertain. "Okay, I'll try it."

"Sam?" Mike asked, looking at me.

"I'm in," I replied. "But I might have to eat crackers and catsup."

Mike laughed. "You can beat that, even if you go cheap."

So we all rode down the street to Ronnie's BBQ, which was a little nicer than Trailside and had a little more class, or at least aspirations of class.

We found a table in a corner and checked out the menu. I figured I could eat a barbecue sandwich with French fries and stay within budget, and Red seemed to have come to the same conclusion, since he ordered the same thing. The waitress wasn't sassy or even very personable, but she was efficient, and we quickly got glasses of water and silverware and orders taken.

"That's a good bunch of kids," I said to Charlene. "They're better behaved than most."

"They were today," Charlene agreed then laughed. "They can be quite different though. When they get excited, they can be a handful. And Roger wasn't there today. He can be quite an instigator."

"Just like his daddy," Mike said.

"Too true," Charlene nodded. "When they're behaving well and listening like today, teaching that class is pure joy."

Mike grunted. "And when they're not behaving, teaching that class can be miserable."

"Just like you're not behaving very well," Charlene said, a little exasperated.

Mike grunted. "I'm behaving fine. You're just not responding well to the truth."

Charlene made a motion as if she was going to bang the table but caught it and stopped. "I'm not responding well to your opinion, not to truth, and you can't tell the difference!"

In the slight silence while Mike thought up a reply, Red broke in. "Your organist was very good. Is she a music teacher?"

Charlene looked at him, made a rather obvious gear change, as if she'd forgotten our presence. "That's Melanie Farris. She's pretty good, but no she's not a pro. She works in Coleman's Hardware Store."

"Well, she's better than some pro's I've heard," he said.

Mike grinned. "She's right cute, too."

Red grinned back. "I did notice that."

Charlene smiled. "You men," she said in mock disgust.

"I'm sure they were talking about her cute personality and beautiful soul," I put in.

Charlene rolled her eyes. "She's in our class, so we know her pretty well, and she is cute. And thank you for getting us off the sore subject," she added, rolling her eyes some more.

"Tell me about Jerry," Red asked. "Is he always that shy?"

Charlene tilted her head uncertainly. "He's pretty shy, but it comes and goes. Sometimes he's a fireball, sometimes he sits in a corner and hopes nobody says anything to him."

"Does he listen in class?"

"Oh, yes. He's the best in the class about listening and understanding. Even when he's in fireball mode and you think he's not listening, he can answer questions about the lesson. And he's such a nice little boy, a really sweet kid."

"Do you know his family?"

Charlene frowned slightly. "His mother lives down in the poor section where things aren't so great. Jerry's father was killed three years ago in a truck accident, and his mother hasn't handled things very well. She doesn't work or even try to."

"Is she a drunk?"

Charlene shook her head. "As far as I know she doesn't drink at all. But she has just fallen apart, no drive and no interest in life."

"She's a sad case," Mike put in. "We knew her slightly before Brad was killed, and she seemed a perfectly normal person. But after that, she seems to have given up."

"That's unfortunate," Red observed.

"And really unfair to Jerry, who deserves a lot better than that," Charlene said.

"That's true," I said, "but you all have to make the best of whatever you get in life. And when one of you falls down, the rest of you have to pick up the slack."

"Well," Charlene said, "there's a lot of slack to be picked up in her case, for Jerry's sake."

Mike looked at me with a raised eyebrow. "You seemed to be excluding yourself in that statement you made. Aren't you supposed to pitch in and help take up slack, too?"

I smiled back. "Absolutely. But we each play a different, unique role. We all have a purpose and each one is distinctive."

Red chuckled. "Well, I hope Jerry's unique helper shows up pretty soon." Then he frowned. "That bruise is pretty bad. I'm afraid it could turn into a blood clot which would be big trouble."

"You a doctor?" Mike asked skeptically.

Red grinned. "No, but in high school I played baseball and was a catcher. So with my lack of size, I learned a lot about bruises."

Just then our food came and conversation slowed while we ate some wonderful barbecue and pretty good French fries.

What conversation remained was mostly the weather—good, with normal temperatures—the sermon, the choir, and the Royals chances—better than last year but don't place any big bets—and trucks—about which Red knew more than I expected.

As we finished and paid, Charlene looked at Mike, "What are your plans for the afternoon? Let me guess—basketball at the park."

"Yep," Mike said, nodding. "We're supposed to play a team from Highland Park."

Charlene frowned. "You take that stuff too seriously.".

"No, we just have fun," Mike said, frowning back. "Would you rather I spent the day working on the truck?"

"No, but why exhaust yourself on something that doesn't matter?"

"That's why. It doesn't matter. Win or lose, we have fun."

"And get scraped and bruised, and—"

"Let's talk about something else," Mike said, angrily and opened the door harder than necessary as he went out.

"It's a beautiful day." Red looked at the sky. "Is the weather always this nice?"

Mike laughed. "Wait till you see our snow," he said. "And the spring floods."

He kissed Charlene good-by, and we headed to his home. On the way, he invited us to come play basketball with them.

Red raised an eyebrow. "I thought you had teams made up."

"It's not nearly that organized," said Mike. "Anybody who shows up and wants to play can get into a game. Usually there are three or four games going on at once."

Red shook his head. "No, thanks anyway. I think I'd rather rest."

"How about you, Sam," Mike asked.

I thought about it a moment, decided I had enough

athletic skills on this trip, and agreed, "It sounds like fun."

So Mike and I—in his shorts and shirt again—spent a big part of the afternoon at the park where, as predicted, three games were going on. It was fun and only once did my borrowed pants nearly fall down, fortunately not when I had the ball.

At the end of the set, we gathered around the water fountain, and there was the normal good-natured joshing and fake insults. Then Mike and I headed back to his house for some reheated canned spaghetti. We did make fresh toast for it. Red suggested trading beds, so I spent the night on the couch while he got the air mattress. I found out the air mattress was more comfortable. But then I didn't have to inflate the couch.

Monday was another day at the Old House Brick Cleaning Company, Samuel Mollock, Prop., on contract to James Benson, Inc. Construction and Remodeling, for minimum wage and a sandwich for lunch—oatmeal cookies from his wife this time, again wonderful—and an orange soda in mid-afternoon.

Again, I walked back to Mike's, this time buying a loaf of bread and some canned vegetables from the grocery which I went by.

Mike and Red showed up about the same time—Red on his bicycle from work, Mike in his big truck from parts and functions unknown, but which had included washing the truck, since it was clean and shiny. Red had a canvas bag full of two sets of work clothes which he said Terry had bought for him during lunch hour.

Mike was glad to get the corn and beans and gladly allowed Red to do the cooking, which involved heating Spam, corn, and beans on the stove, and more garlic toast in the oven.

Over supper, Mike turned to Red, "There's no big hurry, and you're welcome to stay here a while more, but have you thought about a permanent place to live, yet?"

Red nodded past a mouthful of beans. "I asked some of the other folks there about rooms and found out there's one that's cheap about half a mile from the tire store. It's close enough I could walk if I needed to and bicycling is a snap. I rode by it on the way home today."

Mike raised an eyebrow. "Is that Barclay's place."

Red nodded.

Mike made a face. "It doesn't have a great reputation. It's a hangout for drunks, druggies, and worse."

"That's why it's cheap," Red agreed with a shrug. "They rent by the day, week, or month, so when I get ahead enough I can leave it."

"Let's go take a look at it after supper," Mike suggested.

"Good idea," Red agreed.

Then I cleaned the table and washed the dishes. We all piled into the old pickup again and were off to Barclay's Rooms, Day, Week, Month, Reasonable.

We arrived at what had at one time been an expensive stately brick home but was now none of the above—except the bricks. It was in poor repair, and the two semi-conscious residents sitting in the decrepit chairs on the front porch were not conducive to instilling confidence in the place.

We went inside and found Mr. Barclay in an office which had once been a coat closet. Red asked about rooms.

"For how many people and for how long?" Mr. Barclay asked.

"Just me and I expect a monthly set-up would be about right."

Mr. Barclay quoted two prices for two different rooms, the higher price for one with its own bathroom and the lower price for a shared bathroom down the hall.

"Could I see the shared bath one?" Red asked.

"Certainly," Mr. Barclay said and turned to get a ring of keys from a lock box.

He dropped one ring and, when he bent over to retrieve it, I saw a pistol tucked into his waistband, giving me even less reason for confidence in the clientele.

But the room was reasonably nice, at least as good as a room in Mike's trailer, and considerably larger.

"It's a lot nicer than I expected," Mike whispered.

"I'll take it," Red told Mr. Barclay.

"Great," said Mr. Barclay, who seemed to be a lot nicer than most of his renters. "Every month's rent paid in advance and a deposit equal to one month's rent."

Red counted out the agreed on amount and handed it over, then we went back to the office and he signed three places on two sheets of legal stuff.

"You know how to drive?" Mike asked Red on the way home.

"Everything from Charlene's beetle to your rig, and licensed for all of them in Texas."

Mike nodded. "Then you need to save and buy a car. Then you can move to a better place."

"My idea exactly," Red agreed.

Then back to Mike's where we laughed at Andy, Barney, and Goober, and another day was over.

❧❧❧

Tuesday started out the same and was the same until Red and Mike showed up at Mike's at the end of the workday, again at nearly the same time. Red began to pack his very small amount of belongings, all of which had been stuffed in the numerous pockets of his rather tattered old army field jacket. Mike had told me that I didn't need to bring any groceries, and I found out why when Charlene showed up with the fixings for lasagna, which she set about making. Red volunteered to help her and, while they cooked, chatted, and laughed in the kitchen, I helped Mike fix a plumbing problem in the bathroom, during which I found out that I had come over with considerable knowledge of plumbing, and so I wound up doing most of the work and showing Mike how. I guess the Boss pulled another fast one on me.

Shortly after we got the pipe joint sealed again, Charlene called us to supper. We washed up, giving the pipe another check by doing so, and it passed all of the tests.

We sat at the table, Mike blessed the food, and we dug in. Charlene had made some quite good lasagna and, for a while, conversation was limited to "This is good!" and "Umm-hmm," and a groan of contentment from somebody, maybe me.

Like humans, all of us are different, with distinct likes and interests, and a keen appreciation of the Boss's very pleasurable way of gaining energy, that is to say eating, has certainly been one of my greatest pleasures. Even bad food is interesting—well, maybe not that meal of insects—and this was very good food. I've got a major sweet tooth, too, and was looking forward to the cake Charlene had brought, angel food, interestingly.

Everybody but Charlene got seconds of the lasagna, with Mike getting an even bigger portion the second time around. For a while the conversation concerned everybody's day at work.

Red had worked out an efficient way of doing his cleaning duties so that he could spend all but a couple of hours learning about shop operations. Charlene had several funny stories about three year old misunderstandings and mispronunciations.

My big news was that the pile of rubble was getting

smaller while the pile of cleaned bricks was growing larger. Not very exciting.

Mike and Charlene seemed to be about to get into another argument, but Red got them distracted by telling a joke he had heard.

"Tomorrow's Wednesday, church night," Charlene announced. Nobody seemed surprised by the announcement. "The children are having a party instead of the usual class. Mike, can you help out?"

Mike shook his head. "I would have been glad to, but I'm taking a load of seed wheat to San Antonio, and I'll be gone two days."

I hoped he'd run into Charlie who'd been trying to get there.

"What time?" Red asked.

"Six till 7:30," Charlene replied.

"I'd be glad to help out then," he said. "If you'll give me a ride to church."

"Why, that'd be wonderful," Charlene said enthusiastically. "Of course, I'll take you. How about you, Sam. Would you like to go?"

I cocked my head. "Are you having food?" I asked with a grin.

Charlene laughed. "Hot dogs, chips, and lemonade."

"Then I'll come, and, for a hot dog, I'll help out with the party."

"That would be good," Charlene said, although I noticed she had been more enthusiastic about Red's offer of help.

Mike obviously noticed it, too. "I think you're going to have more help than you need," he growled.

Charlene glared back. "With children, it's hard to get too much help. You've helped me out enough to know that."

Mike started to make a testy reply, but Red precluded

it by jumping up. "Let's get the clean-up done. Charlene, since you cooked, Sam and I will clean. You go watch TV with Mike."

So they did and we did. There was very little left over lasagna to deal with, and we got all the washing done in short order.

Charlene left since she had the early duty at Mrs. Bronson's the next day. Red finished packing his very limited baggage. And, while Buck and Roy were pickin' and grinning', we dozed in front of the TV until time for the real thing on the air mattress.

〇〇〇

The next afternoon, Charlene picked Red and me up promptly at six. I am normally an admirer of German engineering, but the beetle's back seat didn't seem to be the finest example of that. Riding in the back wasn't nearly as much fun as the time I'd gotten to drive a BMW over the Alps. I'd come over with full racing driver skills and helped get two anti-Nazi chemists out of Germany just before the war. That was one of my few direct action jobs, Michael's crew gets most of them, but I got that job, and it had been an enjoyable one, both in the sense of what I was there for and getting to drive a thoroughly wonderful car to its limits and a little past.

We got to the church and Ron was already there, and he and his wife Tess were setting up tables in the yard, so we started carrying and setting up. Red started the fire and did the honors on the hot dogs while I helped Ron set up some game equipment. I found out that Ron was retiring from the post office and the national guard at the same time and moving to Arkansas, which was why his Sunday School class needed a new teacher, and the guard needed a new first sergeant.

By that time, the children started arriving, and Mrs. Shilton brought seven kids which about filled up her station wagon. Free food tends to draw a crowd, and at church, a welcome one. Then several games were played which mostly involved the boys running and hollering and picking at girls while the girls screamed back. There was one bloody nose from a collision and a few scrapes but mostly fun and noise.

Then it was time for hot dogs, pimento cheese sandwiches, potato chips, and lemonade. I eventually got a hot dog which Red had done a quite good job on, and a sandwich with one bite missing which one of the children had put back on the tray, and while herding screaming kids isn't conducive to proper appreciation of gustatory delights, I enjoyed it all.

Ron got them all sort of still and quiet—not very—and made a heroic effort at a short lesson. In the semi-quiet, I complimented Red on his work as chef.

He smiled. "Thank you. Not as good as Charlene's lasagna, though. Did you notice Jerry tonight?"

I had to admit that, indeed, I had not, except to notice that he was there. I didn't come over with supernatural vision or anything like that, and other things had claimed my attention.

"All he did was stand around and watch. He never took part in anything but eating."

"Maybe he's just in a shy phase," I suggested.

"He wasn't shy, he was out of it."

Then Ron turned them loose for one last game and pandemonium again descended. I noticed that the bloody nose and the scrapes were back at full throttle. I also noticed this time that Red was right. Jerry was standing to one side, seemingly trying to be invisible and taking no part. Then I saw Red go up to him and say something which made Jerry shrink even further. Red got down on one knee and said something else, but Jerry only lowered his head a little more.

Then, surprisingly, Red grabbed Jerry's arm and pulled his sleeve up. Jerry jerked away and backed up several steps, looking very frightened.

Red stood up and came back over to the grill, looking worried. "He's got a new bruise on his shoulder, even nastier than the one on his neck. And he wouldn't talk at all."

Further conversation was cut off by the arrival of the parents from inside the church, several of whom ate a hot dog or sandwich and then folks began to head home, leaving us to clean up the residue and bask in the glow of a good time by and with the kids. By most of them, anyway.

The week passed quickly. Red said he liked his new residence. I finished the bricks and started removing nails from boards and beams. Mike and I ate more canned stuff, totally forgettable, and on Friday, we watched Blue, Buck, and Sam chase cattle rustlers.

Sunday came and I didn't have to borrow Mike's shirt this time, having made a trip to the second hand store and purchasing my own blue shirt and a pair of black dress pants with only one patched place, which barely showed. At least both of them fit me and were easier to put on than my wings and halo. Mike and I went by and picked Red up, and Charlene again was waiting for us. This time Ron was there so Charlene came to class with the grownups, but I noticed Red watched Mrs. Shilton unload her car full of kids.

Again, church service was a glorious experience of singing, scripture, Melanie's playing, and Reverend Thomas's preaching. Worship is, of course, quite different here than it is on the other side. About like the difference between being up front at a great service or listening to one on a small, poor quality radio with a lot of static. But worship anywhere is always a blessing.

Several times, I noticed Red not being particularly attentive and staring at the second row where Jerry sat with Mrs. Shilton's crew.

Afterward, Red and I were again greeted by a big portion of the congregation and were made to feel part of the family.

For dinner we were invited to Charlene's duplex apartment where she had cooked a ham, sweet potatoes, and beans, all of which were wonderful.

When Mike and Charlene started another testy exchange about nothing, Red again headed it off by saying, "Charlene did you notice Jerry today?"

Charlene shook her head. "Not except to notice he was sitting on the second row again. Why?"

Red considered a moment with a worried look on his face. "He was just completely withdrawn today, even more than Wednesday. And did you see that he had a new bruise Wednesday. An even worse one?"

"No, but I noticed that the one on his neck was healing nicely. Bruises on kids aren't uncommon. They're always getting banged up while they're playing."

Red got a faraway look, then came back. "Kids, yes. But not always the same kid and not bruises like that." Suddenly getting a determined look on his face, he stood up. "Mike, can I borrow your truck?"

Mike got up, too. "No, but I'll take you. Let's go."

"Wait, I'm coming, too," Charlene said.

She went to turn everything off, and we headed out to Mike's truck.

"I'll ride in the back," I offered, climbing into the truck bed. Mike drove us to one of the poorer parts of town and stopped in front of a small, unkempt house that looked as if it should have been condemned.

"That's Jerry's house," I heard Charlene tell Red as we got out.

We saw a group of kids playing in the yard next door, then noticed Jerry standing, watching, taking no part, and keeping his distance.

Red went over to Jerry who cringed a little but stood his ground.

"Jerry, take your shirt off."

Jerry shook his head.

"Please, Jerry. We want to help."

Jerry shook his head.

Impulsively, Red grabbed Jerry, turned him around, and raised his shirt. We all grimaced in shock at the very nasty welts on Jerry's back. It looked as though someone had hit him several times with a cord, very hard. The skin was broken in several places. They were beginning to scab over but a few places were still oozing pink fluid.

"Who did this?" Red demanded.

Jerry was silent.

"Your Mom?"

Jerry shook his head.

"Who, then?"

Jerry shook his head again, looking terrified.

Mike and Charlene started to argue again, but Red didn't play peacemaker this time. He was pulling Jerry by the arm and angrily stalking toward the front door of the house. Mike and Charlene dropped their argument and we followed, a little less angrily.

By the time we reached the porch, Red had knocked loudly on the door and Jerry's mother was coming. When she got to the door, Red lifted Jerry's shirt again. "Who's doing this?" he demanded angrily.

Jerry's mother shook her head. "He plays hard," she said. "It's—"

"No kid plays like that or that hard," Red shouted in his fury. "Who did this to him?"

She just looked at the floor.

Red knelt down and looked into Jerry's eyes. "Who is it?" he demanded.

Jerry shook his head.

I went up beside them, knelt down beside Red, and looked at Jerry. "Jerry, it's going to keep on happening unless you let us help you. You don't have to just let it keep on. Please tell me what happened. Who is it?"

"Jerry, you don't know me yet, but you know Miss Charlene and you know she would never hurt you," Red said then. "Can you tell her who it is?"

Jerry looked up at Charlene and, after a moment, started to cry. "I'm scared," he whispered.

Charlene started crying, too. "Jerry, we want to help you. We want to stop it. But you have to help us."

Jerry wiped his eyes, sniffed, and silently pointed at a house across the street, two doors down, even more decrepit than Jerry's.

His mother groaned and shook her head.

Mike went to the door. "Who is that?"

She closed her eyes and leaned her head against the doorjamb. "He's sort of my boyfriend. Used to be. I told him to go away and stay away after the last time he—I'm scared, too. He's mean."

I turned to look at the house again and was surprised to see Red halfway there, carrying Jerry, and even from the back I could tell there was fire in his eyes.

He went to the door, set Jerry down, and started pounding on the door with his fist, very loudly. Just before we got to the edge of the street, a large man, even bigger than Mike came to the door. He was big, about thirty, and overweight.

"Jerry, is that him?"

Jerry nodded very slightly.

To everyone's surprise, Red threw open the door and hit the man as hard as he could with his fist, knocking him down. Then he went in, grabbed the prone man, and hit him again. Then, to my total surprise, he hauled him out and threw him off the porch where the man landed with a thud. Red jumped off the porch and, as the man tried to get up, Red hit him again with all his might, knocking him back down. Red kicked him hard in the side and then started to kick him in the head. But by then, Mike and I had run up. We each grabbed one of Red's arms, pulling him away, out of reach. He started to fight us, too, but suddenly the fire and wild look disappeared, and he regained control.

We let go, and Red shook himself off. He went back and stood over the man. Mike and I got ready to grab him again, but it wasn't necessary.

Red leaned over. "Listen, stupid," he said very intensely. "If you ever hurt Jerry again, I'll kill you."

I don't know about stupid, but I was totally convinced.

We went back to Jerry's house, where Charlene hugged Jerry and his mom.

"Ruth, what will he do?" Mike asked.

Ruth shook her head. "I don't know. He's mean and might try to take it out on us."

Charlene hugged her again. "Come and stay with me for a while."

"What if he comes there?"

Red turned back to them. "I'll stay with you, too."

Mike got a sudden skeptical look.

"I'll stay on the couch," Red stated, noticing the look. "I've slept on a couch before."

Mike gave a rueful shrug.

Both Charlene and Ruth were enthusiastically grateful.

The ladies and Jerry went inside to pack a bag, and we

men stood on the porch, watching stupid slowly get up and stagger back inside.

Red shook his right hand. "I'd forgotten how it hurts to hit somebody with your fist. I think I broke something."

Mike smiled. "I think you accomplished something. That certainly looked like hero worship in Jerry's eyes as we came back over here."

Red shook his head. "I don't feel like a hero. I feel like a bum for not doing it a week ago."

Then the ladies came out, and Mike, Ruth, and Charlene got in the pickup cab with the rest of us in the back.

Jerry placed himself firmly in Red's lap and both of them seemed quite content with that arrangement.

We drove to Charlene's and unloaded them. Mike carried the bag into Charlene's half of the house. Mike and I both noticed Charlene was holding Red's arm in a rather possessive manner as she got his charge settled in on the couch.

"...and I'll be his Sunday School teacher from now on," I heard her say to Ruth and I felt a thrill of "Mission Accomplished."

I noticed Mike had heard it, too, but to my surprise, he seemed as pleased as I was.

After making sure all was going well, Mike and I headed out.

"I'll check on you later tonight and in the morning," Mike said to Charlene.

"We'd appreciate it," the reply came from Red.

Mike seemed about to make a testy reply, but stopped, and simply sighed. "Okay."

Mike and I went out to his truck. As he hit the starter button with his foot, he looked at his watch. "It's too late to get to the park and get in on a basketball game. Is there any place you need to go?"

"No. Do you have any particular adventure in mind?"

Mike laughed as he backed out. "No, I think we've had enough adventure for one day. I couldn't believe Red today. I thought he was going to kill that guy."

"Yeah, I noticed. I think he might have if we hadn't stopped him. And he was about to take us on to get back at him."

Mike laughed again. "Yeah, and the way he was going, he might have whipped all three of us. Did you see him throw that fellow off the porch? And he weighs twice what Red does."

"I saw."

"Actually, I have seen such before. In Vietnam, I spent part of my time on a Forward Air Control Team and we spent most of our time with the infantry out in the boonies. One of the fiercest fighters I ever saw was a little bitty, mousy fellow who looked like he would be useless in a fight. But whenever we would get hit, it was like he turned into Audie Murphy and John Wayne combined. Amazing. Something else just took over and—Boom! He turned into super-soldier. But afterward, he went back to little mouse, scared of every shadow. Red today was just like that."

I knew what he meant. I had known a fellow about like that, except the men in his army painted themselves blue and fought Romans naked, which, given Roman arms and armor, wasn't a very good idea. He was what would later be called a berserker. His fellow warriors just called him crazy. But when the fight started, he was worth a whole squad. We're not normally allowed to fight in such situations since we're—at least officially— neutral, but I was a priest with the tribe and travelled with the war groups. The beliefs of that tribe would hardly have passed muster in Mike and Charlene's church, but they had the main ideas right, and it was an important step toward getting the church established in England.

"Then it's a good thing Red didn't have a rifle," I said.

"Yeah."

"Do you think that guy will show up back there?"

Mike considered for a moment. "I don't know. If he gets a few beers in him and gets to brooding, he might. You never know, so you have to be ready for anything."

"Good point."

"I'm considering calling the police and having them check on Charlene's place some, too," Mike said, rubbing his chin.

I raised an eyebrow. "Wouldn't that be an obvious thing to do?"

"Normally, yes. But somebody could make a legal case for charging Red with assault. So I'm not sure we need the law involved."

I shrugged. "Well, we said we'd check on them later tonight. Ask them."

Mike looked uncertain, then he shrugged. "Sounds good. At least it's a good excuse to put off making a decision. How about an early supper at Trailside. I'll buy."

"Sounds great."

We went into the converted filling station to be greeted with "Hi, honey! Come on in and find a seat. I'll be right there." Shirley/Jessica walked past us to another table. "You get a discount tonight, honey," she said to me. "For having to associate with this lowlife." Mike got a big wink in the process. "That won't hurt my tip, will it, honey?" she said with a grin

"No, because I wasn't going to give you one, anyway," Mike replied with a return wink.

Jessica/Shirley cackled and went off to take an order.

We both got "honey'ed" half a dozen more times along with a laughing warning about roaches in the fries. A wonderful steak, fries, and a terrific piece of cherry

pie—Tom's skills weren't limited to apple pie and burgers—were reduced to crumbs and catsup smears.

We went back into the trailer and, for an hour or so,
Mike watched TV and read a magazine, while I got reacquainted with Hamlet in a paperback book on Mike's
shelf. His best stuff is as good as it gets. Someday I hope
to get to watch Olivier play that role.

As it started to get dark, Mike decided it was time to
go back to check on Charlene. We drove back over and
knocked on the door. Nobody answered for a couple of
minutes, then we heard the upstairs window open and
Red's head came out.

"Just making sure it was you." The window closed and
then Charlene opened the door. Inside, they looked more
like they were having a sleep-over party than cowering in
fear. Ruth and Jerry were eating popcorn. A pallet was on
the living room floor in front of the TV, and Jerry was
watching the cat and mice cartoon where one of the mice
was wearing a diaper.

They said they'd seen no sign of any problem.

"Ruth," Mike asked, "you know him best. How likely
is he to cause trouble?"

She shook her head. "It depends on how much beer he
drinks," she said. "Beer makes him meaner."

"How often does he drink?" Mike asked.

"Only when he's awake."

Mike shook his head. "Who's sleeping on the floor?"

Ruth touched Jerry's arm. "Jerry and me."

Mike looked at Red. "What about you?"

"I'll be sleeping in the upstairs hall by the window I
just looked out of, so I can see who's coming up."

Mike looked thoughtful for a moment. "What if the
first thing you know of him coming is his breaking down
the door? Then the ones he wants are the first ones he
comes to, unprotected. I'd suggest Red on the living

room floor, and Ruth and Jerry upstairs, so they would have some warning and could get out the window if they need to."

Red looked around and thought for a moment, too. "Good idea," he said. "We'll do it that way."

He disappeared up the stairs and came back carrying a camping mattress and a baseball bat, which he deposited on the floor by the couch.

Mike looked at Red. "Do you think we should have the police check—"

He stopped when we all heard a car with a loud muffler stop in the street outside and a car door slam.

"Oh, no," Ruth said and Jerry cringed up against her.

"Is that him?" Red asked.

"I think so." Ruth nodded fearfully. "Let me go talk to him."

Mike and Red looked at each other "Do you think—"

"*Ruth!*" we heard in a bellow outside.

Red frowned. "I don't think talking will do any good."

"I'm calling the police," Charlene said.

Red and Mike both nodded.

We heard him yell for Ruth again, closer.

"Let me talk to him," Ruth said, going to the door.

Red shook his head. "I don't think that's a good idea."

"I have to try."

Red and Mike looked at each other again. Mike shrugged and nodded.

Ruth opened the door and went out on the front step, while Red, Mike, and I looked out the window. We could see him in the porch light, standing on the side of the street, a beer bottle in his hand.

"What do you want, Bart?"

"Get in the car. You're going with me."

"No, Bart. I told you to leave me alone."

"I told you to get in the car," he screamed—with a few other words thrown in.

"No, Bart. Go away." And she turned to come back into the house.

Then Bart lost it. He started screaming obscenities and coming toward the door. Red pulled Ruth into the house and he, Mike, and I went outside.

Bart screamed more obscenities when he saw Red. "I'm ready for you this time, you little—"

He dropped the bottle, pulled a large kitchen knife from his waistband, and ran at Red. Mike tried to trip him but Bart caught his balance and kept coming at Red with the knife held up high like an ice pick. Not good knife tactics, but still dangerous. Red blocked the stab with his forearm and hit him in the chest as hard as he could, but Bart tried to stab him again.

I knew it was time for some direct action. I held up both arms and the clear sky suddenly erupted with lightning. Several bolts streaked overhead and the thunder which came simultaneously was deafening. Everybody in the yard stopped for an instant, but it hadn't done the trick. Bart started to make another stab, and Red was about to kick him in a very sensitive place. I threw my arms up again and, this time, only one lightning bolt flashed, but it struck the ground right between Red and Bart. It made Red take a few steps backward, but its effect on Bart was terrific. He flew backward three or four feet and landed in a heap on the ground. He was making a habit of that.

For a few seconds, everybody simply stood still. Then Mike looked incredulously up into a clear sky, in which the brighter stars shone dimly through the city lights. Then he and Red both went over to Bart. Mike picked up the knife and threw it toward Bart's car. Red checked to see if Bart was breathing, which he was, but unconscious.

Then a police car came up with lights flashing and took charge of the situation. But not before Charlene came running out of the house to grab Red in a very enthusiastic and passionate embrace which lasted quite a while. Then she checked him out carefully to see if he was hurt and found a small cut on his left forearm where he had not completely parried the knife.

She pulled him inside to clean and bandage it.

Mike shook his head, half amused, half hurt. "I'm fine, too, thank you," he called after them. "Nice of you to ask."

The policemen's work took most of a half hour and an ambulance took Bart off to the emergency room with a police guard.

After the police left, we all went back into Charlene's living room, where Jerry had the hero-worship look again and sat on Red left side.

Charlene, with a similar look, but opposite polarity, sat close on his right with her arm intertwined with his.

Mike noticed it but tried to ignore it. "Well," he said, "I hope that's a happy ending."

"If not an ending, at least a break," Red put in.

"Red, I guess you won't be needed here tonight. Do you want a ride to your room?"

"No," Charlene said quickly. "It's too late. He can still stay on the couch."

Red looked at her, a little surprised. "I guess I'd better go to my room. There's no need for me to be here now."

"Then I'll drive you," Charlene said, jumping up and getting her keys.

"Okay," Red agreed a little uncertainly. Then he smiled, real big.

Mike and I went to his truck and, as we pulled away, he turned to me and with a fatalistic shrug said, "I think I

just got beat out for my girl by a hitch hiker I picked up."
He chuckled. "Well, I guess I saw it coming."

"You have to admit, the two of you didn't seem to be too happy together since I've been here."

Mike nodded. "True, and as I told you before, I…Well, I won't say I don't care, but really it's as much a relief as hurt."

I laughed. "Then you should take that as a good sign. And I don't think Red is going to stay a hitch hiker or even a janitor for long."

Mike nodded. "I think you're right, there. He's got a lot on the ball. He's going to do well in life. And in spite of his stealing my girl, I think we'll be good friends for a long time."

"I'll bet you're right. I hope you're right."

"What about you? Are you going to stay a brick cleaner?"

"Nope, I've finished that job. I guess I'll be moving on again before long."

"Where to?"

I shrugged. "Second star to the right and straight on till morning."

Mike laughed. "And I get the idea that you'll keep on finding Lost Boys."

"Probably, but you seem to be doing a lot of that yourself. By the way, I noticed you seemed unperturbed by Charlene's announcement that she'd be taking the Sunday School class."

"I never was opposed to her taking it. I think she'll be great at it. I wasn't bothered by the disagreement as much as by our way of dealing with it. I just wanted her to decide to take it on her own, instead of taking it because other people expected her to. I wanted her to be sure just who was calling her to take it."

I nodded. "Good thinking."

"When are you leaving? You're staying tonight, aren't you?"

I thought about it. "What's on for tonight?"

"The last two honey buns and a John Wayne movie."

"Then I'm staying tonight."

So I did. We laughed at Goober's antics again, and after Davy and Colonel Travis died heroically, I lay on the couch and, when I heard Mike start to snore, it was all gone.

CHAPTER 4

EDDIE AND KURT

The field was a very peaceful scene with the green grass under the mostly sunny sky. The trees in the fencerows moved gently in the June breeze, and the long rows of white crosses contrasted nicely with the bright colors of nature and the red, white, and blue of the American and French flags flying in the distance.

Down one row of crosses, an elderly man slowly made his way, stopping often to read the inscribed names and sometimes reaching out a hand to touch the letters. The equally elderly lady with him watched him carefully and a little anxiously and several times patted him on his shoulder. Somewhere near the middle of the row, the man stopped completely and spent several minutes just looking at one of the crosses. Then he touched the gravestone, this time tracing out each letter slowly. Then he knelt in front of the gravestone and, gripping it with both hands, bowed his head until it rested against the marker.

His wife said something, but the man seemed not to hear until she shook him slightly. Then he raised his head to look at her with tears running down his face. He took her hand, kissed it, and said something. She smiled a little uncertainly and walked off toward the shady area where a concrete bench had been placed under a beautiful oak with a good view of the graves and the chapel.

The man put his head back on the marker for a while. Then he sat down on the grass and leaned back against the stone with his eyes closed. He sat completely still for several minutes, then his head leaned forward, and he slept.

ℰℑℰℑ

The jolt of coming across wasn't nearly as severe this time, since I wasn't really flesh and blood, but coming into space and time is always a shock, and it still took a moment to orient myself. I was a typical human male in appearance, but without any discernable weight and my boots made no imprint in the dirt under my feet. I could walk but it felt like I could just as easily have floated. I was wearing an American military uniform which was quite worn and rather dirty. I was in a field with tree-lined fencerows, very much like the one where the old man slept, but this one was misty and everything was indistinct. The field had been a pasture, but no animals were present, and they would have been disappointed in the forage anyway since most of the field had been torn up by tanks and half-tracks. Only one remained, a single Sherman tank, and it sat in the field facing the road.

I walked toward it and, as I came up closer, I could see one man sitting in the commander's hatch atop the tank, looking intently down the road. He was speaking into the tank's communication system and trying to talk to the tank crew, but getting no response since he was alone in the tank. Although I made no noise walking, my movement caught his eye and he turned to look at me. His first impulse was to grab at the controls to swing a machine gun in my direction, but he recognized my uniform and stopped.

"Hello, Sergeant Harrod," I called out. "Mind if I come up?"

"Sure, come ahead," he responded.

I climbed up and stood beside the turret so we could talk. He looked at my captain's bars.

"Sir, what's going on? I must have been knocked unconscious because, all of a sudden, I find myself here on my tank with all my crew missing and nobody around."

"It's a little confusing, isn't it?" I responded and gave him a friendly smile with reassuring overtones. "But at least you can be glad you didn't come to with a bunch of German tanks coming down that road."

He frowned. "I guess that's right. I know I've seen them coming down that road before, but it seems like a long time ago."

"If you think about it for a while, I believe you'll figure it out. How many times have you been here waiting for them to attack you?"

He frowned. "Just once but it didn't end up like this."

"Lots more than once," I prompted. "Think where you were just a moment ago."

He glanced around. "Getting shot and—" He stopped with a very confused look. "No, I was…I can't…" He looked at me very strangely then smiled. "I'm dreaming it again, aren't I? That's why you asked how many times I've seen this. The answer is so many times I've lost count. But always in a dream, except for the first time. Then it was real. But it always ends up the same. Old Betsy here explodes, Eddie dies, and then the rest of us get shot as we try to get out."

He looked around us at the misty, subdued indistinctness of our surroundings. "But I've never been aware of it being a dream before." He laughed softly. "It's a little strange to be able to know I'm in a dream. This place is the same place, but it doesn't exactly look real. Nothing seems solid except, me, the tank, and—" He reached out and touched my shoulder. "—and apparently you, too. Except you're new. You weren't here then, and you've never been in any of my dreams before. Who are you?"

I smiled and looked down at my uniform. "Just like it says here, I'm Captain Samuel Mollock. And you're right, I wasn't here that day. And this is the first time I've been in a dream."

That was certainly the truth. I had never done anything like this before. I had been over here in human form many times, several times in the wings and halo form, and once as both at once—a flesh and blood angel with giant chicken wings on my back and a yellow neon halo when I came into eighth century Saxony. I was there to tell one of the tribal chiefs to not kill a Frankish missionary and to let him teach. The Saxons being Saxons, I had made my point by wrestling their champion, throwing, and pinning him, and then flying treetop high in the first ever victory roll. It hadn't helped that the monk had been more afraid than Aethelbert and had fainted and then hadn't been able to speak coherently for a week afterward, but he eventually came out of it and did a lot of good preparing the Saxons for the church and civilization.

But *this* was a first for me. To come over into a human's dream was just plain weird, even for us. Appearing to somebody in a dream is one of our standard methods, but our appearing is the entire dream in those cases, and we just stand by their bed while they're half awake. Here, I was going inside of his dream, which I had never done before.

But the Boss's ideas always have a good reason behind them. It's just that sometimes—like this time—He doesn't explain it all to me. So this was new to both of us.

"I'm confused," he said. Then he grinned. "But

dreams usually are confusing. Why are you the only solid thing besides me and the tank?"

"Because I'm a real person."

"How can you be real when you're in my dream? You have to be something from my imagination."

I laughed. "Normally, you'd be right. But as you've figured out, this isn't a normal dream. And I'm a real person, not a figment of your imagination."

"How can you be in my dream if you're real? And why am I asking you? If you're my imagination, you can't know anything I don't."

"I'm a real person, but I didn't say I'm a normal person. This is a real dream but not a normal one. You're about to see a lot of things that aren't normal, but which will be real."

He stared at me for a moment. "I think you're trying to explain this," he said, "but I'm just getting more confused. Who are you and why are you here?"

I grinned and floated up away from the tank until I was about twenty feet above the ground then uncovered. The light brightened, and I transformed into the wings and halo garb. Sergeant Harrod's face took on a look of amazement, wonder, fear, and awe but with a big smile.

"Arthur Harrod," I said in the Authoritative Voice with Stabilizing Undertones, "you are receiving a visitation." Then I lowered myself to the tank and resumed the appearance of the army captain again. "How's that?" I asked. "Did it explain things?"

Sergeant Harrod laughed. "I don't know if it explains things or confuses me more. What's a visitation? Why me? Are you really an angel? What—" He stopped suddenly and looked at me skeptically. "Do that again."

I laughed and sprouted wings that glowed in the mist, flapped them a couple of times, then went back to normal.

He shook his head. "So I'm getting a visit from an angel in a dream, or maybe dreaming about an angel, and it concerns the time when Eddie died and I got wounded. Have I got it right so far?"

"Yep. Keep going."

He shook his head. "I'm through. It's your turn. Explain."

I shook my head back at him. "No, you have to figure this out for yourself."

"Okay, what am I supposed to figure out?"

"Start by telling me what happened here that day."

He shrugged slightly. "We had fought our way through the hedgerows for about a week, and we were trying to get to the crossroads village about a mile away when a bunch of German armor counterattacked and caught us in the flank. Our company was set up in this field to defend against the German tanks, which we expected to come down the road. They did and, when we fired on them, we got hit from the right side over there by tanks and scout cars. One of their tanks hit our tank in the side right below the turret. I barely saw them before we got hit. It gets a little fuzzy after that. There was an explosion, and I was thrown halfway out of the commander's hatch. I told the crew to get out before the fuel started burning and everybody got out but Eddie who was in the gunner's seat.

But before we could get behind the tank for cover, we were all hit by machine gun fire. I was hit in the leg and side and fell off, but I was able to crawl over behind the tank, and the rest of the crew jumped into a half track from the infantry platoon with us. Just then a P-47 flew over and hit the German tanks with rockets and knocked a couple out and then the battalion got its stuff together and drove the rest of the Germans off.

"An ambulance came by, picked us all up, and took us

to a field hospital where I spent two months and then I was assigned to Sixth Division in time to cross the Rhine with them."

"Sounds like it was pretty tough," I said sympathetically.

"Yeah, it was. And add in artillery going off and burning tanks, and gunfire, tanks and half-tracks moving around. And screaming."

I winced. "Was there a lot of screaming?"

"Oh, yeah. I was really loud."

"But you're leaving something out, aren't you?" I asked.

He continued staring straight ahead and said nothing.

"Tell me more about Eddie," I prompted.

He looked down and shook his head.

After a minute's silence, I asked again and he just shook his head, closing his eyes.

Another minute of silence. "It's not just the German tanks you dream about, is it?"

His head sank a little lower and after a few moments, he looked at me. "Why are you doing this to me?"

"Why did you come back here?" I responded.

He shook his head and closed his eyes. "I don't know. Maybe I shouldn't have."

After a short pause, I said, "Since you did come, you know that I'm not doing it to you, you're doing it to yourself. Whose grave did you stop at?"

He turned quickly and looked at me with anger. "Whatever I'm doing, it's my doing and my business. It's hard enough without you rubbing my nose in it all." He slumped with his anger spent and we were silent a while.

Then he smiled a little and looked at me. "I never expected to see an angel, but if I had, I wouldn't have expected it to go like this. Aren't you supposed to bring fire and brimstone, or make an important announcement?"

I laughed. "That's not my job this time. I'm just here to nudge you along."

He sighed. "Nudge me along to what?"

I didn't answer.

"To someplace I don't want to go, obviously. Are you a real angel, or am I just having a weird dream?"

"Both. I'm a real angel, and you're most certainly having a really weird dream."

"Well, if you're real, I'm willing to do this, but if this is just a dream, then I'm just pulling scabs off a wound to no purpose."

I reached over the turret and clasped his shoulder. "I think you have already answered that one yourself. Where are you right now physically?"

He rubbed his face. "Several miles west of here, sitting on Eddie's grave. I think you're right. Somehow I believe you and that you're for real, so okay, here goes.

"When we got hit, the explosion of the German shell threw me most of the way out of the tank. I was still connected to the intercom and told everybody else to get out, since we were completely out of action. I saw Pete come out the loader's hatch and Johnson and Davis getting out of the front. I looked back in at Eddie, and he wasn't coming out but he reached both hands out at me and said something I couldn't hear but I know exactly what he was saying and it was, 'Help me.'

"I reached in for his hand, but before I could pull, there was another explosion inside and that knocked me completely off of the tank. When I got back up on it, the whole inside was on fire and all I could do was get off.

"So Eddie burned to death because I didn't try harder to get him out. He was my crewmate, my gunner, and my best friend, and I let him burn up. That's what I dream about—Eddie burning in the tank and I didn't do anything."

He put his head down on the gun mount and was quiet for a while.

Then he looked up. "Is that what you wanted, to make me relive it. It's not like I haven't relived it many, many times in my mind and my dreams, but I've never told anybody else about it, not even my wife. So now Captain Samuel the Angel, what do I do? Did you come to judge a coward? That's what I am and if I hadn't been, I would have gotten Eddie out—"

"No, I'm not here to judge anybody. That's not my job. As I said, I'm just here to nudge you along."

He wiped his eyes and smiled faintly. "Well, you nudged me into telling that story for the first time ever. I've heard that talking about things helps, but telling that story didn't make it quit hurting. In fact, it hurts worse now. Was that your purpose?"

"No, but we're not done," I said.

He started to reply but stopped when we both heard the sound of something coming down the road toward us. He looked at me, puzzled. "What—"

Then an open topped jeep driven by another soldier came into sight and pulled into the field through the gateway in the fencerow by the road. The driver stopped, turned the engine off, got out, and walked toward us.

Sergeant Harrod straightened up suddenly. "Holy cow! It's Eddie!"

And, with that, he was up out of the tank, reached the ground in two jumps, and was grabbing Eddie in a bear hug, which was enthusiastically returned. I followed a little more sedately, floating most of the way, since this was a dream, after all.

After a while of bear hugs, shoulder and back pounding, and some incoherent, half shouted exclamations, Art stepped back and looked from Eddie to me and back. "All right," he said, "is this for real? This isn't just another silly dream, is it? I've dreamed about seeing you so many times, but never like this. Are you really Eddie? Captain, is this real?"

I laughed. "Remember that I told you that you were going to see some things that weren't normal? This is one of them. It's quite real. The real Eddie is in your dream, just like I am. He's not your imagination."

Art suddenly stopped and got a fearful expression, looking at me. "Are you here to take me away?"

"No." I smiled. "I'm not the death angel. You'll make it back home and see your grandchildren again."

With great relief, Art whooped, grabbed Eddie in a big hug again, and lifted him off the ground. "It's so good to see you. There's so much I want to know, but—but—"

"I know," Eddie answered, straightening his shirt which had gotten disheveled during the welcome. "We've got a lot to talk about. But first, it's been a long time since you've been on a tank. Let's take a look at her."

Art turned and looked at the Sherman. "Sure, but is she real?" he asked me.

I smiled. "Not physically. Most of old Betsy went to the Renault factory and was made into cars. But this one is more than just your memories. It's a perfect replica of your tank the day of the battle."

They both went to the tank, walked around it with big grins, chattering like boys out of school, and climbed all over it. After several minutes of examining the outside, they climbed inside and took their normal positions with Eddie in the gunner's seat and Art just behind and above him in the commander's position. I climbed in and stood on the turret floor where I could see both of them while they worked all the controls and looked through the telescopes and, in general, got reacquainted with their old machine.

After a good bit of that, Eddie reached into the cargo

pocket of his pants. "I'll bet you remember these," he said, bringing out a cardboard box.

"K rations!" Art exclaimed. "I haven't seen them in years. I haven't missed them much either."

Eddie laughed. "But you still have to eat some for old times' sake." He opened the box and revealed another box which opened, revealing several paper packages and a can. Opening one of the paper wrapped packages, he chuckled. "Here have a biscuit." He handed Art what looked like a big, soft cracker.

Art took a bite and smiled. "Now I remember why I didn't like them very much, but it's good to remember."

Eddie reached across the gun breech with another package. "Here, Captain, have a chocolate bar."

I remembered K rations from a time in the Philippines when I had gone to help a priest escape from a prisoner of war camp. I had to convince a Japanese soldier to check the other side of the building while we sneaked from the barracks to the supply shack. That job had been helped by his disapproval of the way things were going in the camp and his humanitarian impulses. We had managed to take a few cases of captured K rations with us, as we sneaked out through a tunnel which the Philippine resistance had dug, and they were all we had to eat for a week. But after three weeks in the camp living on a handful of raw rice a day, the K rations seemed wonderful, at least at first. So it was a trip down memory lane for me as well as for Art. Also, like Art, I could remember why we had gotten tired of them. The chocolate was rather hard and stale, but not bad.

After a brief discussion of the rations' lack of gustatory merit, Art sighed. "All right, Eddie, you and Captain Angel didn't come here just to eat war rations, play on a tank, and make me remember. What are you up to?"

Eddie swiveled in his seat and looked up at Art.

"You're right. There's a bigger purpose than that. I've come with a message for you."

"From who?"

"From me."

"Okay, what's your message?"

"You need to quit worrying and let go. Quit feeling guilty. Most importantly, I didn't die because you didn't get me out. That German shell had taken my legs off at the hip. I wasn't trying to get out of the tank because I couldn't. I was in deep shock and I was bleeding to death. I wouldn't have lived more than a minute, no matter what."

Art looked shocked and perplexed at the same time. "But—But I—"

"No. You didn't have anything to do with it. When our ammo exploded, it knocked me unconscious, and I never felt the fire. You're not a coward, and I didn't die because of anything you did or didn't do. You did everything that you could or should have done."

Art's shocked look got bigger. "But I saw—"

Eddie laughed. "You saw me die, but it wasn't your fault. Now you know and you've had it confirmed by a voice from beyond the grave."

Art looked over at me and I nodded. He looked back at Eddie. "I've spent years and years thinking you died because of me, and that you would hate me for it."

It took some doing because of the cramped turret, but they managed another bear hug, along with a couple of bumped heads.

After they sat back down, Art wiped his eyes. "I'm in my twenty-four-year-old body again, but I'm obviously still an old man with less control of my emotions. I haven't cried this much since—"

Eddie laughed. "I'm not an old man and I'm crying too."

Art looked at me. "That's a big load off of my heart. But why did you wait so long, Captain?"

I shrugged. "Some things aren't for understanding, just for accepting. This is one of them."

"But you're not done yet," Eddie said, "There's another burden you've been carrying for too long."

I touched Art's arm. "You remember that job offer you got in '64? You turned it down, even though it was a really good opportunity. Why?"

Art looked down, mumbled a little, then looked up at me sharply. "I guess there's no point in lying to you, is there? It was with a company that was a subsidiary of a German corporation and my job would have required me to deal with Germans on a pretty regular basis. Given my experience with Germans and my feelings about them, I wasn't about to take the job."

"Let's go outside," Eddie said.

Art looked puzzled but climbed out and down to the ground, followed by Eddie and me. We stretched a little and then, once again, we heard a vehicle driving, but this time in the field next to us. It slowed to negotiate the chewed up break in the fence row, which had been opened by the German tanks, then drove up and stopped. Eddie was grinning, but Art looked very distressed. "That's an Opel armored scout car just like the ones that hit us from that direction," Art said.

"Yes," I said, "but remember that the war was a long time ago, and Germany and America have been staunch allies ever since. I'll use one of our old standards. 'Fear not.'"

The driver's door of the scout car opened and a man in a German army uniform got out, carrying a small bag. "Guten tag, gentlemen," he said in a thick Saxon accent.

Eddie nudged Art. "Come on, Sergeant Harrod. Let's go meet him."

We did and Eddie shook his hand. "Howdy, Kurt," he said. We all shook hands, but Art was very reserved about it.

"Art," I said, "Kurt was a captain in the Wehrmacht, and, after the war, became part of the West German Bundeswehr reserves and retired as a colonel. He was a refugee from the eastern zone and owned an appliance store in Hesse. He was also a hard-line anti-communist, and an elder in the Lutheran church."

"Und I continued driving Opels all my life," Kurt said with a grin. "But not armored ones. Hauptman Kurt Eberhardt Weber, at your service," he said, with a verbal flourish and a bow.

"Art," I said, "let's help him unload some equipment."

We all went to the back of the scout car, with Art looking very skeptical about it all, and opened the rear door. Kurt handed out a field table and camp stools, and we carried them to a grassy spot just in front of the tank.

"French made," said Kurt. "We had a lot of captured French stuff."

Eddie put his box of K rations on the table, and Kurt took a loaf of hard rye bread and a sausage from his bag. We all sat on the stools, Kurt blessed the food in German, and we passed the sausage and bread around.

With a big grin, Kurt reached into the bag again, looking at me. "Samuel, Frau Schneider made me bring this for you," he said, producing an ancient style of crock. "Blutwuerst."

I laughed. She had been Fraulein Kruger when I had known her in thirteenth century Schwabia, and all of the young men in Grusselsheim had been in love with her, and with her cooking, too. I had been there to help preserve some manuscripts treated as relics in the village church, and I had developed a real fondness for Fraulein Kruger's bloodwurst, and the village priest's son Ludwig had developed a greater fondness for the bloodwurst maker. He'd won that competition and with their help, the manuscripts had made it safely to the library in Stuttgart. They're still there, still being studied by historians.

I passed the crock around, and we all ate big chunks of bread which Kurt cut, using his combat knife, and some of both kinds of sausage. We spent some time praising the food and comparing the K rations to the German stuff, most unfavorably. Art took no part in the conversation, was even hesitant about the food, and had made a point of sitting across from Kurt, not beside him.

"Art," I said, handing him another piece of bread, "Kurt is like you and Eddie. He's a war veteran, and he's also a veteran of the battle right here in this field."

Art looked at Eddie, who nodded and grinned past a mouthful of sausage.

"Ja," said Kurt. "That day, I led my company in the counterattack on your battalion. I was in the lead tank and it was my tank that fired the round that took your tank out. And it was my machine gun that wounded you and your men as you got off the tank."

Art looked shocked and leaned back, speechless, unable to respond.

"Calm down," I told him. "I've already told you that Kurt is a perfectly nice fellow who was one of the good guys after the war, even by your standards. And he raised two very nice children."

"Und four grandchildren," Kurt added proudly.

"Now tell me, Art," I said. "What would you have done the day of the battle if you had a minute's warning that you were about to get attacked from the right flank?"

Art raised an eyebrow. "I'd have shifted and fired on him."

I smiled. "And…"

"And nothing!" Kurt laughed. "Your seventy-five-millimeter shell would have bounced off the front armor of my Tiger. But if you could have gotten behind us and put one into my engine—"

"Then that's what I'd have done," Art said, a little testily.

"Right," Eddie replied. "So what you're telling me is that you would have done to Kurt precisely what he did to us."

"Exactly right," Art responded, a little more crossly.

He started to say more but suddenly stopped, looking uncertain and a little puzzled.

Eddie laughed. "Now you see what I mean about carrying a burden too long. You've been carrying way too much guilt and anger, and it's all for no reason. Kurt did nothing to us that we weren't trying to do to him and his soldiers."

Art looked around at each of us for a few moments, his expression a study in puzzlement. Then the puzzlement hardened into anger.

He abruptly stood up and quickly walked around behind the tank and out of sight.

After a few moments of silence, Eddie looked at me. I shrugged. Kurt issued a "Humpff" which he managed to make sound very Teutonic.

I decided that it was an occasion calling for some intervention. I switched over to the robe, wings, and halo, grew to nine feet tall, and floated up over the tank, putting on my grim, determined, but inviting expression.

Art noticed the glow from me and looked up. I settled to a few feet off of the ground just in front of him. He looked surprised and a little fearful.

"Arthur Harrod," I boomed in a voice loud enough to ensure attention, if my appearance hadn't done so. "You know who I am. You know who sent me, and who sent

Eddie and Kurt. You should be able to figure out that He didn't send us here to you so you could stand there and act stubborn. There is an important purpose behind this message to you that you need to change. You can be a part of His purpose or you can keep on hurting yourself and miss out. Choose!"

Art narrowed his eyes and looked like he wanted to argue. But before he could say anything, to my surprise, Eddie and Kurt came around the tank and stood by Art. They just stood in silence for a moment.

Then Art sighed. "It's too much, too much. Everything at once, it's just too much."

"It's a lot," Eddie replied, "but it's needed. You've been so wrong for so long that it's hard to let go. But you'll be better off if you do. And it's not like you've been an awful person. You've just had this one part of your mind and soul that's been shriveled up by hate and guilt, but it's all misplaced. You need to let go and get past it."

"I'm not sure I can. That's been such an important part of me for so long that I wouldn't be me any more without it."

Eddie laughed. "Sure you would. You'd just be a better you. You believed me that my death wasn't your fault and that your guilt was misplaced, so why won't you believe us that your hatred of Kurt and Germans is misplaced, too."

Art was silent for a moment. "I don't think I want to give it up." he said slowly.

Eddie snorted. "You like your pain too much to let it go?"

"I don't know. I don't—"

Before he could say anything else, I put plan "B" into action and, from just out of sight in the rear of the tank, came a very loud "Gott in Himmel! Wieder der krieg?"

"No, it isn't the war again," I called out in English. "Come meet somebody."

Around the tank hobbled an old man. He was reaching to his hip, but found nothing since his pistol had long ago been melted into cookware. He did a big double take when he saw me but then smiled. "Yes, now I remember. In my dream, you told me to be ready for this, but I wasn't sure it was real." He spoke quite good English, with a high Bavarian accent.

I smiled. "Yes, it was real, and it seems you are needed. Leutnant Helmut Stahl, meet Sergeant Arthur Harrod. Helmut, show him your scar."

Helmut looked puzzled, but lifted his shirt, revealing a nasty red scar running from his right hip up to his armpit.

"Art," I said, "you don't recognize him as an old man, but you remember Helmut from his actions in the war. He was one of the German infantrymen who ambushed your platoon three days before your battle with Kurt's company. You and your tank crew broke it up by running your tank over the fencerow that Helmut's squad was behind. Eddie fired the machine gun right into their position, and you used your heavy machine gun to destroy their gun. One of your shots hit Helmut. "

"It was you!" Helmut shouted. "I've always wondered who you were." He hobbled over to Art, grabbed his hand, and shook it enthusiastically. "At our reunion in '85, we had several American soldiers from your division as guests, but I never expected to find out who was in the tank that got us. I am very pleased to meet you."

Art was totally dumbstruck. Eddie nudged him. "Now you see how it should be done."

Art whirled, looked at Eddie, then back at Helmut, then up at me, then at Kurt. He grabbed his head and started backing up with a frightened look on his face. Then he went back to Eddie and grabbed his arm. "Did

you come back from the grave just to torment and confuse me?" he asked angrily.

"No," Eddie replied calmly. "I came back to be your
friend, once again. You've missed out on too much that's
good because of the guilt, hate, and sickness in your
heart. And you're going to keep on missing out until you
decide to let go of that pain. It's hurting you terribly, but
you're holding on to it like it was your lifeline."

Art closed his eyes and rubbed his temples.

"It's too much," he said again. "It's too much all at
once."

"No, it isn't," Kurt said in his best German officer
tone of voice. "It is no more than you faced the first time
in this field, and you stood up to that test quite well. And
this time you can not only stand up to the test, you can
win this one. Losing here the first time hurt you badly
and wounded your body and your soul. But as long as
you go on being bitter at Helmut and me, you are con-
tinuing to lose and lose and lose."

"What you're doing is hurting you and nobody else,"
Eddie said.

"We do not come here to torment you," Kurt interject-
ed, rather forcefully. "We come because you are given a
very special chance to make some badly needed changes
and become a better part of something great and wonderful. Und so far you only come part way. You are given
here a very unusual chance to be better and to see an angel, and you call it torment." His German accent got
broader as his emotions grew. "Leutnant Stahl, how many
of your men were killed when this tank ran over your
squad?"

"Four dead, three wounded," Helmut replied.

Kurt turned back to Art. "So you hurt him more than I
hurt you, but does he hate all Americans? No!"

"I was leader of German-American Friendship Club in my hometown," said Helmut.

Kurt turned back to Art. "You just saw that he not even hate you. But you act like you the only one who lose friends in the war, and so you hold grudge forever.

"Every week in church, you and Helmut pray 'Forgive us our trespasses as we forgive those who trespass against us.' Do you cross fingers in church when you pray that? What you really pray is 'Forgive me like Helmut forgave me but not like I haven't forgiven Helmut and Kurt. You listen to Samuel und Eddie and let change happen, or…or..." Then he grinned. "Or I shoot you again."

We all chuckled at that, and even Art smiled.

"You lose a great opportunity now," Kurt went on, "because you act like a kanooklehead."

Art looked quizzically at Kurt then looked at Eddie who also raised an eyebrow. "Like a what?" Art asked.

"A kanooklehead. A dumkopf."

Art looked shocked, almost like Kurt really had shot him again and then suddenly, to my great surprise, Art and Eddie broke into laughter.

Eddie reached over and rubbed Art's head. "Yeah, Art. Quit being a knucklehead."

Art turned to Eddie. "Is that another voice from the grave?"

Eddie grinned back. "No, Pete is still quite alive and well and living in Tulsa."

Art smiled. "Good." He rubbed his face and broke out in a grin. "Well, I certainly don't want to be a knucklehead," he said ruefully.

I could feel the great change, and I knew that the Boss had done it again, but I didn't understand how. Kurt and Helmut were looking puzzled, too. I went back to human form, but forgot to go back down and remained a foot off the ground.

"What was that all about?" I asked.

Art turned back to me. "Pete Runnels, the loader on our tank called people 'knuckleheads' whenever he thought they weren't performing up to standard. We all picked it up and called each other that when we felt it was deserved. Kurt and Eddie seem to think I deserved it then."

"You did," Eddie said.

"So Pete is still in Oklahoma. I'm glad. He certainly talked about it enough."

"And Helmut is still around, too," I said.

"Yes, indeed," Helmut put in. "Long retired and living with my daughter in the Bavarian hills. I went to sleep in her big chair and found myself here."

Just then Kurt looked at me surprised, and I noticed I was still walking on air so I lowered myself, even though it didn't seem to matter in a dream.

"So it seems I am forgiven?" Kurt asked.

Art laughed. "No. The question is 'Am I forgiven?'" he said. "I need it for holding on to hatred for so long. You are right. I have been praying that prayer without meaning it. Just now I prayed it sincerely for the first time."

Kurt nodded. "We have all needed forgiveness for something."

Art laughed. "Well, now I know what it's like to be forgiven again and to have a big load lifted. Thank you, all of you."

He grabbed Eddie in another bear hug, and shortly they grabbed Kurt, Helmut, and me, and we all had a big group hug.

"I'm going to eat some more of Giselle's sausage before I go back," I said after we broke. "Come and help me."

We sat back at the field table and started in again on

the food, after getting another stool for Helmut who looked around at everybody then at me, smiled, and in mock indignation said, "Herr Angel. Everyone else is young again. Why am I the only old man here?"

Everybody laughed.

Art looked at me. "You said there was some great purpose in this. What purpose?"

I shrugged. "I have no idea," I said and took a bite of bloodwurst on rye.

Art looked surprised. "You don't know either? But I thought that you would know, being—"

I shook my head and swallowed. "I know what I need to know, but like you I often don't know the ultimate purpose. I don't know why we were all sent here to you, but I know who sent us. That's enough."

"It doesn't matter," said Kurt. "'All things work together.' Our part is to do the best we can."

"Sometimes we know, sometimes we don't," Eddie said.

Art shook his head. "I'm not sure how I'm going to explain this to my wife Ellie—" He sat up straight suddenly. "Ellie! She's back at the cemetery—"

"Relax," I said. "Time works a little differently in a dream. By the time she notices you went to sleep, you'll be awake. Don't worry. Or once again I can say, 'Fear not.' It's all part of the plan."

He relaxed. "But I want to ask so many questions. What, and why, and how, and what's it like, and—But really right now those questions don't seem as important as I would have thought." He looked at Eddie and me then at Kurt and Helmut. "I guess I found that some things are more important than questions."

I nodded. "As I told you, some things aren't for understanding but just for accepting. Getting to see Eddie again and having Kurt, Helmut, and me come here are that sort of thing."

Art reached across the table and shook Kurt's hand then Helmut's then took Eddie's. He started to say something, but before he could speak, it all disappeared.

❧❧❧

The elderly man woke up with a start. He looked quickly around but then smiled and leaned back, contentedly. He stood up, patted the gravestone once, and headed toward the bench where the lady was sitting, walking much more stiffly and slowly than he had been walking in his dream. The lady met him and asked him something. His response was a laugh and a wave of his arm. She asked something else and pointed at the rows of crosses which he hadn't yet visited. He shook his head, gave her a contented-looking smile, and arm-in-arm they walked back toward the waiting car.

CHAPTER 5

ALL TOGETHER NOW

I came out in a thick grove of cedar and had the usual moment of disorientation and shock. But this time, my shivering wasn't all from the transition. It was cold, very cold, and there was about a foot of snow on the ground. I had on a heavy coat, but the cold bit right through it. I looked around and could see nothing but juniper trees, since it was almost sundown and dark cloudy, and the little bit of red glow from the west didn't help much. The trees were thick right there, and the only indication that I hadn't come over in an unpopulated wilderness was the sounds of a superhighway coming from the east.

I shivered again and set out walking in that direction. I soon came out of the juniper thicket into what seemed to be a pasture. I looked around for any cattle and didn't see any. I didn't expect to since I had checked it out closely from the other side, but I still hurried across the field because I didn't want to meet a mean bull in the dark. I've been skittish about bulls ever since that time in the 1600s just outside Seville when I went in to help a local farmer decide to be the assistant teacher in the parish catechism class. He owned a huge bull, which took an equally huge dislike to me and twice chased me around the field—much to the amusement of the farmer and his daughter. It worked out right in the end. With the daughter helping me apply pressure to the farmer, he took up the catechism class, and one of the boys in the class later became a missionary and the bishop of Manila. Also, the daughter married the local butcher, and the butcher wound up with most of the bull hanging up in his shop window.

I reached the highway without meeting a bull or even a calf and, as I was climbing over the fence onto the highway right-of-way, the wind picked up. It started to snow, hard. I could see the large gas station and truck stop, which was my goal, about a mile away to the south, so I crossed the ditch and headed that way. By the time I'd gone a quarter mile, the snow was noticeably deeper.

The cold and wind were uncomfortable enough that I was quite glad when a car stopped and the driver motioned for me to get in. I gratefully sat in the warm car.

"Thank you," I said to the driver.

Then I stopped and looked back, trying to not do an obvious double-take, but the driver helped me out by saying, "I'm only going to the truck stop up ahead, but if you have any sense, that's where you're heading, too. It's where you belong with this blizzard that's coming."

With that as my excuse, I looked at him and, while the lights from his dashboard weren't very bright, I could see him well enough to recognize him. I didn't know yet if they still called him Red, because his hair was pure white on the sides, and completely gone on top, but even though he was a good bit older, I still recognized him as my old hitch-hiking partner from Omaha. He was a lot better fed now, though—still skinny, but he didn't look malnourished any more.

"The truck stop will be fine," I replied. "Anywhere out of the snow and above freezing."

He chuckled. "We keep it a little warmer than that."

"Oh? Do you work there?" I asked.

He nodded. "I'm the head mechanic, and building maintenance man."

"This seems a good night to hole up somewhere and stay in," I said, watching his windshield wipers fight a valiant battle against the snow, but at best fighting it to a draw.

"Yep," he said, a little distractedly as he carefully negotiated the tracks through the growing snow.

I took the hint and didn't talk, letting him concentrate on his driving as we went up the exit ramp. Then we were into the parking lot of the truck stop, and, even though the snow was deep there, it was more level, so he was able to relax a little. "Oh, we'll stay warm here tonight," he said.

"Good," I said, "At least as long as the electricity stays on."

"No problem," he said. "We've got a generator with enough fuel for weeks. So our power will stay on, one way or another. And there's back up gas heat."

He drove to the back of the building and pulled into a parking place next to a twenty-year-old pickup truck. "I'm Sam Himmel," I said, reaching out my hand.

"I'm Red," he replied, taking it at looking at me curiously. "Sam, huh?"

I nodded. He appeared to be thinking, but then seemed to drop the thought and opened his door to let in a swirl of cold air and snow.

I had wondered why I was sent over with a different last name this time, and now I knew why. I had on some other occasions seen the same person on two trips, but usually it was on purpose—a return trip.

It was a lot less common for the same person to just happen to show up—so I knew to be watching for the

Boss to be getting sneaky on me again. He tends to do that.

"Come on in with me," he said, leading me through a door that said *EMPLOYEES ONLY* and into the office section of the place. We came into a hallway that looked like the hallway to a truck stop office area with a few office doors. Red opened one of the doors on the left and went into a small but highly organized looking office. The far wall was glass and looked out on a shop floor with four maintenance bays, two of which had trucks in them. One of the trucks had the hood up with a man leaning over working on the engine. Red looked at the mechanic, who was wearing a coat, and grunted.

He put some papers which he had carried in with him on the desk and started his computer. While it booted up, he went across the hall and opened a door and we went into another office.

The old pickup truck outside should have given me a clue but I was still surprised to recognize another old friend, Mike. He had aged even more than Red, with thin, gray hair and saggy skin, and he still was a little overweight, but not much more than forty years ago. His office was bigger than Red's and had the look of a disorganized mess which had recently been cleaned up. It had a sitting area in it with a couch and a few comfortable looking chairs. That area was, in contrast, very neat and had obviously been set up and maintained by a lady.

He was talking on the telephone, telling someone "...we're in fine shape, so if you have troubles, come on over. Yes, ma'am, that would be fine, too. You're welcome. Bye."

He looked at Red with a brief glance my way. "Mrs. D'Amico is worried about the power going out. So am I."

Red grunted. "I had Charlie check out the generator Tuesday, and it's fine, and the fuel tank's full, so we should be just dandy. But the shop's cold. I guess that vent finally went down, so I'm going up to check it out. Oh, this is Sam…"

"Sam Himmel," I said, going up and shaking hands. "Red picked me up on the interstate and brought me here."

"Your car get stuck?" Mike asked.

I nodded. I didn't look like a hitch hiker this time. I was dressed in nice clothes, with a nice overcoat and looked about like an insurance adjuster, which was my cover story.

"Have you heard from Greg?" Red asked. "If that vent has fallen, it will be a two man job to get it fixed."

"Yeah," Mike replied. "He was on his way to Taylorsville, and he's now holed up in a motel half-way there."

Red groaned. "And none of the night crew knows beans about ductwork."

Now I knew why I had been sent with HVAC knowledge. "Red, I know that work and have done it before," I piped up. "Can I help out?"

I had done it before, but not this trip. I had come over just a couple of years earlier as a heating and air conditioning repairman in the Ukraine where I had been sent to help the priest in a small town church persuade the local civic leaders to approve a church school. Since most of the town council members were holdovers from the previous era, they weren't too sympathetic. But it worked out when the women of the town decided to get involved.

Red looked hopeful. "Are you certified?"

I shook my head. "No," thinking that my Ukrainian papers had expired, and had a different name on them, anyway. "But do you want a certificate or heat?"

"Good point and, for that matter, I'm not certified either, but I'll have Greg check it out and sign off on it when he gets back."

He looked at my clothes a little skeptically. "But you're liable to ruin your clothes and my coveralls would be way too small for you. Mike, can he borrow yours?"

Mike gestured at a door. "In the closet. Help yourself."

I did, and Red and I went back to his office. Red got on the phone while I changed into Mike's coveralls, which were way too big for me but they would work, so I put them on, rolling up the sleeves and legs.

"Hi, sweetheart, I made it in," Red was saying into the telephone. "Yeah, it's getting bad, and I expect I'll be here at least all night. No, don't even think about coming in. It's getting too bad out, and Henry can handle it, at least as long as Louise is here to keep him straight. I will. Gotta go. I love you. Bye."

He hung up and started putting his coveralls over his clothes. "That was my wife Charlene. She's the manager of the restaurant here, but she's staying home tonight, like most smart people."

He led the way out onto the shop floor where we looked up at the exposed ductwork. It was obvious where the problem was and, when we got a ladder on each side and climbed up to look at the damage, it turned out to be a simple repair. A piece of duct had worked loose and fallen and was blocking the airflow to the whole shop. It was a pretty simple repair job to drill into the concrete ceiling, put a brace on the duct, and clamp the whole thing into place. There were several times when the job took all four of our hands but we were done in half an hour, half of which was spent gathering tools and hauling stuff up the ladders.

We went back into Red's office, where I got out of Mike's coveralls and back into my own clothes.

"You certainly know ductwork," Red said. "How come you're not certified?"

"I could have been, but I left that job for another one."

"Well, you were certainly a big help up there. Thanks a lot."

"I'm glad to help. In fact, I'm still in your debt for bringing me here."

"No, I think you more than repaid that just now. Well, I think I'll go out and double check the generator, in case we need it, and make sure everything else is going all right out there." He went out the door into the shop area, and I went across the hall to Mike's office, knocked on the door, and heard him say "Come in," so I did and put his coveralls away in the closet.

As I closed the closet door, Mike studied me. "Do I know you from somewhere?"

"I don't think so," I said. "This is the first time I've been through here."

"You ever been in Omaha?"

I nodded. "Yeah, but not for over twenty-five years." Actually it was a little over forty years, but I was trying not to give away too much. I wasn't sure how much I was supposed to let them know and figured that the best way to handle it was straightforward undercover, unless I had clear indications otherwise. The Boss has good reasons for what He does, but sometimes, those good reasons aren't at all clear. Frequently, we're as surprised by His work as humans are.

"Me, too. Maybe we ran into each other there. Were you in the trucking business then?"

I shrugged. "Sort of. Around the edges of trucking and construction. Were you in trucking there?"

"Yep. I owned three rigs and drove one of them."

"Hmm. Isn't it a pretty big jump from three trucks to a truck stop?"

Mike smiled. "Yeah it is. And it took a lot of hard work and some lucky breaks. But Red is a very hard worker, and I try to be."

"Oh, is Red your partner?"

"Yeah. Back in Omaha, I had those three rigs and was thinking about expanding. Red was managing a tire store for his cousin Terry and was thinking about going into some kind of business as a sideline. Terry got wind of this place coming on the market, so he put up a big part of the money. Red and I put all of ours into it and bought this place half and half."

"No, fifty-one/forty-nine," Red inserted, opening the door. "Mike is a much better manager than I am, and I didn't want to be tempted to try and take over. I'm a maintenance man and mechanic, not a financial manager."

"And Terry owns the equivalent of thirty percent in non-voting stock."

"Mike also has a truck line with fifteen rigs, that I'm not a part of, but we do all of his trucks' maintenance here so it's a decent base income just from that."

"And the fuel pumps are basically money machines."

Red laughed. "He says that because he doesn't have to keep them operating and fix the busted ones."

"And the restaurant has been doing really well since we hired Tom Jr. as head cook. He didn't want to move this far away from home, but Red's oldest daughter convinced him."

"Oh?" I asked, "How'd she do that?"

"By marrying him," Mike said, grinning.

"My wife Charlene has been the restaurant manager for the last two years and has done a really good job, but she's making noises about wanting to do something else and letting Tom take it over. I think mostly she misses working with children and teaching."

"She's a teacher?"

Red nodded. "Thirty years teaching third grade at Glenside Elementary and about that long in the primary

Sunday school class at Mill Run Baptist. She retired from third grade to manage the restaurant, and I'm convinced she's regretted it ever since. She won't admit to having made a mistake, though."

"How many children do you have?" I asked.

"Four," Red answered. "Jerry the oldest, who's up the road teaching at Shiloh Seminary. He's married with two kids. Marlene, who's married to Tom, Jr., Betty who lives in Texas with her husband and kids, and Jo Ann who's in college."

I felt a thrill at that. Of course, I remembered Jerry and was very pleased to hear that he seemed to have turned out all right. But Red claiming him as his son was a surprise. Well, maybe not.

But before I could ask, the intercom buzzed, and Red was called out to the shop floor to deal with a problem with the pneumatic system. Mike decided to check on the kitchen, so I went out into the public part of the truck stop and wandered into the restaurant. The crowd was growing, with more and more people deciding to take shelter from the snow storm. Through the window, I could see traffic moving very slowly on the highway.

I decided it was time for me to indulge my sweet tooth, went to the counter, and sat next to a young man who looked like he had been a little down on his luck. His clothes were a little ragged, and he needed a haircut, but he seemed to have tried to look as presentable as he could under the circumstances.

He was eating the cheap hamburger and had a glass of water. I ordered a piece of the homemade apple pie, which was offered on the menu card and on a sign above the counter, and coffee.

While I waited for it to come, I turned to the young man. "I'm glad we're inside instead of out there on the highway right now."

He turned, looked at me, and smiled. "Yes. It's a lot warmer in here."

I glanced around the room. "It looks like we're probably going to be here all night at least."

He smiled again. "There seems to be plenty of room left."

"I'm Sam," I said with an inviting expression.

"I'm Josh," he said.

"Do you live close by?"

He shook his head. "I'm out seeing the world, at the moment."

"It's a good world to see," I agreed.

Then my pie arrived, and I found out that Tom Jr. had inherited his father's cooking talent. It was a wonderful piece of pie. Josh took the opportunity to leave the counter and go into the store. He had been polite and likeable, even if a little vague. Well, I certainly couldn't complain about that since, when we operate undercover, we raise vague answers to high art.

That had caused me trouble once in twelfth century England. I had gone in to help convince a local bad boy not to become an outlaw but to stay on as the cattle herder for his village. He'd had several conversations with one of the outlaws in the forest and was thinking about joining them. When the village sheriff didn't like my vague answers as to who I was, where I'd come from, and what my business there was, he had locked me in the jail. It worked out in the end.

Jack never joined the outlaws, but that was more the work of a village lass who had taken a shine to him, and her arguments apparently were a lot more convincing than mine.

I had spent the time in the dungeon with another traveler and was able to convince him to go to the monastery in the next county where he wound up the groundskeeper and the founder of a family which became big supporters of Thomas Cranmer.

The pie was soon reduced to a stray crumb or two. I paid and wandered around a while.

I found a small snack shop at the other end which worked out of the same kitchen as the restaurant. I had a nice visit with a newlywed couple named Hal and Sherry from down further south who were enjoying the snow since they saw so little of it. So I visited with them for a while then wandered back out to the front. I noticed Josh was sitting on the floor against the wall close to the door, so I went over and sat beside him.

"Rather nasty business out there," I said in a conversational gambit.

He smiled. "I've seen worse."

"I suppose so." So had I. Like that winter in a yurt in Siberia. At least here the sun was going to come up in the morning.

Then the door opened and three people came in. One was Mike and the other two were an older couple, the man pushing the woman in a wheelchair. Mike was telling the man something, but I didn't hear. I was too shocked to listen because I recognized Bob and Bonnie Dunn whom I'd worked with very recently. This job was really turning into old home week.

Bob looked casually in our direction, looked away, then did a quick double take and stopped, looking at Josh and me with recognition. Then he frowned and went on.

I didn't know what that was. I know he didn't recognize me, since I looked completely different this time. Maybe he knew Josh from somewhere.

Bob, Bonnie, and Mike disappeared into the store part, and I talked with Josh a little more about nothing much. Then I saw Red come through the doorway, look around, and head straight for me.

"Sam, do you know anything about plumbing? We've got a broken pipe in the pump house. I can fix it but it's a two man job. Could you help again?"

"Sure," I said, getting up, "but I'm not a plumber."

Red turned and headed back toward the offices. "You'll do."

I followed, thinking fast. This was a good opportunity which looked too sweet to be coincidence. Sure enough, the route we took was leading us right by Mike, Bob, and Bonnie, so right as we passed them, I said, "But there's probably a real plumber in this crowd."

It worked just like I hoped. Bob heard me and turned around. "I'm a plumber," he said. "Can I be of some help?"

Red stopped and turned to look at Bob. After a moment's consideration, Red shook his head. "There's no need. I expect we can take care of it." He looked at Bonnie. "Don't you need to stay with…"

Bob shrugged slightly. "Somebody needs to stay with her, but it doesn't have to be me."

"I would be glad to sit with her," we heard someone say behind us. We turned to see Josh standing there with a smile. "I don't exactly have anything else to do," he said. "We can sit in the restaurant where we'll have lots of chaperones."

I had a strong urge to go with this one, so I said to Red, "That sounds good and a real plumber would be a good idea. When it comes to plumbing, I'm just a pipe holder."

"I'd be glad to help," Bob said, "and I'm like this gentleman, nothing else to do."

"Okay," Red agreed with a smile. "Mike, if you will help these folks to the restaurant, we'll go fix a pipe."

Bob gave Josh some instructions which basically consisted of keep her upright, and then Mike led Josh and

Bonnie off to the restaurant. Red, Bob, and I went back to the offices where Red gave each of us a heavy coat.

Outside, the snow was falling even heavier, and the wind had begun to blow. Red led us past the truck fuel pumps to a small building. We went inside of it, where the shelter from the wind was welcome, even though the building was unheated. Inside there was a maze of pipes, tanks, and pumps. The floor had about a quarter inch of water on it which was in the process of becoming ice.

Red took us to the end of the room where a pipe joint was emitting a fine spray of water, fortunately spraying toward the wall where it was making an interesting array of ice formations and stalactites.

"Yep, we've got a corrosion problem," Bob said, "but I think it'll be a pretty simple repair." He followed the pipe back to a pump and looked at Red. "Will it hurt any-thing if I shut this pump down for a few minutes?"

Red shook his head. "This pipe feeds the water faucets on the truck fuel islands. I don't think they'll be getting much use tonight."

Bob hit a switch and turned the valve where the pump fed into the leaky pipe. The spray of water slowly dimin-ished.

"Where are your tools?" Bob asked.

Red led us to a bench by the door where a tool box and peg board with some rather strange objects resided.

Bob looked the display over, opened the toolbox, and checked out the contents. "You have first class tools, here," he said. "Mostly better than I have. That's great."

"Yeah," Red agreed. "I found out a long time ago that cheap tools can be the most expensive kind."

Bob gestured at a rather large appliance hanging on the peg board with two handles and an incomprehensi-ble—to me—maze of arms. "I've always wanted one of them and now I wish this job needed it."

Red laughed. "That's one tool I'm not sure was cost effective. I've used it twice in ten years."

Bob smiled. "But when you need it, you need it real bad."

He picked up the tool box and headed back to the leak. "But everything we'll need is in here and—" He picked up a roll of something off a peg. "—and this."

He took a small gas torch, lit it, and applied it to the joint. He and Red began a discussion of brands, sizes, temperatures, and even flame colors of various torches, then branched off into pipe wrenches, spanner wrenches, thread cutters, and eventually left the English language altogether—all the while cutting the pipe and grafting in another joint and a short piece of pipe while I performed my promised function of pipe holder.

Then the conversation shifted to baseball. It turned out both were ardent fans of the Royals—them again—and the conversation went to on base percentage, ERA, and again they soon ceased to speak standard English, but they both seemed to enjoy the whole conversation immensely.

As Bob cleaned off the tools and returned them to their appropriate place, Red thanked him profusely. "You were right, Sam. Having a real plumber helped a lot. I could have done that job, but it might have taken me all night instead of forty minutes."

"Well, I'm glad we weren't out here all night," I replied. "My feet are already freezing."

We went back out into the snow and got back to the offices, where we stomped the snow off our feet and put the coats back in Red's closet.

"Since you both have been so helpful, you're both welcome to hole up back here in the offices if you would like. There are more comfortable seats and free coffee."

Bob considered the proposition for about a tenth of a

second. "That would be great. Bonnie has always been a little sensitive about being on public display among people she doesn't know, and I think she would be a lot more comfortable back here. I'll go get her and bring her here. Thank you very much."

He then headed out to the front. Red and I went over to Mike's office, where he was just hanging up the telephone and making a face at it.

"Bad news?" Red asked.

"The snow storm is intensifying, and now the forecast is for twenty more inches by morning."

As if on cue, the lights chose that moment to go out.

"Uh-oh," Red moaned. "Let's hope—"

Then the lights flickered several times and came back on.

Mike breathed a sigh of relief, and Red pumped his fist once. "Great, the generator kicked in just perfect."

Mike grinned real big. "Yeah, and it's always a relief when it does, Little Fellow."

Red grinned back. "You should have more confidence in my work, Big Fellow. But now, I'm going to go check on everything and reset all the automatic timers." He started out Mike's office door but stopped and turned back. "I told Sam and Bob the plumber who fixed the leak that they could stay back here with us."

Mike nodded. "Sure." He gestured at his sitting area. "Lots of room."

So I sat on Mike's couch while he made another phone call, this time to the kitchen, but I changed my mind and went over to look at a shelf with some trophies and pictures on it. They were church league basketball trophies, all at least ten years old, with team pictures beside them, with Mike in each of them, looking older as the pictures looked newer.

I turned toward Mike when he hung up the phone and,

from that perspective, I could see the pictures on his desk. I looked at the largest picture and laughed. She was forty years older but still very recognizable as Shirley/Jessica, the sassy waitress from Trailside Diner. In the smaller pictures beside it were two younger versions of herself, both of whom had the same sassy smile, and a skinny younger copy of Mike but with "Shirley's" grin. Next to them was a group shot of five grade school age children whom I suspected were Mike and Jessica's grandchildren.

Mike cocked an eyebrow. "Are my family pictures humorous?"

I laughed again. "No. I recognize your wife, I think." Actually, I knew exactly who she was but I figured that I shouldn't reveal that. "Wasn't she a waitress at Omaha, named Shirley, in a little converted filling station that was a dump, but had great food?"

Mike smiled. "You have been to Omaha, haven't you? Yep, that's her. But her name's Jessica."

"Oh, I thought it was Shirley."

Mike laughed. "She always wore a name tag that said Shirley. I don't know why. We've been married thirty-seven years and, still, all she will tell me about that is to say it was 'to confuse the police if I ever get arrested for serving this slop.' Personally, I think she did it because she's a nut."

I smiled. "I'll bet she said 'serving this slop, honey.'"

Mike chuckled again. "Yeah, you do remember her, don't you? When we bought this place, she worked as a waitress here, too. And bookkeeper, and cook, and janitor, and sometimes even mechanic's helper. She's been a hard worker and a big help. Some weeks in the early years her tip money was all we had to live on."

I pointed over at another picture on the other side of his desk. "Who's the first sergeant?"

He swiveled in his chair to look at the picture of the man in uniform. "That's my baby brother, Harry. Ex-hippie and anti-war protestor who changed his mind. He wound up going to Desert Storm, the invasion of Afghanistan, the invasion of Iraq, and back to Afghanistan where a bomb under the road blew up his gun truck and killed him and his driver. His gunner survived minus a foot, and Jessica and I have sort of adopted him. He has no family, so he lives in the apartment over our garage, and we drive him around until his physical rehab is over. He works for Red in the shop, too."

"What changed your brother's mind?"

"He went to San Francisco and saw the protestors spitting on soldiers coming back from Vietnam. He walked straight from the terminal to a barber shop then to a recruiting station. He found out he liked military life and stayed in. Thirty-four years of service."

"Did he have a family?"

"Divorced. One son. His wife took off fifteen years ago and never had any communication with Harry, and we don't know where she is. I've tried to find them, off and on, but had no luck. I would love to see Harold, Jr. Maybe someday."

Just then there was a knock on the door and Bob brought Bonnie in.

"Still snowing?" Mike asked.

Bob parked her wheel chair at the end of the couch and sat beside her. "Harder than ever," he replied. "I saw on the TV in the lobby that it's supposed to snow until about three a.m. and then start getting even colder. It's going to be nasty. I'm sure glad we got in here before it was too late."

Mike nodded. "Yeah. Me, too. You'd have a hard time with your wife if you were still stuck on the highway."

Red came in then and reported that all was well with the generator and the automatic machinery.

"Great," I said. "We were just discussing how glad we were that we were in the warm instead of stranded out on the roads."

"I was just out front and could see the highway from the front windows," Bob said, "and nothing is moving, so there are several people who are stuck out there."

Mike nodded thoughtfully. "Yeah, and we need to try and get as many of them in here as we can, don't we?"

"Right," Red put in. "And we've got Jimmy Rennert's six-by-six dump truck that he brought in for new rings. It'll hold up fine for what we need, and I've already told Lance to get some snow chains on it."

Mike laughed. "You're ahead of me again, Red. Who's going?" He looked around the room.

Bob and I both said "Me," at the same moment.

"The nice young man who sat with Bonnie while I worked on the pipe might go," Bob added.

Mike looked at Bonnie. "Then who'd sit with Bonnie?" he asked.

I remembered Hal and Sherry, the nice couple whom I'd met in the snack bar and had been rather impressed with them. "I think I know someone," I said. "I'll go ask them."

"Great," Mike said. "I'll get the truck and bring it to the front door and all of you meet me there. Red, see if there's another young healthy fellow who'll go with us."

We all left the office, except for Bob and Bonnie. Fortunately, Hal and Sherry were still in the same booth, and they were quite happy to have something useful to do, so I led them back to Mike's office where we all introduced ourselves and Bob gave them some instructions.

Then he and I headed out to the front, where Red had brought some heavy coats. He also brought a young soldier from the army post just up the road who wanted to help. So we all bundled up, but still were short of warm clothes.

Red shook his head. "That's all we've got here, and it's not enough. I guess we'll—"

"I've got an idea," Sergeant Roy Cole said. He walked into the restaurant and loudly shouted, "Some of the men are going out to bring in folks that are stranded on the road. They're short of gloves, hats, and scarves. Can any of you help them out?"

We were immediately overwhelmed with offers of gloves, scarves, coats, galoshes, thermoses of coffee, furry caps, and other less practical things—one man offered his watch and pen. I guess he meant well.

I took a furry cap and a scarf from a Mr. Robertson, and some overshoes from Mrs. Kerns who had big feet— the overshoes were a little too big for me—so I was well set up. The rest of the rescue team was equally well equipped, and we went out into the cold after Roy said good-bye to his wife and three year old daughter.

"You be careful out there," Mrs. Cole said.

"I will," he promised. "And this time I won't be gone a year and nobody is out there with guns. And besides—" He turned and pointed at me. "—Sam is going to take care of me. Right, Sam?"

I nodded. "I'll be his guardian angel, I promise." Once again, I cracked myself up. Sometimes I can be downright hilarious.

We went out to the truck. I was immediately glad to have all the warm clothes I had and, very shortly, wished for more.

We loaded up, with Mike driving and Bob and Red in the cab with him, and Josh and Roy with me in the bed of the truck where it was very windy and cold. Lance had apparently swept the snow out of the truck when he put the chains on, but it was already filling back up with an inch or so of snow. A lump under the snow in the bed turned out to be a pile of wool blankets which we quickly shook out and wrapped ourselves in.

Mike started off. The snow chains made an odd grinding sound as they rolled over the snow, but they worked, and we were able to get out of the truck stop and down the access ramp with little trouble.

As soon as we got on the highway, it was obvious that it was going to be difficult to maneuver around all the stopped cars and that lots of people were glad to see us because several car doors opened and people got out to flag us down.

The first car we came to was one that tried to flag us down. We jumped out of the truck bed to see about them.

The driver met us "I'm glad to see you folks. We were just about to try to walk up, in spite of—" He pointed to the just-opened passenger door where the passenger had an obviously brand new cast on his leg.

"That would have been difficult," Roy said. "Close the door for a minute to keep it dry." Then he went to the truck. "Is there a garbage bag or something like that in there?"

Red looked around and then looked behind the seat. He reached into the area there and pulled out a roll of thin black plastic. "Will this do?"

"Great!" Roy said. "Is there any string or rope?"

Red looked and shook his head, but the driver of the car grinned. "I've got a ball of butcher's twine in the trunk," he said, going back to it. He rummaged around and came out with a small ball of twine.

Roy and Josh opened the car, wrapped the cast in the black plastic, and then tied it in place with the twine. Then Roy motioned to me. We picked the young man up, while Josh took hold of the leg in a cast to keep it from getting banged around. We carried him around and sat him on the lip of the truck bed, then got in and helped him the rest of the way.

The other man climbed in and we were off again, but went only about fifty yards when we stopped again to check out a car with a light showing inside. Two middle aged ladies were in it, scared half to death. It took all of my persuasion power and Josh's help to get them to agree to get into a truck with several strange men. Roy and Josh were very gentle and circumspect in helping them aboard, which elevated the ladies' confidence in us.

So we headed on down the road.

The next vehicle showing any signs of life was a red pickup truck that contained an almost frantic young man and his wife who looked to be about ten months pregnant. When he saw that, Red got out and we put her into the truck cab, out of the cold. Her husband calmed down a lot after that and pitched in to help.

We seldom went very far without stopping to pick somebody up. We stopped and investigated any car showing any light inside, most of which had people in them, all of whom wanted to go with us. Several of them were either elderly or sick and needed help getting into the truck. Three of the ladies in particular needed a warm place, being a combined twenty-two months pregnant, and they displaced Bob and Red in the truck cab. Their husbands all helped out in the back. We needed the help. Pretty soon in the proceedings, Red, Bob, Josh, Roy, and I were cold, wet, and tired. Bob and Red helped out a lot, in spite of their gray hair.

We had one very scary moment when an old man in an old, very rusty car—and who clearly wasn't normal even in the best of times—totally freaked out when Roy opened the door of his car. The man jumped out of the car so fast that he knocked Roy down and then started running through the snow as fast as he could, screaming. But Roy, who was a lot younger and in much better physical condition, jumped up, quickly caught the man, and tackled him. The old man tried to fight and get free, but Roy had him in a hold he'd learned in Ranger School so the old man could do nothing more than wiggle.

Josh went running after them. He caught the old man's head between his hands then put his face right up against the old man's, saying something too soft for me to hear, but it worked.

The old man quit struggling. "Okay."

"Let him go, Roy," Josh said.

Roy did. The man stood up, very calmly retrieved his hat, and climbed onto the truck. When we got going again, he went over to Josh. "Thank you, young fellow. Very much."

Josh just smiled and patted him on the shoulder.

I wanted to ask what he had said to the old man, but we reached another car and went back to work.

In just over half an hour, we had all we could carry, so Mike turned around—very carefully—and followed his own tracks back to the truck stop while Red, Bob, Roy, Josh, and I held on and rode on the running boards since the truck bed was completely full.

Red shivered. "I haven't been this cold since I left Omaha."

"Not since military cold weather training in Alaska," Bob put in.

I could top them with the story of the winter I spent in an Inuit village in northern Canada in 1792 where I convinced the village to not kill one of Alexander McKenzie's scouts who had gotten lost. It worked and they adopted him into the tribe. When the first missionaries arrived on the Fraser River, they found one village with an established church with a pastor named McLeod.

While they compared cold weather experiences, I did some thinking. I was convinced that this rescue mission was crucial to my purpose in being here, but as of yet, I didn't know what my specific job was to be—aside from helping old people into the truck. I thought over each of the people we had found but I hadn't gotten any nudges about any of them. But the more I thought about it, the more I was sure that the truck trip and getting people out of the stranded cars was crucial to what the Boss had sent me here for. So all I could do was keep going.

We unloaded everybody at the front door of the truck stop, took a couple of minutes to go in and get some hot coffee into us, and then we headed right back out for another load. Mike followed his own tracks to where we had turned around then resumed honking the horn and flashing the lights, just in case anybody didn't notice the two-ton dump truck driving around. We found several more cars with people who wanted to go in, and a few who, unwisely, decided to wait it out in their cars.

In one place we thought for a moment we were stopped, because somebody had left their car sideways at the edge of the road, completely blocking it. While Bob and I discussed the possibilities, Mike solved the problem by using the truck bumper to push the car into the ditch.

Bob laughed. "That's one way to get it done," he said.

"I hope the car owner has good insurance," I replied.

"I hope *we* do," we heard Red say as he came up behind us with a middle aged couple to put on the truck and under blankets.

For forty more minutes, we rounded up strays and stopped when we met another truck coming from the other direction, on a similar mission. It was being driven by Mike and Red's competitor—and friend—from the next exit. They had a truck load of refugees as well. Mike and Red went over and talked to them for a minute and they decided that they had picked up everybody in that section who wanted it, so we turned around and again headed back.

I was thinking fast, now. Something was wrong. I was still convinced that the rescue run was a key to my mission but was equally convinced that none of the people we had gotten was the one I was looking for.

Since our load wasn't quite full this time, there was room for all of us on the bed of the truck, so I made my way to the front and banged on the cab roof.

Mike rolled his window down a little. "What?" he yelled.

"Stop and wait," I said.

"Wait? What for?" he asked, sounding a little annoyed, but he stopped.

"Just wait," I responded. "Everybody be quiet a moment."

The conversations stopped.

I looked around, hoping to see something, but all I noticed was Josh watching me expectantly.

One of the men started to ask something, but I held up my hand for silence then got the nudge I had been expecting. I turned to the west and pointed at a patch of woods, just past the fence which bordered the highway. "In there."

I climbed over the side of the truck, jumped down, and started walking toward the woods, but before I got very far, we heard someone yelling.

"Wait! Wait!" the voice called.

I stopped. Shortly, a man came running out of the woods and rather frantically started climbing the fence.

"Slow down and be careful," I called to him. "We're waiting for you."

He didn't slow down much and was soon coming up the bank to the truck. Mike got out to help him up the last little bit. "How'd you know he was out there?" Mike asked me as we helped the man up over the tailgate and into the truck.

I just shrugged. "A hunch, I guess," I said.

"Well, I'm glad you had it," he said as he headed back to the driver's seat.

I swung myself up into the truck bed to be met with sincere and effusive thanks from the man, who on closer look in the dim light turned out to be rather young and short, with distinctly oriental features. He was not dressed for a nighttime trek through the snowy woods and who would have been in a tough spot had we not stopped for him.

The truck's engine and grinding of the tire chains made conversation impractical but I took a good look at our late arrival to make sure I would recognize him once we got back to the light and warmth.

We were able to make it back without any great crisis. There was a bit of a scare when, trying to get back up the access ramp, the truck hit a drift which stopped it momentarily, but Mike backed up and, with a running start, hit it hard and broke through.

Red cheered. "I'm glad we made it, but even if we hadn't, we could walk from here."

Again we got off at the front door and trooped inside, with Bob and Red carrying an elderly lady, and Josh and Roy each assisting a limping person. I helped the folks down from the rather high truck bed, with the latecomer helping from inside the truck. Mike helped the second set of pregnant ladies down from the high cab and safe into the arms of their husbands.

As we watched the last of the people dismount, Mike and I heard a tractor come around the corner of the building. It was outfitted as a construction tractor with an enclosed cab, and a digger arm on the back. "Oh, for crying out loud!" Mike muttered as the tractor pulled up beside the truck. The tractor cab door opened and a well-remembered face poked out.

"Hey there, honey. Need any help?" Jessica said with a big grin.

She had aged quite well, a few more wrinkles, but I suspected her lack of gray hair came from a bottle. Just past her I saw another face from the past. Charlene was now completely gray and rather plump, but otherwise about what you would expect after forty some years.

"You two don't have a lick of sense, do you?" Mike said, but with a grin.

"Nope," Jessica responded. "Otherwise why would we have married you two?"

"What are you doing here?" Mike asked.

"We were sitting at home by ourselves and decided we would be more useful here. I didn't think my truck would make it in so we came in this. No problem."

Mike chuckled and shook his head. "Well, go put it under the shed by the mower and come on in."

The tractor door closed, the tractor drove away, Mike remounted the truck cab, drove away to the back, and we all went inside, cold, wet, and miserable, but safe.

❧❧❧

We all took a couple of minutes just to soak up the warmth and light. Then I found the nice folks who had loaned me the warm clothes and returned them, with sincere thanks. Bob and Red headed back to the offices, but I felt the urge to stick around out front for a bit, so I did. I felt like company anyway, so I wandered around talking to people and helping a few get situated, even though there was no lack of help available. Everybody was in a good mood, happy to be off the road and in a warm place.

Then Mike came out and announced that there were five coin operated clothes dryers in the shower area, if anybody needed to get dried off, and a good number headed that way. That cleared out the front enough that I could go looking for the man who had been the last to get on the truck. I found him sitting at a small table in the snack bar with a hot dog and some coffee. I sat down across from him and introduced myself. "I'm Sam," I said. "I was on the truck that brought you in."

He smiled back. "Yes, and thank you. If you hadn't stopped when you did, I would have been in trouble. I'm Richard."

"Well, I'm glad you found us anyway. So what do you do when you're not stuck in a truck stop?"

He tilted his head uncertainly. "Right now I work in a men's clothes store. It's not a bad job, but I don't think I want to spend my life doing that."

"Then what do you want to do?"

He shrugged. "Good question, but I don't have any answers. I graduated from college last June, but I'm not at all sure about my next step."

"You're young," I said. "There's still time to find out. What about your family?"

He drained the last of his coffee. "Mom and Dad are both immigrants. Dad was Burmese and Mom was Montagnard. They met and married in Vietnam and came here at the end of the war."

At that, I sat up straight, and if human ears could perk up, mine would have. It sounded just like the people I had been with my last time in Vietnam. "What's your full name?"

"Richard Seng."

"Yep," I said, "That's a Burmese name. Jingpo isn't it? How did he wind up married to a Vietnamese?"

Richard smiled. "Don't call Mom Vietnamese where

she can hear you. Her people and the ethnic Vietnamese didn't like each other much. She's from the Jarai tribe. Dad's family was part of a group of refugees from some ethnic warfare in Burma where the central government tried to establish control over the Kachin region. Granddad and the surviving family got away and wound up in North Vietnam, very near the Laotian border and the DMZ. They were allowed to stay, but Dad says it wasn't a very good situation for them. They were tolerated but not accepted. He was drafted to be a porter on the Ho Chi Minh trail and went into South Vietnam that way. Mom was a cook for her village's militia which was led by an American, Sergeant Johnson, and their job was to try to disrupt the delivery of supplies to the Communists in the south. Mom got captured by the soldiers guarding Dad's pack train and they planned to kill her, but Dad and a couple of others escaped with her and got away. Mom led them back to Sergeant Johnson's troop, Dad joined it and they spent the next few years fighting the Communists. Dad was adopted by Mom's village, and they got married."

That was certainly Seng and the Jarai lady I had known. This job was really a trip down memory lane. A long trip. I wondered what the Boss was up to. He likes to be devious at times and this certainly seemed to be one of those times.

Well, everybody seemed to be together now, and all I had to do was figure out what my part in it was. It was centered on Richard, but obviously, the Boss had something bigger in mind than just him.

"How did they get to America?"

"When the Communists took over, Sergeant Johnson was in Manila, assigned to the embassy. He technically went AWOL, hitched a ride on one of the last flights into Saigon, stole an army truck, and drove to Mom and Dad's village. All of the survivors loaded up in the truck and drove to the coast where they stole a fishing boat and headed out to sea where Sergeant Johnson found a US Navy ship, the captain of which had been a pilot who got shot down and Sergeant Johnson had led the rescue team in that got him out. So the captain was willing to bend the rules and take aboard a dozen refugees. They got off of the ship in Manila, and Sergeant Johnson used his embassy connections to get them all visas, but they got the names mixed up and Dad's personal name became our family name. So Mom and Dad wound up in Alabama, working in a grocery store. Now they own two stores and have seven American citizen children and five grandchildren so far, all with MP-3 players, cell phones, and computers."

"Just your everyday American success story," I said, grinning.

"Yeah." He chuckled. "And every day I say a prayer of thanks that I'm here instead of in a re-education camp there. And another prayer of thanks for Sergeant Johnson and still another for his Alabama church which took in a village of foreigners and made them welcome."

"But in spite of living the American dream, you're still not certain what to do with your life?"

"No. But retelling that story puts it in perspective. Compared to what could have happened, spending my life selling suits and socks in Birmingham isn't bad at all."

"Very true, very true," I agreed. "What's your dream job?"

He hesitated, thinking about it. "I don't know."

"Well, the last time you thought you knew, what was it?"

He hesitated again. "I thought I was going to be a pastor, but…"

"But…" I prompted.

"But now I don't think that."

"Why?"

Another hesitation.

"Too personal?" I asked.

"No, no." he said quickly. "Just…painful."

"Oh. Sorry. A bad church experience?"

He nodded. "While I was at college."

"What happened?"

He shook his head. "But it wasn't all their fault. It was mine, too. That makes it worse. If it had been all their fault, then I could feel righteous and superior. I can't, because I know I was part of the problem."

"So now you're having a faith crisis?"

"No, not about the usual stuff of a faith crisis, but…yeah, a crisis of faith in myself. If I can't handle that, how could I handle a church? I know such things are going to happen again. We're human beings, not angels."

I smiled. "Most of us, anyway."

He looked at me funny and I said, "Don't get discouraged. The trick with doubts is don't give in, keep going anyway."

He grunted noncommittally.

Just then Mike and Red came out from the back, and Richard excused himself to go and thank them. They talked for several minutes while I went around and did a little visiting.

Then Mike announced that he was turning off the lights in the snack bar and he would leave the door open so folks could go in and sleep in there. Several people went in and some others were already laying down in the main part. Richard was standing at the big front windows, looking out over the highway which was now dark and still. I thought he was lost in thought, but he turned and beckoned.

"Mike, come look at this."

Mike went over to the window and I tagged along. Richard pointed. "Watch that spot just past the car carrier, on the other side of the highway."

We looked and, in a few seconds, saw a yellow glow on the snow which blinked three times, a pause, and then blinked three times, a pause, and on and on. "That's the low place in the right of way," said Mike. "There's something down in it that we can't see from here. That's what's making the light."

"Well, I think there's somebody in a car out there," Richard said. "And I think that's a signal."

"Maybe, but it could be an abandoned car with flashers still on."

"But then it would blink steady, not on and off."

Mike looked thoughtful. "You're probably right. I expect a car has slid off into that low place."

Richard turned around. "Can I take the truck out to see?"

Mike raised an eyebrow and looked amused and skeptical. "No, but you can go with me if you want to."

We went back to the offices and found Red. "Red," Mike said, "We think we've found a car load we missed the first time. Richard and I are going to go check it out."

Red nodded "I can go, too."

Bob and I both said, "Me, too," at the same time.

Mike shook his head. "There's only one car, so we don't need many and, given the risk, the fewer people along, the better."

So Red outfitted Richard with his insulated coveralls, parka, and overshoes, since they were about the same size. Mike suited up, too, and they headed out.

Bob lay down on the couch to try to nap, and Red and I went out to the front to watch from the big windows.

Since just about everybody out there was trying to

rest, Red turned several of the lights out, leaving enough on to see to get around, and we took chairs to the window. The truck made it out of the truck stop with no problem, but the drift that had made trouble for us as we came in earlier was worse and stopped them. They both got out and shoveled for a while, then Mike got back in and, again, got a running start and broke through. They made it about half way there then had to stop and shovel again. It took longer that time, but again, the truck broke through.

Another time, the truck slid a little toward the ditch, making Red and me both hold our breaths for an instant, but Mike got it back under control.

Then they were there, and we could just make out Mike and Richard as they got out of the stopped truck, crossed the highway, and disappeared into the low spot. They stayed out of sight for about ten minutes, long enough for me to wish for miraculous powers to do something from a mile away, but I hadn't been sent over for that kind of thing this time. I seldom do much along those lines, since those jobs tend to go to Michael and his crew, but I have done a couple. Once in fourteenth century Scotland, I got to make a wide ditch appear suddenly, keeping an English noble from catching a runaway serf who kept on going and whose grandson was a big supporter and protector of John Knox during the Reformation. But here, all I could do was watch and hope.

Something must have worked, because we eventually saw four figures come back onto the road and get into the truck cab. Mike carefully backed up between two snow covered lumps which I assumed were cars, turned the truck around, and headed back.

This time, the way through both drifts was still clear enough to get through and the return trip was lacking in excitement, fortunately.

Instead of coming to the front Mike drove to the back, so Red returned to the office section to see Mike and Richard come in with their prizes, but I had a sense that I should stay in the front, so I did.

Most of the people in the lobby were settled down for the night with the hold out night owls congregating at the counter in the restaurant.

I went to the window for a moment and watched the snow fall, but the peaceful moment was interrupted by a shout behind me. I turned to see Roy Cole spring up from his blanket, run over, and grab another man's wrist.

"Let it go," Roy commanded.

Then I noticed that the other man was holding what looked like a lady's billfold.

The noise roused everybody and my guess as to the identity of the object was confirmed by a middle-aged lady who exclaimed, "That's my wallet!"

At that, Roy twisted the man's arm around behind his back and, with some footwork, had the man immobile, face down on the floor. Roy handed the wallet back to the lady and then looked around, seemingly unsure what to do next, having a prisoner and no idea what to do with him.

Fortunately, Charlene and Jessica came out of the kitchen, drawn by the commotion, and Charlene took charge. "Let him up, please, Sergeant Cole," she said, looking at the rank and name tag on Roy's uniform. "I don't think he'll run very far in this storm."

Roy released him and they both stood up, but Roy stayed close and alert.

Charlene faced the suspected thief, who was average height, average build, shabbily dressed, and with several tattoos. "I suppose you have a good explanation?" she demanded.

With a surly look, the man replied in an equally surly tone, "She dropped it and I was about to give it back to her."

Roy shook his head in a negative and Jessica snorted. "Yeah, I'll bet," I heard her mutter as I worked my way closer through the people sitting up watching.

Charlene gave Jessica a dirty look, then turned back to the man. "What's your name?" she asked.

He rolled his eyes, then looked at the floor. "Frank," he said in a tone which inspired great confidence in his ability to prevaricate.

Charlene looked out the window. "With the snowstorm I don't think we'll get the sheriff to come out—" She looked around at the people bedded down on the floor. "—so I'm not sure what to do with you."

Jessica stepped in front. "I do," she said. "Frank, you come back into the kitchen with us and work the rest of the night, and we'll forget the whole thing and act like we believe you about returning the wallet. Okay?"

Frank and Roy both looked skeptical, and Frank smirked at the same time.

Jessica, noting the smugness added, "Otherwise, we turn Sergeant Cole loose on you."

Frank looked back at Roy who was a good four inches taller and fifty pounds of muscle heavier and the smirk disappeared from his face and came onto Roy's. Frank seemed to think for a moment. "Okay, but no cops at all, right?"

Charlene rolled her eyes but Jessica got a mean grin. "If you didn't do anything wrong and were going to give it back, what difference would it make about police? Never mind. Come on."

Roy looked distressed. "Ma'am, are you sure that's safe?"

Jessica smiled at him. "Henry will take care of safety.

And Henry's bigger than you and has a rougher background. It's safe enough."

"Okay," Roy said, "but first—" He stepped toward Frank and got his arm in a lock again. Roy's hand slipped into Frank's back pocket and came out with a large folding knife. He tossed it to Jessica. "You don't want him to have this."

"Thank you. Come on," she said to Frank, and they went through the doors into the kitchen.

I watched the doors close behind them and considered things. At times, when we're here as straight flesh and blood, the Boss gives us the ability to see things beyond the physical world, and I had gotten that sense with Frank. Something definitely was not normal about him. There was some kind of evil presence about him that wasn't his, but I couldn't place what it was. There was a cloud of spiritual darkness around him that only I could sense. He seemed almost to be possessed, but I can recognize that easily, and this wasn't it. But I was definitely getting a heads up from the Boss, so I knew to pay attention.

So I headed back to Mike's offices to see who they had brought in. The new folks were a young lady about twenty to twenty-five and an elderly man who looked eighty or ninety, but was getting around just fine. I had just gotten the door closed when it hit me with a big jolt. The elderly man was another person I knew from a past job. He had seemed twenty five or so when I worked with him in his dream, but I had also seen him in the cemetery. It was Art Harrod, who had met his old army friend and some former enemies, too.

Mike had sat both of them in chairs next to a gas heater and put blankets on them.

The relief of getting everybody in safely, along with the late hour, had everybody a little giddy and there was a good bit of laughing, joking, and good natured banter.

Mike made introductions all around.

"And I'm Art Harrod," Art said, "and this is my granddaughter Debbie. And believe me, we are both very glad to meet all of you. When the car slid off of the road, we were very afraid. Especially when we decided to check out the other cars and found them all deserted."

"Well," Mike said, "somehow we missed each other. We had been by there in the truck twice, but we didn't see you, or your blinkers. Richard here is the observant one who noticed your signal."

"That was Granddaddy's idea," Debbie said. "It was certainly a good one."

"It worked anyway," Mike said.

Then Jessica swept in like a Nebraska tornado with a pot of coffee, followed by a very large man who looked like another of Mike's reclamation projects—at least the long jagged scar running from his mouth to his ear looked like a knife wound and attested to some period of his life in a less sedate setting than a truck stop kitchen. He was carrying a tray with a sandwich apiece for Art and Debbie. "Here, honey. Roast turkey sandwiches and coffee, straight from Henry's grill, and he makes a good grilled turkey sandwich." She filled two styrofoam cups with the coffee and put packets of creamer and sugar on a table next to Art, along with a stack of cups. "And here's more cups if any more of you want some coffee."

Henry handed the plates to Art who thanked him, handed one to Debbie, and hungrily took a big bite.

A smile followed. "These really are good," he said to Henry, a sentiment echoed by Debbie but less articulately around a mouthful of sandwich.

"Thank you, sir," Henry said with a nod, then he left the room just ahead of the flying tornado that was Jessica, who was certainly being Shirley tonight.

"What were you doing out on the road tonight?" I asked.

Art made a face. "We certainly shouldn't have been, should we? We just flew back from Germany and were in a hurry to get home, and kept going past what we should have."

"Germany?" I asked, surprised, but pleased. Apparently, the visit that Eddie, Kurt, Helmut, and I had made had accomplished something.

"Yes," said Debbie. "Granddaddy is the retired admissions director at Shiloh Seminary."

Mike laughed. "Maybe I'll retire if I get a trip to Europe out of it."

Art laughed back. "Not quite. I still keep my hand in things there at the school and a year ago, I started up an exchange program with Evangelische-Luther, a seminary that's in Brandenburg. An acquaintance of mine who had been an appliance dealer in Hesse left the seminary there some money, and we're using some of it to set everything up. "

My ears perked up again. "Who was that?"

"He was a German, Kurt Weber. I knew him slightly, but didn't know about the bequest until I contacted the Brandenburg seminary with the idea, and they had been thinking along the same lines, so everything just kind of fell together. Debbie went with me because she's a student at Shiloh and a student assistant in the admissions office, a job she got due to sheer nepotism. But she has kept the job by being an excellent worker."

Bob and Red had been in the corner deep in a discussion of power tools, but when Red heard Art mention Shiloh Seminary, he came over. "Do you know Jerry Ross who teaches New Testament and Greek?"

Art smiled. "Certainly I do. Everybody knows Jerry. He's not only one of our star teachers, he's a wonderful person that everybody loves. Do you know him?"

Red nodded. "He's my son."

Art stood up, letting his blanket drop and went over to Red. "I would like to shake your hand and congratulate you on a wonderful job of raising a wonderful person."

Red shook his hand with a big grin on his face. "Well, actually he's our foster son, but he lived with us since he was six, when his mother was institutionalized."

"Then he's your son. Same thing. And he truly is a wonderful person."

"I think my wife Charlene gets most of the credit," Red replied.

Mike stood up and stretched. "I hate to break up the party, but I'm an old man and I'm going over to Red's office to get some sleep."

Art laughed. "I don't think of you as old."

Mike smiled. "I feel very old right now. When you folks wind down, there are some pallets in Red's office and a couple more in my closet. Good night."

He went out the door, followed by Red. Bob, Josh, and I got Bonnie out of her wheel chair and laid her on the couch. I certainly couldn't tell, but Bob said she was comfortable and asleep.

Josh stretched. "I think I'm going out front for a little," he said, and went out. Richard and Debbie were sitting in two chairs in the far corner, whispering with their heads close together. Art and I spread a blanket apiece and laid down on the floor, while Bob went over to the corner with Richard and Debbie.

I wasn't really sleepy since, as most always, I'm a perfect physical specimen, and my day had started at sundown, while all the others had spent a day at work or travel before that. I listened for a few minutes, but then got the urge to step outside which I took as instructions from the Boss, so I put my shoes, hat, and coat on and went out into the cold. I looked around for whatever opportunity the Boss wanted me to take, and saw Frank over by the kitchen back door, huddled against the dumpster, smoking a cigarette. I went over and huddled, too. "How's kitchen work going?"

He gave me a curious look and shivered. "Better'n jail. An' the company's better looking than the bunch in the drunk tank. 'Cept for Henry. And they're all a lot nicer."

I chuckled. "I can imagine." I said. "What do they have you doing?"

"Washing dishes in the dishwashing machine," he said. "It's not bad."

"You could do worse," I agreed, "and as you pointed out, you're dealing with nice people."

He shrugged, but stared into the horizon.

"You know that your life would be a lot better if you got a regular job, even washing dishes, and looked for good people to hang around with."

He shrugged again, but this time he seemed to be shrugging in agreement.

"You need to find good folks to associate with and find a job doing something useful. You'll live better and be a lot happier than trying to be a thief."

He turned to look at me. "I expect you're right, and I think I'll give it a try." He smiled and flipped his cigarette away into the snow. "But I'd better start by not freezing to death here." Then he went into the kitchen.

But I needed some time to think so I went back to Mike's office, sat, pretended to sleep, and thought it over. It was clear that the Boss was being cute here by getting all of these people I'd worked with before—or who were connected with a former job—together in one place. But so far, I had no idea what my role in this was to be. I had learned that Richard was at the center of it, but how the rest of them fit in was still a mystery.

I spent several minutes trying to fit it all together but got nowhere.

The only connections I could see with everybody was my having worked with all of them before, and that they were all here at the truck stop.

After twenty minutes or so with my mind racing like a runaway truck engine, I gave it up and listened in on Bob, Debbie, and Richard having their conversation. After a few moments, I wondered if maybe I shouldn't join it. They were talking about the seminary Debbie was attending and while Richard was interested in it, he wasn't jumping to apply, given his uncertainty about his professional future in that field.

"But that doesn't matter as much as you seem to think," Debbie told him. "A lot of the students there aren't sure about their future. In fact, a good many of the students come there just to see if they have a vocation. Some find their dream there. Some don't and leave. Either way it's a great experience and a good way to learn Greek."

"You're still young enough to spend some time trying new things," Bob said. "It's difficult to waste a year at your age, and a year in seminary would be a good way to learn if you want to do that."

"But," Richard said with a grin, "if I go and decide not to stay, I'll have learned Greek to no purpose."

Debbie giggled. "Then you can always impress your friends with your Greek Bible."

"No," Bob said, "learning something is never a waste of time. I wish I could go to college, even at my age."

"Richard, I think you should try it," Debbie said. "When the roads open, come on by and I'll show you around. And you can talk to some of the students and teachers."

I rose up and looked at them. Richard was thinking seriously and I could tell the idea of being shown around by Debbie was a very interesting one.

I figured I wasn't needed there, after all, and that Debbie had some more powerful and persuasive arguments than I could muster, so I got up, put my shoes back on, and went out into the hallway.

I wasn't sure where I was going, but when I went by the door into the kitchen, I had the clear impulse to go in, so I did. Just inside the door was a cardboard box with hairnets, pairs of thin plastic gloves, and a rack of what seemed to be lab coats, so I helped myself to one of each, washed my hands at the sink, and went looking for adventure, or at least for something useful. It didn't take long. I saw Frank stacking plates from a rack on wheels onto a shelf. I noticed that the rest of the kitchen crew was in the front, so I stopped and helped. Frank looked at me funny, but didn't try to run me off, so I said, "How's the work going?"

He snorted. "Minimum wage and hard work. How do you think it's going?"

I frowned at him. "You should be grateful. They could have put you out into the cold."

He shrugged. "I been cold before."

"But you'll admit, it's better in here, isn't it?"

He smiled slightly. "Yeah, I guess."

Just as we finished, Jessica came back. "Break time. Come on and have some coffee." She looked quizzically at me and clearly was about to ask, "Who are you and what are you doing here?"

Which I forestalled by holding up my hands, showing the gloves. "I've been helping Red out and came in here to check on Frank."

Both Jessica and Frank looked a little surprised and skeptical, but Jessica just turned and left with a gesture that seemed to mean to follow, so I did. We do have a tendency to inspire trust, since people sense our unfallen natures—at least good people do, and Jessica seemed to qualify, at least tonight.

She led the way to a break area in one corner of the kitchen with a table, microwave, coffee pot, and a television, which was turned off. We each got a cup. Jessica poured coffee for each of us and for Charlene who came in and sat.

"Where are you from, Frank?' Jessica asked as she poured his cup.

"New York," he replied, reaching for the sugar. "And Chicago. And Minneapolis. And Philly."

"A big city boy, huh?" she asked, sitting down across from him.

Frank managed to nod and shrug at the same time, apparently agreeing.

"What kind of work do you normally do?" Charlene asked.

"When you're not stealing," Jessica added, earning a dirty look from both Charlene and Frank.

"I usually work as a messenger and delivery man for a store supply company."

Drug runner, I thought. Or such like.

"Is that a pretty good job?" Charlene asked.

Frank shrugged. "I guess. It's hard work, long weird hours, and…a little dangerous. But it pays pretty well, and has good possibilities to move up."

I noticed Jessica roll her eyes at his mention of moving up, but this time she kept quiet.

"What all do you do as a messenger?" Charlene asked.

"Carry messages," Frank replied with a grin. But it was a friendly, joking grin, not the smirk. Frank was being friendly but not very forthcoming.

"By foot, or bicycle? Car?"

"Any of those, depending on how far I have to go and the priority."

"So living in those places, I guess snow like this is something you're used to."

Frank laughed. "I hate cold and snow."

Charlene and Jessica had both been to New York a few times and, for the next few minutes, they discussed some of the famous sights there. I had witnessed part of one of the most famous sights in New York which was General Washington's evacuation of Manhattan. I only saw a small part of it, having come over as a traveler staying at a country inn, and my job was to persuade a British squad leader not to burn the inn.

That one was an easy job, since the sergeant was very unhappy with his orders so he just burned an old, empty shed and kept going.

The inn was later the place where a church met and was the scene of the conversion of a young Mohawk who became a missionary to the Indian tribes in the Ohio valley.

There was a pause in the conversation, so Jessica filled in. "Is drug running hard work?"

Frank took the bait without thinking. "Yeah. You have to pay careful attention and you risk—" He stopped suddenly and narrowed his eyes. "Hey, you—"

Charlene tried to suppress a giggle and failed. Jessica didn't even try to suppress hers.

Frank just shook his head and stared into his coffee cup.

There was a short pause which I ended by saying, "There's a purpose to your life, and it's not what you're doing with it now. You'll be much better off and a lot happier if you find your purpose and get with that program."

After another short pause, Charlene nodded. "Why do

you live on crime when there's a better life being honest and working hard?"

"And a lot more pride," Jessica put in.

Frank snorted derisively. "Honest people are just rabbits to get eaten by the hawks," he said with a smirk that clearly stated that he thought of himself as a hawk.

Just then Henry came around the end of a rack of cans. "Have you ever been in prison, Bud," he asked in his booming voice. He stood up to his full man-mountain size and flexed his impressive muscles. "In there, hawks like you are little people and folks like me are lions who eat hawks alive."

With a glare at Frank, he turned and stomped back toward the stoves. Somewhere in there, Frank's smirk disappeared to be replaced by uncertainty.

Charlene smiled a little then turned back to Frank. "Besides that, there are good reasons to be a good productive member of society. Like—"

"Like self-respect from doing a good, honest job," Jessica interrupted, standing up. "Which you're about to do. So let's get back to work."

So we all washed our cups and headed back to our regular functions, them to the kitchen, and me to find Red.

As I was closing the kitchen door, the outside door opened and Red came inside, along with a gust of cold air and a flurry of snow.

"Getting colder," he said. "But the snow is slacking off."

"I thought you went to sleep," I said.

"Too worried about things," he said. "I've just been out checking the generator again. If it goes out, we'll be sitting in the dark and a lot cooler."

"I thought you said you have gas heat."

"We do, but the fans are electric. We wouldn't freeze,

but we would get a little chilly in here. But not danger-ously so. A lot warmer than outside."

"Did the generator seem to be working okay?"

"No problems. But I plan to keep a close eye on it. There are several drivers out there in their trucks and five or six motor homes with folks in them. If the generator went out, we might all have to try to crowd in with them."

"Oh?" I asked. "Some folks didn't come in here?"

Red shook his head. "They're as well off in those as we are in here. As long as their fuel holds out and their engines work, they've got light and heat as good as we have."

I thought about it a moment and realized that he was right.

"So now I am going to sleep. Good night."

I looked at the clock. "'Good morning,' you mean."

Red chuckled, shrugged, and went into his office. I made a quick check of the folks in the front. Everybody was sleeping or trying to, except for Sergeant Cole's daughter who raised her head to look at me. I smiled at her, she smiled back, and laid her head back down on Mama's belly.

I went back into Mike's office, just in time to hear Richard promise Debbie that he would think about com-ing by campus for her guided tour.

"Great," she said. "I'll be looking for you. But right now, I've had a long, rough day, and I'm going to sleep." She lay the blanket out on the floor and very quickly exe-cuted her plan, while Bob and Richard continued a whis-pered conversation. I lay back down and, instead of sleeping, I listened in on their discussion.

Bob, being not well acquainted with seminary, didn't continue that discussion but began to quiz Richard about his life direction.

I pretended to sleep while I listened to them talk. Bob was trying to convince Richard that he should consider trying seminary and that his bad experience should be a learning opportunity instead of a roadblock. Richard was resisting on the basis of his own response during his bad experience, but his resistance was getting less and less.

I tried to figure out if I should approach Frank further and what I should be focusing on. After a couple of minutes of minimally productive thought, I heard Jessica open the door quietly. She looked in, checked out who was present, and frowned. I went out into the hall with her.

"What's up?" I asked.

"Have you seen Frank? He's disappeared."

"Not since coffee break a while ago."

Jessica frowned again. "Henry said he thought he saw him out around the motor homes by the generator shed about five minutes ago, but he wasn't certain."

"I don't know. I hope he hasn't run off."

She just shook her head and headed back into the kitchen, mumbling "…can't help some people…"

I went back into Mike's office, sat, and thought again for a few minutes then drifted into a doze where I could still hear but things got confused.

We were all suddenly brought back to clarity when someone loudly slammed the outside door open and yelled, "One of the motor homes is on fire out here!"

With that, we all jumped up and went out to look.

A fire was blazing in one of the motor homes and, to make it worse, it was parked next to the generator house, threatening to catch it on fire.

Mike quickly took charge as usual. "Bob, come with me to get the big fire extinguishers. Josh, Sam, and Richard, go see if anybody is still in there."

Josh, Richard, and I ran toward the fire while Mike,

Bob, and Red went off in a different direction. Jessica and Charlotte came out of the kitchen door and followed behind us.

I had dealt with fires before—several times, in fact. One of the worst was a time I had gone to the Philippines to work with the guerrillas. The mission sent us into a Japanese-held area to bring out a young priest who, for several reasons, chiefly involving threats to his family, was a collaborator. We sneaked into the town undetected and had loaded up with Japanese ammo and explosives, when the priest found us. I was able to convince him that if he would join us, we would take his entire family out with us, but while we were discussing it, we were discovered by a Japanese soldier, whom the priest had befriended. The soldier shot at us and missed, hitting a kerosene lamp instead, setting the fire, which wound up burning half the town. One of the guerillas shot the soldier, but too late to do any good. The guerrillas and the priest, quite rightly, took off for the hills while I stayed behind with two men to get the priest's family out in the confusion. It worked.

We moved the soldier's body to where it would look like he had died in the fire, hopefully—and successfully—avoiding reprisals. And, in the chaos of the fire, we got his mother and two sisters away to the hills, but at the price of their losing everything they owned, as well as the father and two brothers already lost to reprisals. The priest wound up being an excellent chaplain to about a brigade's worth of guerrillas—and a very proficient guerrilla himself—and was quite forgiven for his earlier collaboration.

Richard reached the burning motor home first and kicked out the window in the door. He then reached in and opened the door. Smoke billowed out, driving him back, but he got down low and crawled in. I tried to follow, but before I could start in, Richard reappeared, dragging a woman by the ankle. Josh and I helped get her out, and Jessica and Charlotte took over and sat her on the running board of a parked truck.

"We'd better get her inside," Jessica said.

"Then help me get her up," Charlotte responded.

They got one of the woman's arms over each of their shoulders and started toward the door into the offices.

Just then Mike and Bob came up with the fire extinguishers. Mike used his to break out a window and started expending it into the motor home. The heat drove him back a moment and he looked over the top of the burning motor home to the roof of the generator house which was beginning to burn, too. "Bob! Use yours on the generator house roof!"

But before Bob could do so, the dump truck came roaring around the corner of the truck stop with Red at the wheel. It headed for the burning vehicle. Red slowed and put the bumper of the truck against the back of the motor home then started moving. At first, we thought it wasn't going to work and that the motor home was frozen in place, but then it started to move, with its tires skidding in the snow. Red pushed the burning vehicle away from the generator building, ending that threat, and then backed away and used the truck's fire extinguisher on the smoldering roof of the generator house.

Just then, the woman that Jessica and Charlotte were taking inside came to and started screaming, "Robbie's still in there! Robbie's still in there!" She broke loose from their grip but was still woozy and fell into the snow.

Charlotte tried to get her to tell her who and just where Robbie was, but she only kept screaming. Jessica and Charlotte both tried to calm her down and get her to talk rationally, but it didn't work.

Then I heard an engine start and noticed motion over

by the burning vehicle. I looked that way to see the tractor with a loading bucket on the front and a backhoe on the back come out of a low shed with Richard at the controls. He drove close to the burning motor home, then turned around, so that the backhoe was toward the fire. Then the seat swiveled, and Richard moved the backhoe arm next to the burning motor home, lowered it, and then, extending it, tore a section of the roof away. He then jumped from the seat to the backhoe arm and climbed out on it until he was over the hole in the roof. He paused for a moment when we heard Jessica raise up from questioning the woman from the motor home. "He's in the back section!" she yelled at him.

Wrapping his coat around his head, he jumped onto the roof then dropped down into the interior.

"That crazy fool is going to get killed," Mike said, going in as close as he dared and then trying to see into the burning vehicle. Then things changed. Or actually my perceptions changed, and I could see both the physical side and the spiritual aspect of events. Not just a hint like before with Frank, but clearly. It had happened to me before but rarely when I was in full flesh-and-blood human form.

Time slowed to a crawl, and I could see from both sides at once. I was immediately aware that, from this new perspective, the fire changed dramatically. It was no longer just a physical phenomenon but a living being—a being of such malevolence, rage, hate, and destructiveness that I recoiled and took a step backward.

In spite of it being made of fire, it seemed to me to be a vast darkness, looming above everything, threatening to destroy everything in sight. It wasn't a new experience for me, since I had faced such demons before, but it was never fun. Or safe.

At least now I understood why I had sensed the evil

presence around Frank which had been this evil being working on him to start the fire. This one was a class of being that was especially powerful and dangerous. Tolkien named them well—Balrog, an Anglicized version of the Latinized version of the Grecized Hebrew for "master of evil." But just then I wasn't thinking linguistic derivations. I had realized the target of his presence and fury—Richard. And Richard had just gone straight into the heart of the fire and darkness.

I also knew what its target was. Not Richard's soul, the Boss had it safely in His hands for all eternity where no demon could ever touch it. But obviously the Boss had big plans for Richard, and the evil one was here to keep Richard from fulfilling those plans, either by destroying Richard's dedication and, thereby, taking away Richard's future dedication and effectiveness in the Boss's work or, even worse, by getting him to do something that would cost him his life.

Both intellectually and from prior experience, I knew that this demon's power was greater than mine, but I wasn't sent here to watch it take Richard, so I pushed back with as much strength as I had, knowing it wasn't enough.

But then another unusual event happened and my senses took on yet another dimension. I became aware of the power of some of the people around me, as if they had begun to glow with an inner light. Mike, Red, Charlene, and Bob all had the light about them, and I knew that they could help. For an instant, I was confused but quickly grasped the secret and fell to my knees.

"Help me," I shouted so they all could hear and folded my hands, as if in prayer.

Mike looked back at me, startled and confused, but then he looked surprised and turned back to the burning motor home. Soon the light emanating from him took shape and reached toward the fire. Then I saw three other beams come from behind me and knew that Red, Charlene, and Bob were joining in. Then another joined us and, in surprise, I looked back to see that one of the truck drivers was praying with us in the spiritual battle. In the same glance I noticed Jessica come out of the building and had a flash of hope that she could help but could only feel fear and uncertainty from her as her power shrank and withdrew. Disappointed, I turned back and pushed harder. But it still wasn't enough. Our combined efforts were having an effect, but I could feel Richard's confusion slipping into the darkness of despair and uselessness. And in that situation, it could even get him killed.

Then suddenly I heard a very physical, earthly contralto shout of "*No! No!*" and I immediately felt Jessica's strength come back into the fight, the light shining brightly out of her, and it made a big difference. I made one last push of desperation and was very gratified to see that with Jessica providing the missing piece, our combined power grew greatly, and immediately threw the evil force out of space and time back to his fire hole.

Everything went back to normal senses, and the fire became just a fire again, but still deadly. I fell to my hands and knees in the snow, momentarily exhausted. I looked around and saw that Mike, Red, Bob, and Charlene all looked a little dazed, and Jessica was on her hands and knees in the snow like me. A wave of joy washed over me, and I felt a little giddy over the victory. But underlying the joy was a definite undercurrent of sadness and grief because, beneath the fire, darkness, and evil, I had recognized the being as one who had once been a close friend and brother. But I had learned to deal with that grief. I put it aside and got back on the job.

Mike took a step toward the fire but the heat was about to drive him back when a window opened and

Richard's head appeared, followed by his arm putting an unconscious boy of about five years over the side. Mike ran the rest of the way in, grabbed the boy, then ran back. After a quick check, Mike announced, "He's out, but he's breathing."

I looked back at the hole in the roof of the motor home where Richard jumped for the roof and was pulling himself up when the roof fell in, dropping Richard back into the flames. But Red, unnoticed in the excitement, had gotten to the tractor controls. He moved the digger arm to a point right over Richard, who jumped and caught it with one hand. Red moved the arm to get Richard away from the fire. But just as we started to breathe again, Richard's grip slipped, and he fell back toward the flames.

Then, seemingly miraculously, a hand reached down from the digger arm, grabbed Richard's hand. and pulled him out of the fire. Unseen by anybody, Josh had climbed out on the arm and was ready to help. Richard, fortunately, didn't weigh much, and Josh held him as Red moved them over a deep snow bank where they dropped into the waiting arms of Jessica and Charlene, who began rolling them in the snow to extinguish their clothes, which were smoldering in several places each.

Red revved the tractor engine and picked up a scoop load of snow which he dropped through the hole in the roof, extinguishing the fire inside. Then he put another scoop full on top of that for good measure.

Everybody then threw snow onto the generator shed roof which quickly stopped the smoldering there, too. That was followed by a big cheer by all the participants, along with several onlookers and truckers who had come over to help.

While they were dealing with the generator shed, I took a moment to reflect. The kind of power I had just seen in my friends wasn't at all unprecedented, but it was rare, and to have that many of them with it in one place for one purpose had clearly taken a lot of really cute work on the Boss's part. I was gratified to have been able to play a part in it. Of course, the humans weren't completely aware of what had happened, and they all thought they had just been praying, which was correct, but not all of the story. I realized that several of my jobs had been a part of that long range plan, and I again smiled at the Boss's skill at making a plan come together. It also showed that Richard had a really important place in the plans, and that both sides were taking a major interest in him.

Then everybody went back inside, while Red returned the loader to the shelter.

Everybody went into Mike's office with lots of chatter and laughter. Bob used the first aid kit to treat several burns, none of them serious, fortunately. The worst were on Richard's hand and shoulder, and on the woman's arm, but Bob's army medic diagnosis was that if they would keep them clean and treated with burn ointment, they would heal fine.

Mike called the emergency room of the county hospital where his friend worked as an emergency room nurse, who told Bob that the best treatment which was available to us for smoke inhalation was oxygen, so Bob got two tanks and masks out of the emergency supplies and hooked them to the woman and her son.

Mike called Henry to the back and told him to take the lady and her son up and give them a good breakfast, on his expense account.

Then Richard became the center of attention. We all made him tell us about his rescue efforts and how he found the boy.

He told everybody about seeing the backhoe in the

shed and using it to open the roof and to get into the back of the motor home.

"When I got inside, I couldn't see very well for the smoke, so I lay on the floor and was able to see the boy's hand where he had hidden under a cabinet. So I grabbed his hand and pulled him out and hoisted him over the side where I was going to try to throw him away from the fire, but Mike came up and grabbed him.

"So then I tried to climb back up on the backhoe arm, but my grip gave way, and I fell back in. I thought I was dead, but it seemed like a hand from heaven reached down and grabbed me and pulled me out of the fire. But I knew it was real because Josh's grip hurt, and the flames hurt even worse."

"How'd you know how to operate the backhoe?" Red asked.

"Weekends and summers in construction work while I was in college," Richard replied. "I learned how to use one very similar to yours, and it all came back to me when I needed it."

"Weren't you scared?" Debbie asked.

"Yes, terrified, but…something was there with me. It was…well, it was a strong sense of divine presence, that everything was going to be—No, that wasn't it. I didn't have any sense of invulnerability, or even protection. Like I said, I was scared to death and the fire was burning me and it hurt. And there was something there trying to make me just give up. But something else was there with me, too. It was a sense that the fire and my getting the boy and myself out was very important, but that its main importance was not here and now, but in some greater, spiritual perspective. In a bigger sense, I knew that it was critically important, and in a larger, greater background I knew everything was going to be all right. Even if we had died in the fire, it was going to be okay in a greater way.

"I'm having trouble explaining it, but it's crystal clear in my mind. I could see myself as one link in a long chain, back to Vietnam, Burma, and lots of people back then and more on up ahead that I can't see. I'm important to that chain and what I do has ultimate significance, but only if I go with the plan behind the significance and not against it."

"It sounds like you had a heavenly perspective for a moment there," Bob said.

Richard nodded in excited agreement. "Yeah, that's it. Exactly. Here in this life, we have to struggle, and we even fail, but from that greater perspective, the end result is all under control. So it's not that here and now doesn't matter. In fact, it matters even more because it makes a difference in an ultimate sense, not just in terms of our lives here."

"'Whatsoever you do in word or deed...'" Debbie said.

Richard nodded at her. "Right! Right! That makes more sense to me now. I felt something giving me a sense of peace, but spiritual peace, cosmic peace. Even though right then and there, I was scared to death and my hands were getting blistered."

"Did it change your thinking about anything?" Bob said.

Richard smiled. "It gives me a new perspective on everything. If nearly dying in a fire can be seen as less than greatly significant, then hurt feelings become totally insignificant. So, Debbie, I plan to be taking you up on that offer of a guided tour. But only as long as you're the guide."

Debbie squealed, jumped up, ran over, and hugged Richard. Then she looked a little embarrassed, but Richard just grinned.

As has often happened to me, I get sent to persuade,

and a pretty face proves even more persuasive. Oh well, the Boss has a big variety of means to accomplish things. Sometimes us, but a lot more often, just plain folks are His main tools.

"How did you get out there on that arm?" Red asked Josh.

"I was there all along. You just couldn't see me because you were looking somewhere else. That's not unusual," he said with a wry smile. "People often don't see me because they're not looking for me or they're looking in the wrong place."

Since it was now about normal waking up time, we all decided to go into the restaurant for breakfast. As we were trooping out, Lance came into the hall from Red's office and had a whispered conversation with Mike, which Mike ended by saying, "Call the sheriff's office and tell them all of that. And tell them that the kitchen folks can give them a good description and maybe they can get some fingerprints."

Lance left and I asked Mike what was up.

"Lance checked out that motor home, and he's convinced that the fire was set on purpose. But the law enforcement people will have to handle that."

I nodded. "How are the restaurant's supplies holding out?"

"No problem," he said. "We have enough for a week's normal operations, and could stay in business for three weeks without a supply run. The menu would get pretty limited after the first week or so, but we'd eat just fine."

"That's good to hear," I said, "because I've worked up quite an appetite."

Mike laughed. "I've watched you, and I think you always have an appetite. And a major sweet tooth."

I laughed back. "Guilty on all counts, and I am willing to undergo an ordeal by pancake to prove my guilt."

So I did exactly that. Mike and Red moved several tables together, and we ate in a group, celebrating the end of a long, cold, hard night. We had high powered waitresses since Jessica and Charlene came out to take orders from our group. Jessica even had on her old "Shirley" name tag from Trailside and she also put on her sassy Shirley act, calling all of us honey.

She brought my pancakes with, "Here you go, honey, those dark specks are just cigarette ashes. Won't hurt you."

I grinned. "Did Tom drop them on the kitchen floor?"

She responded with a big grin. "Honey, if he dropped them on that floor, you'd never find 'em again," she said and followed it with a big wink. "I can still sling it, honey. Mike told me you remembered me from Trailside." Then she started sassing Bob. Charlene was a lot more polite to her end of the table.

I sat between Debbie and Red and we had a delightful time, along with pancakes, sausage, and coffee. Richard was now interested in hearing all about the school programs and seemed especially interested in the exchange program with Brandenburg.

During the meal, I noticed Bob and Josh sitting together and engrossed in some private conversation.

After everyone finished, we put the tables back, and most of the folks went to separate parts of the truck stop, and I moved my coffee to an empty booth, but before I could get started with any deep thoughts, I saw Josh and Bob go out the side door, with Bob pushing Bonnie in her chair.

I briefly wondered what was up with them, but, with no guidance from the Boss on the subject, decided that they were all capable of handling their own lives.

Jessica came out of the kitchen, drying her hands and when she saw me she came over and sat in the booth with me. She looked at me intently and said, "Just what was it you did out there?"

I put on a questioning look with confusion. "I mostly stood and watched," I said.

"That's not what I mean and you know it," Jessica said, shaking her head. "There was more to that than what meets the eye, and you were at the center of it. So what happened?"

"What do you think happened?"

She got a look of concentration. "I could feel some prayers going out and then I prayed, too. But there's more to it than that, isn't there?"

I smiled. "You've heard that 'prayer changes things.' Don't you believe in prayer?"

She smiled. "More now than ever."

"Then there's your answer," I said. "I'm glad you decided to join in with us out there."

She looked a little skeptical. "Me, too, but…Well, I have to get back to work. But I think you know something you're not letting on about."

I shrugged. "Don't we all?"

She headed back to the kitchen. I went to the coffee pot for a fresh cup, where I was met by Hal and Sherry who had sat with Bonnie during the truck rescue run.

"I'm glad to see you," Hal said. "I need to go see Mike and…" He hesitated, looking a little sheepish.

"He needs some moral support," Sherry put in.

"Yeah," Hal said, with a rueful half-smile.

I raised an eyebrow. "I'm not sure what support I can give, but I'll gladly help you find him and be there when you talk to him."

An unexpected development, but encouragement is the stock-in-trade of all of us who are members of Uriel's crew, so I went along to encourage. And give moral support.

We went back to Mike's office which was, for the moment, empty of everyone except Mike.

"Mike," I said. "Hal would like to see you a moment."

Mike looked up, obviously tired. "If it's about your bill. I'll be happy to take an IOU and you can mail the payments later."

Hal shook his head. "No, sir, that's not it. We paid cash and were sensible. It's about the picture on your desk."

Mike looked at the picture of Shirley/Jessica, raising an eyebrow. "My wife?"

Hal turned a little pink. "No, sir, the other one, the soldier. I noticed it when we stayed in here with Mrs. Dunn."

"Oh," Mike turned a little to look at his brother's picture. "What about Harry?"

Hal looked at the floor. "He's my father."

Mike raised both eyebrows and his eyes got big. He didn't look tired any more. "You're Harold, Jr.?"

Hal nodded, looking back up at Mike.

Both of them said nothing for a few moments, then Mike got up, came around the desk, and wrapped Hal in a big bear hug, which was returned. Mike raised one arm and brought Sherry into the hug, too. Then they were all three crying, and I decided my moral support wasn't needed any more so I went back out to the booth where I had moved my coffee, got a cinnamon bun, and thought about things.

It was all making a lot more sense now. Mike and Red had provided a safe haven for us all and had spearheaded the rescue effort. Richard had been one of the rescued, but without my intervention, might not have made it. Without Loc having saved his parents' lives, Richard wouldn't have been born. Then he was the one to notice Art and Debbie's signal and went to rescue them. Bob and Debbie had been able to talk to Richard and prepare him for the Boss's revelation to him in the fire. And now Richard was interested in the German exchange program, which wouldn't have happened without Eddie, Kurt, and me working with Art. I still didn't understand everything, but I very seldom know all the details, and it doesn't matter. I understood who sent me and who got us all together, and that was enough.

By then there was a little bit of light appearing in the east, and I started to wonder again about Bob, Bonnie, and Josh. They had been outside for quite a while. It was long enough and cold enough that I was beginning to get a little concerned, but then I saw Bob come back in by himself and look around. He saw me sitting at the booth alone, came over, and sat down across from me. It was then I noticed his face. It had that look, the one where the person has seen a vision and something of the other side shows in their face. I was intrigued and pleased for him, but puzzled.

Before I could say anything, Bob looked up at me. "He told me who you really are. I had already suspected it, but it's good to see you again, Sam."

I put on a puzzled frown. "Oh? Who am I really and who told you?"

Now Bob looked a little puzzled. "Josh told me."

"Oh?" I asked, more puzzled. "And who does Josh think I am."

Bob looked even more puzzled. "He knows who you really are, of course. He knew all about the last time three years ago when we helped Roger and Audrey and Darrel. Why wouldn't he?"

Now I was completely shocked and confused. "How would Josh know anything about those people?"

Now Bob looked totally confused, too. He turned and looked outside but apparently didn't find what he was looking for and looked back at me. "Are you telling me you don't know who Josh is?"

I just shook my head.

Bob quit looking confused and just smiled real big. "Think about it. Josh, Joshua, Yehoshua. Yeshua. Jesus."

I started to look puzzled but then the light came on and I felt my eyes get big. "Josh is—"

Bob nodded, grinning. "The Son himself. You really didn't know?"

I shook my head. "No. I guess He closed my eyes, too. He can do that, although He normally doesn't with one of us. I guess that explains Richard's sense of divine presence out there tonight. And yours, too." Then I smiled when I realized why our power had grown so great when we were facing the balrog. Josh had focused it. But we had helped. We all had a role to play in the Boss's work and plans. When we do our part, the Boss makes something even greater out of our efforts. He even makes something good out of our failures, like my mission with Loc.

Bob got the beatific look back. "Well, it was wonderful. He left with Bonnie."

Another light came on in my mind, and I knew why Bob had come back in alone. "She must have been a very special lady, then," I said.

Bob nodded. "She was. He took us outside, but it wasn't cold. We went over behind the pantry shed and, suddenly, Bonnie could talk and move again. We all talked about her life, our kids, and—and—and then Josh said that they had to go." Bob's eyes were somewhere else now and a tear leaked out. "He told me I could go with them if I wanted to. I wanted to go, I wanted to go so bad, but Bonnie told me that I still had a lot to do here. I asked Josh what I should do, and he just said it was my choice, but that if I stayed, he'd be talking to me again about some things. But Bonnie insisted that I stay. So here I am." He looked back at me again. "It would have been so nice to have gone together. But I expect she's right, and I've still got some things to do here." He wiped his eyes with a napkin. "Then they left. I could feel them go and it was a healing, not a leaving. I could feel all of her pain and hurt fall away, like it was happening to me, too. It was wonderful. He 'shall wipe away all tears from their eyes.' That's what Josh did for Bonnie. Now I know what that means, because I felt it happen, too."

I handed him another napkin. "I'm thinking that it's not just Bonnie who's a very special person."

We sat in silence for a few minutes, then I remembered something and decided to satisfy my curiosity. "When you and Bonnie first came into the truck stop, you stopped and looked at Josh and me like you knew us. What was that all about?"

Bob took on a thoughtful look for a few moments. "I thought I knew you both and my first response was that it was you, Sam Mollock. And Josh had the same…light, or aura, or…something…about him. I don't know what it was that I saw, but I knew the two of you were something different. But when I looked again, you clearly weren't the same person I'd known, but I kept a suspicion."

I laughed. "Well that's twice you've discovered me. "

Bob chuckled. "No, that's once I discovered you and once you were given away. Oh, Bonnie gave me a message for you."

"For me?"

"Yeah. She said thank you for the perfume. After you gave it to me and suggested it, I kept putting some on her every day. I didn't know if it mattered to her, but just now she told me that it made her feel good, and was about the only thing that made her 'feel like a woman and not just a blob of malfunctioning flesh,' as she put it. She said to tell you thanks for getting it started."

I laughed. "Well, I'm glad to have been useful."

Bob watched me eat the last of the sweet roll. "Now satisfy my curiosity. Isn't gluttony a sin?"

I laughed but stopped, nearly choking on the roll. "Gluttony is a sin. Feasting is a blessing. It's gluttony if it goes on too long. I don't get to eat like this very often." I told him about that meal of raw insects and about the time in Baluchistan where I had lived for two weeks on nothing but goat cheese and very sour goats milk and way too little of both. But I had helped a Russian soldier escape from a warlord by persuading a guard to go visit his girlfriend and then helped the soldier get back to a Soviet position. He had later played an important role in the reestablishment of the church in Tula, his home town in Russia.

"So, what were you here for this time?" Bob asked

I shrugged. "I'm not really sure. Something about Richard, and I'm guessing that getting him back on track into the ministry was part of it, but you and Debbie did more there than I did." I grinned at him. "Both times I've worked with you, you've taken over and done my job."

Bob smiled. "Well, I'm glad to have been useful, too. But I think Debbie had more to do with it than either of us."

I nodded. "I think so, too. That's the never-ending story—and one of the greatest things in creation. I never get tired of watching young folks fall in love."

"Old folks, too, for that matter," Bob replied.

"True, true." Then I got the okay, so I said, "You're not the only repeat visit I'm making this trip. I've also worked with Art, Mike, and Red, and with Richard's parents before."

Bob's eyebrows shot up. "Is something big going on?"

I shrugged. "Probably. But then one thing I've learned

for certain is that everyone and everything is significant in the Boss's eyes."

I told him briefly what had happened with each of the other people he'd met during the night.

He sighed. "Well, I can certainly say that you work with a wonderful class of people."

I nodded. "In these cases, and yours, that is certainly true. But it's not always like that. There are evil people out there, and I've worked with them, too. You're all his children and sometimes even the evil ones can remember that."

So I told him about working with the Brazilian pirates off the coast of Venezuela and Guiana whose major trade was in the captured ships' crews who were sold into slavery. My persuasion hadn't worked, and I was put in with the intended slaves, one of whom was a skilled burglar who got the door open, then three of us got out and swam to shore where we enlisted the help of a Prussian ship to attack the pirates at the same time the captives came out and attacked.

The prisoners were freed and were landed in Lisbon, and the surviving pirates wound up in a well-deserved Danzig jail awaiting trial.

"How long will you be here?" he asked.

"Just till sunup."

He looked out at the growing light in the east. "Well, that's in just a few minutes. Now, I guess I have some authorities to notify and talk to. Sam, it was a great blessing to get to work with you again. When I told you before to keep an eye on us, I didn't really expect that you would come back, but I'm glad you did."

"I'm glad, too." I said. "And how is one L Darrel doing?"

Bob smiled. "He's doing great. He gets off probation next month, and he's got a job with a locksmith there in town. And once again he's a regular member of my Sunday school class, so I'm keeping an eye on him, too."

"That's good to hear."

"I guess you're going outside to disappear on us."

"I guess so. But I want to see Mike and Red before I leave."

So we both went back to Mike's office, stopping on the way to watch the first snow plow make its way down the highway in the pre-dawn twilight, followed slowly by a long string of again-moving traffic. We went in and saw Mike and Red talking to Hal and Sherry, and I heard Mike say, "…I've kept your dad's insurance money in a separate account for you and your mom, in case you ever turned up, and the interest has been invested into the truck stop, so you and Sherry are part owners here with some substantial non-voting stock holdings. So you're not the penniless newlyweds you thought you were."

He passed a sheet of paper to Hal whose eyes got big. "Oh, wow! That's more money than I expected to make in my life!"

Mike chuckled. "Maybe not that much, but it's a nice start."

"What do I do with it? Can I leave it invested here?"

"Sure. Or I'll buy it from you and you can invest the money somewhere else. It's yours—your choice. Except the stock issue requires that if you sell, you are to give Red, his cousin Terry, and me first option on buying it at market value. But you shouldn't rush. This isn't a decision to make in a hurry, and you need somebody besides me to advise you about it."

Then Mike looked at Bob and me.

"Snowplows are coming through, now," I said, "so I'm heading out."

Mike, Red, and Hal came over to shake hands. I turned to Bob to shake his, but he grabbed me in a big hug, instead. "Keep watching," he said.

"You're always being watched over," I replied.

"Yeah, I know."

I started to leave but got another message and turned back to Bob. "You remember that very pregnant lady in the red pickup truck? She just started labor, and you're the closest thing to a doctor here. She's in the snack bar."

Bob grinned. "Life goes on," he said then turned to Mike.

Mike shrugged in mock resignation and grinned back. "Bring her back here. My office has been a motel, I guess it can be a delivery room."

I headed out through the front, but when I saw what was on the television in the lobby, I gave in to the urge to buy a honey bun and watch a few minutes of Goober and his hilarious antics. I laughed until my sides hurt, and the honey bun was gone, then I went out into the snow, delayed leaving again for several minutes to watch a beautiful sunrise, then…

EPILOGUE

BETTY AND BOB

The hospital room was dimly lit and the middle-aged lady sitting in the chair was watching the old man in the bed. The close attention probably wasn't necessary. That morning, his third stroke in two days took away the last vestige of consciousness and left no hope. She was crying softly into a wad of damp tissues. She had turned the television off several hours earlier, tired of the unending tennis matches, golf games, and twenty-four-hour news reports of riots in the Mediterranean.

She shredded the tissues, threw them away, and pulled another handful out of the box, starting the process all over again.

"Oh, Daddy—" she moaned very softly, but didn't finish the thought, at least not aloud, not that it would have mattered to the unresponsive man in the bed.

She cried that clump of tissues into a soggy mess, discarded it, and started another. She took a deep breath as though she were going to speak again, but stopped in surprise when a strange golden light shone briefly on her father's face, and he opened his eyes. Her eyes opened wider when she saw that his eyes seemed to be focused on a spot just below the ceiling on the opposite side of the room, and she jumped when he smiled and spoke.

"I wondered if it would be you. I hoped it would be anyway. It's good to see you again, Sam."

He seemed to be listening for a moment then smiled again. "I know. You told Art that you weren't the death angel, but I'm glad you got to do that at least this once. I've been looking forward to this ever since I got so sick."

He listened again as the daughter looked on in shock and wonder. "Yeah. But I'm glad I stayed these last couple of years. Bonnie was right, I had some very important things to do."

He listened again and gave a puzzled frown. "What one more thing?"

Then he suddenly turned his head, looked at his daughter, and gave a gasp of surprise. "Betty!" he said delightedly and tried to hold out his arms to her, but only the right one worked, and not very well.

That was enough and Betty was out of the chair and into his hug, giving her own enthusiastic two armed hug in return. They both held on and wept for half a minute and then Bob drew back to look at her.

"Betty," he said. "It's so good to see you."

She nodded, sitting back down and giving the tissues another dose. "Oh, Daddy, I'm so sorry. I'm so—"

"No, no, no," Bob cut her off. "This isn't the time for that. This is a joyous reunion, and we're going to keep it happy. It's such a wonderful blessing to see you." He got a distant look for a moment, remembering, but then banished the thought and smiled again. "How have you been?

"I've been really bad, and it's made my life really rotten, Daddy. But I've been a lot better since a year ago." She beamed broadly at the last statement.

Bob raised his eyebrows with a look of happy expectation. "Did you—"

Betty smiled happily. "Yes, Daddy, I did. I did it just like you taught me in Sunday School, Bible School, and at home and—and it worked, just like you said. As Grandma would have said, I got religion. It didn't fix everything, but it fixed a lot of things inside of me."

Again, Bob held out his arm and the hugs and tears got another workout.

"Thank you." Bob said when they could speak again. "It's worth dying to hear that. But why didn't you tell me?"

"Because as I said, it didn't fix everything, and I was too ashamed of the mess I'd made to come to you. That was so wrong and I'm sorry, Daddy, but I let the guilt and shame and the doubts hold me back."

Bob shook his head. "Yeah. I know about doubts. I lived my whole life with them, until your mother died. That took away all of my doubts. Honey, don't let fear, guilt, shame, and especially not doubts, ever stop you again. Those things aren't even real. What's real is you, me, your mom, your brother Ben, the grandkids, the love we all have for each other, and the ultimate source of that love. Doubts are just unreality trying to take away your reality. Don't let them."

Then he looked back at the ceiling. "You told Richard something like that, Sam. Remember?" Then he looked back at Betty. "Can you see him?"

"See who?"

"Oh. Well, anyway, I wish I could introduce you to my friend Samuel. He's an angel."

Betty looked confused. "An angel is your friend?"

Bob smiled. "I know. It sounds crazy, but it's true, and not a bit crazier than a man in my condition talking to you. But I wish you could see him."

In response, the dim room became filled with a beautiful golden light, and Betty gasped in shock as Samuel appeared, in full robe, wings, and halo with a wondrous Heavenly light of holiness shining through him.

Betty put up her hand, as if in defense, but stopped, simply gaping in wonder. Then the vision faded until all that remained was the dim hospital room, which now seemed unbearably dull.

"Yeah," Bob said. "Pretty amazing, isn't it?"

"And that's your angel?" Betty managed to gasp.

Bob laughed. "No, he's not my angel, he's Heaven's angel. But he is my friend. We worked together twice."

Betty looked at her father in astonishment and respect. "You—You—"

Bob nodded. "Yep. When you come up, I'll tell you all about it. But I hope that's a long time away. So—we don't have much time—I guess…" He looked up at empty space and listened. "I didn't think so. But how are you?"

"Daddy, I'm married. It's to somebody you wouldn't approve of. There are several things about him I don't approve of, but now he's trying. Really. He's got a job now, and he even comes to church with me sometimes. Please pray for us, Daddy." She looked up at the ceiling. "And, Mr. Samuel, you pray for him, too. Please." The golden light flashed once again. "Thank you, thank you." She cried into the tissues again.

"Do you love him?" Bob asked softly.

She nodded, but with an uncertain look in her eyes. "Yes, Daddy. I do. Most of the time, anyway. And he really is trying. He just has a ways to go yet."

Bob squeezed her hand. "Then with your love and your faith to help him, he can do it." He nodded toward the ceiling. "And there's all the power either of you need."

Betty giggled. "Is this what you meant when you said you lost all of your doubts?"

Bob smiled. "Something like this. But even better."

He listened to nothing again, then nodded. "Okay. It's been great to see you, Betty. Thank you so much for coming back. You too, Sam. Every time I see you, it seems I have a miraculous last conversation with one of my women folks. And it has truly been a blessing each time. Thank you both very much."

He looked back at Betty. "Goodbye, Betty. I love you." He seemed to be about to say something else, but his head dropped and his grip on her hand fell away.

Betty sat alone in the room and cried, but the worst grief had gone away with Bob and Samuel, leaving tears of mostly happiness, and hope.

About the Author

Ray Sutherland grew up a farm boy in Kentucky, then joined the army where he was sent to Germany. He graduated from Western Kentucky University and got a doctorate in Bible from Vanderbilt University in 1986. Since then he has taught Bible in the Religion Department of the University of North Carolina at Pembroke. He was pastor of South Laurinburg Baptist Church and was an instructor in the US Army Chaplains' School at Ft. Jackson, as a reservist.

Sutherland is married to Regina. They have two sons and four grandchildren.

www.ingramcontent.com/pod-product-compliance
Lightning Source LLC
Chambersburg PA
CBHW070438120726
47910CB00003B/830